Everyone loves Sammy Keyes!

"An intelligent, gutsy, flawed, and utterly likable heroine."
—*Booklist*

"Humor, romance and adventure;
this story is an absolute blast."
—*Chicago Tribune*

"Think a combination of Carl Hiaasen's *Flush* and Janet
Evanovich's Stephanie Plum books, and you'll be
right on target." —*School Library Journal*

"Van Draanen offers such an explosive combination
of high-stakes sleuthing, hilarity, and breathlessly paced
action that it's impossible to turn the pages fast enough."
—*Kirkus Reviews*

"The sleuth delights from start to finish."
—*Publishers Weekly*

"A high-quality, high-amp mystery series."
—*The Horn Book*

"The most winning junior detective ever in teen lit.
(Take that, Nancy Drew!)"
—*Midwest Book Review*

"Sammy Keyes comes armed with attitude."
—*Orlando Sentinel*

"This funny, clever series is NOT for kids only. I challenge
the most seasoned mystery reader to guess 'who done it.'"
—*Cozies, Capers & Crimes*

Also by Wendelin Van Draanen

How I Survived Being a Girl

Flipped

Swear to Howdy

Runaway

Confessions of a Serial Kisser

The Running Dream

The Secret Life of Lincoln Jones

Wild Bird

WENDELIN VAN DRAANEN

SAMMY KEYES

AND THE Power of Justice Jack

A Yearling Book

All rights reserved. Published in the United States by Yearling, an imprint of Random House Children's Books, a division of Penguin Random House LLC, New York. Originally published in hardcover in the United States by Alfred A. Knopf Books for Young Readers, an imprint of Random House Children's Books, New York, in 2012.

Yearling and the jumping horse design are registered trademarks of Penguin Random House LLC.

Visit us on the Web! rhcbooks.com

Educators and librarians, for a variety of teaching tools, visit us at RHTeachersLibrarians.com

Library of Congress Cataloging-in-Publication Data is available upon request.

ISBN 978-0-307-93060-6 (pbk.) — ISBN 978-0-307-97407-5 (ebook)

Printed in the United States of America

13 12 11 10 9 8 7 6 5 4

First Yearling Edition 2012

Dedicated with gratitude and fond memories
to Robin and Ben, who have always taken in strays
and let them stay in their "hot pink" trailer.

Special thanks, as always, to Mark and Nancy—
my very own Justice League

SAMMY KEYES

AND THE Power of Justice Jack

PROLOGUE

The city of Santa Martina has some odd ducks swimming in its waters. There's Madame Nashira, the fortune-teller who lives in the Heavenly Hotel. There's the Elvis impersonator who works nights at Maynard's Market. There's the Psycho Kitty Queen, who used to be a beauty queen but now has a gazillion cats and looks like a ninety-year-old Barbie.

We've also got a cockeyed taxidermist, a whole school of pro-wrestling maniacs, Dusty Mike, who hangs out at the graveyard, and a hunched old lady who likes to walk her two-hundred-pound pet pig.

And that's not even taking into account all the bikers and gang guys and— Oh yeah! How could I forget?

Heather Acosta.

So, really, I thought I'd seen it all. I thought this crazy town couldn't surprise me with anything new.

And then I met Justice Jack.

ONE

Dot DeVries is Dutch.

Well, at least that's her heritage. She was born here, but her parents are from Holland and they speak with an accent and say *ja* a lot.

And even though Dot acts like an everyday ordinary eighth grader most of the time, when the calendar flips over to December, the Dutch girl in her cannot be contained.

"Here!" she said before school on Tuesday, forcing a small chunk of what looked like black rubber into my hand. "Sinterklaas came last night!"

According to Dot, Sinterklaas is the Dutch version of Santa Claus. He's a big man with a long white beard and he brings gifts to good boys and girls, only instead of using eight reindeer and a sleigh, he rides just one big white horse, and instead of putting lots of presents all at once under a tree, Sinterklaas gives a few little presents spread out over five days, and he puts them in your *shoes*.

Dot gets *way* into Sinterklaas, but this was the first time she'd shared anything from him with me. "What is it?" I asked her, staring down at the rubbery black nugget.

"Dutch candy!" she says, popping one in her mouth. "It's delicious!"

"Really?" I ask, 'cause, honestly, it looks like someone diced up an old tire.

"Really!" she squeaks. "Yesterday was the first of December, so before bed we put our shoes by the fireplace, left apples for the horse, and sang the Sinterklaas song, and this morning we had treats in our shoes!"

I still wasn't convinced, but she was so excited, I figured, What the heck? and put it in my mouth.

It was rubbery.

And bitter.

And *bleeeechhhh*.

"You don't like it?" Dot says, 'cause *bleeeechhhh* is written all over my face.

I look around for someplace to spit it out.

"Give it a second!" she says. "Really! It's delicious!"

But I can't take it another second. It doesn't just taste like something that's been inside a shoe, it tastes *like* a shoe! I hock it like a big black nasty loogie into a bush and wipe my lips on my sweatshirt sleeve. "You seriously *like* that?"

"Your teeth are black," she says, zooming in a little on my mouth.

"So are yours!" I tell her, inspecting hers, and we both hurry to the water fountain to swish our mouths out before class.

Then on Wednesday she comes up to me looking kinda sheepish and says, "Mom thinks you'll like these better."

I arch an eyebrow at the little paper-wrapped cube in her hand. "What is it?"

4

"Hopjes," she says. "It's coffee candy."

"*Black* coffee?" I ask, picturing my teeth turning all icky again.

"No, no. It's sweet. It's really delicious."

I just stare at it, 'cause coffee that's been in a shoe sounds about as appetizing as tar. "You said that last time."

But she forces it on me, and when I unwrap it, what I see does look edible.

It's caramel-colored.

Shiny.

Like a piece of real candy.

So I pop it in my mouth, and after a few seconds Dot says, "Well?"

My eyes bug out a little. "This is the best candy I've ever tasted!"

"Told you!" she squealed.

Then on Thursday she brought a package of what looked like little waffle cookies. "They're *stroopwafels*!" she said. "My favorite!"

They were also delicious, and since our friends Marissa and Billy and Holly were all there wanting to try them, they went fast.

"So, wait," Billy says. "You sing a song at night and in the morning you get cookies in your shoes? Do you have to be Dutch to do this?"

Dot grins at him. "You have to be good!"

He laughs. "Well, that eliminates me."

"And if you're *not* good, you don't just get a lump of coal. You get put in a sack and taken away by Sinterklaas's helpers!"

"Seriously? They kidnap you?"

"Uh-huh!" she says, and her eyes are all sparkly. "But if you *are* good, then on the last day, Sinterklaas comes and throws *pepernoten* through the roof and leaves presents at your door."

"Pepernoten?" Holly asks. "What are those?"

"Little spice cookies!"

I squint at her. "He throws cookies through the roof? How?"

Dot grins. "He just does! He's Sinterklaas! You look up and see them falling from the ceiling."

"Don't they break?" Holly asks. "Don't you get crumbs everywhere?"

Dot shakes her head. "They're little, and they're hard. They crash through the roof and scatter all over the house and the children race to pick them up. They're delicious!"

Marissa squints at her. "You eat them off the *floor?*"

Dot shrugs and smiles. Like, Yeah, that's what we do. Then she adds, "We keep it going because Anneke and Beppie are still little, and I'm glad—it's the most fun holiday ever!"

"Who's Anneke and Beppie?" Billy asks.

"My sisters."

"A double dose of mischief," I tell him, because last New Year's the rest of us spent the night at Dot's house and they were like a couple of nosy mice, spying on us everywhere we went.

"Wish I could be a fly on your wall," Holly says. "That's got to be wild."

"It is! Especially because Troy and Stan go into combat mode and try to raid my stash of *pepernoten*."

"Let me guess," Billy says. "Brothers?"

Dot nods. "They think they're so smart, but this year I've got a satchel ready and they're going to have to tackle me for them."

Marissa shakes her head. "So little hard cookies come through the roof, you guys collect them—"

"We dive for them!"

"—and put them in *satchels* so your brothers can't steal them—"

"Well, I steal theirs, too. And they steal them back!"

"—and after they've crashed through the roof, scattered all over the floor, and endured an epic battle between you and your brothers, you *eat* them."

Dot grins from ear to ear. "It's tradition!"

Billy laughs. "Can I get a skybox seat?"

The rest of us laugh, "Me too!" and then the warning bell rings so *we* all scatter off to class.

Then on Friday Dot comes racing up to us before school, all out of breath and rosy-cheeked. "Guess what?" she pants, but this time she doesn't have Dutch cookies or candy or little tabs of tar.

She's got an invitation.

"Mom says you guys can come over for Sinterklaas tonight!"

We all look at each other, and finally Billy says, "Really?"

Dot nods like crazy. "No skybox seats, though. You have to get in and be part of it. Wear heavy socks and come ready for battle." She gives a little grin and shrugs. "At least that's what Troy and Stan say. Mom says as long as you don't blow it for Anneke and Beppie, you're welcome to join us."

"Well, I'm in!" I cry, and Billy goes, "Me too!" and right away Holly and Marissa say they'll go, too.

"Invite Casey if you want," Dot says, looking at me. "The more boys we have to go up against Troy and Stan, the better."

If I had to choose one word to describe Dot DeVries, it would be *nice*. Of all the people in our group, she's the one who's the bubbliest and sweetest. Sometimes I feel like she gets left out because the things the rest of us get into are a little, uh . . . rough around the edges? But I actually think it's more that she has a big, tight family to do stuff with and the rest of us don't. I live with my grandmother in a seniors-only building—which is top-secret because it's illegal since I'm only thirteen. Holly lives in an apartment with two women—Vera and Meg—who rescued her from being homeless. Billy covers up his home life with jokes and stuff, but there's nothing funny about how afraid he is of his dad. And Casey, well, his family's a mess, and Marissa's is, too. Which boils down to the fact that all of us except Dot are either trying to patch a family together or in the middle of watching one fall apart.

So not only is it nice of Dot to invite us over to her family's Sinterklaas party, her thinking to include Casey is really . . . thoughtful.

"You guys are still together, aren't you?" she asks me, 'cause I'm just standing there staring at her.

I nod, then turn to Billy and say, "You think you could tell him?" because, to make a long story short, Casey's mother thinks I'm evil and has forbidden him to see me.

Billy and Casey are best friends and Billy's used to being our messenger service, so he says, "No problem-o!"

Dot swings off her backpack and produces copies of a map. "Here," she says. "It's been a while since you've been over, so I thought this might help. Mom says be there by seven."

"You're out in Sisquane?" Billy asks. And he's right—getting out to Sisquane actually *is* a problem. I don't have a bike, and Marissa's was run over by her father, and it's quite a ways to skateboard . . . especially at night. I look around at the others. "I bet Hudson will give us a ride."

"Good ol' Hudson," Marissa says, because even though Hudson Graham is seventy-three, he's so unbelievably cool that his house has become our headquarters.

"Brilliant!" Billy says. "Let's meet at the old chap's!"

Everyone laughs and agrees, and then off we go to class, excited for the day to be over so we can invade Dot's house, where cookies are said to fall through the ceiling.

TWO

Hudson Graham drives a 1960 Cadillac that he's named Jester. It's obviously ancient because nobody makes cars with pointy taillights, whitewall tires, and huge steering wheels anymore, but Hudson keeps it sparkling so it *looks* brand-new, and there's no missing it when he's cruising the streets of Santa Martina because it's *lavender*.

When Hudson drove it around front, Billy practically peed his pants. "Dude, that is awesome!" And before he can even finish bouncing up and down, he grabs Marissa's hand and calls, "We got shotgun!"

Now, Marissa and Billy aren't shy about being "together." But when it's the five of us, I don't like to make Holly feel awkward, so Casey and I just act, you know, *normal*. Which is sometimes hard because he's a freshman at Santa Martina High so I don't see him during school, and because of his mom and demented sister I'm not allowed to see him after. So it's not always easy to just be all hey-how's-it-going when I *do* get to see him.

Anyway, Marissa and Billy slide in front while Casey, Holly, and I pile in back, and then off we go to Sisquane.

Sisquane used to seem like the boondocks, but it's not

that far outside of Santa Martina, and it's been built up a lot recently, so people don't think of it as being shacks in the woods anymore. It even has a golf course and gated communities.

The DeVrieses don't live in any of the new developments, though. You pass right by those and keep on going until you find a bunch of mailboxes on a post and a dirt road that has a crooked sign that says MEADOW LANE.

"It's down that way," I tell Hudson when I spot the sign. "But we can walk from here."

He turns onto Meadow Lane anyway, but stops. Besides the big potholes ahead of us, the road is kinda overgrown with weeds, and scraggly bushes on both sides are sort of choking it off. Plus, about thirty feet away there's a big branch sticking out across the road like one of those safety gates at a railroad crossing.

Hudson looks over his shoulder at me. "Are you sure?"

"It's not far," I tell him, and we all scoot out.

"Wow! This *is* the boonies!" Billy cries like he's just arrived at Disneyland.

Hudson rolls down his window. "You're sure you have a ride home?"

I nod. "Dot's dad. Don't worry. We're fine."

"You want me to keep the lights shining?"

I look back at him and smile, 'cause usually he treats us like we're mature and responsible and smart, but right now he looks like he's setting loose a litter of kittens.

"We're fine, Hudson. Really. It's right around the bend."

So we all wave and holler, "Thanks!" and he drives away. And then it's dark.

Dark dark.

And as we move past the big branch sticking across Meadow Lane, we start hearing noises.

Like rustling.

And crunching.

And hooting, and whooshing, and *croaking*.

"I feel like I'm in the *jungle*," Marissa whispers as she clings to Billy.

"I don't remember it being this overgrown," Holly says, pushing a sprig of a bush aside. And even in the dark I can see that her eyes are cranked wide and roaming around all over the place.

"I'm pretty sure it's just a little ways around this bend," I tell them, but right then there's a huge crashing, crunching, mega-rustling sound in the undergrowth to our right.

"Ohmygod!" Marissa squeals, and actually jumps into Billy's arms.

Holly jumps back, too, but before I can grab onto Casey, a flying *haystack* knocks me flat.

The haystack's got paws.

Big furry ones.

And a big, hot, slobbery tongue.

One that's soaking my face!

"Aaaah!" I cry, pushing back.

"Nibbles!" Dot shouts from somewhere in the dark.

"He's right here!" I shout back.

"That's a *dog*?" Billy asks, and then cries, "The Abominable Furball!"

Dot appears with a flashlight and yanks Nibbles off of

me. "I'm so sorry!" she says. "He chewed through his rope. He's had to be out all day because"—she glances over her shoulder and drops her voice—"we've been cleaning floors." She drags Nibbles along and says, "I guess I'll put him in the basement until after Sinterklaas comes."

So she goes around the side of the house and locks the Abominable Furball away, and races back to the porch, where we're waiting for her.

"Shoes off today," she tells us as she kicks out of her clogs. So we all get down to stocking feet, and then we step inside.

Now, Casey had never actually been inside Dot's house before, and since this was Billy's first time anywhere near it, neither was prepared for the Land of Blue. At first their eyes just go a little buggy, but when we enter the kitchen, Billy cuts loose with, "Whoa!"

It was actually very polite, considering. I mean, knowing Billy, he might have said something like, Blind me with blue, why don'tcha! because the wallpaper, the counters, the linoleum floor, the dishes and pots and pans . . . *everything* is just bursting with blue.

"Dad says it's a cross between the sky and the deep blue sea," Dot explains, then laughs. "And who doesn't like the sky and the deep blue sea?"

I almost say, Well, if you're *drowning* . . . , but for once I keep my big mouth shut.

Mrs. DeVries' head pops in through a doorway, and she whispers, "Are we ready?"

Dot hands us each a paper lunch sack. "Everyone's here!"

Mrs. DeVries smiles at the rest of us. "If it gets too wild for you, just step aside, *ja*?"

We all nod, and I can tell Billy's about to make some crack and *ja* back, so I jab him in the ribs with an elbow.

"What?" he says, pulling a stupid puppy dog face.

"Don't even," I tell him through my teeth.

"Don't even what?"

"I know you, Billy."

He gives me his impish grin. "*Ja!* You do!"

I elbow him again even though Mrs. DeVries is gone, and just as I do, a really loud cracking sound thunders through the house.

"Holy smokes!" I cry, and Dot squeals, "Anneke! Beppie! Sinterklaas is here!"

We look at each other all bug-eyed, then scramble out of the kitchen and into a wide hallway by the family room, where Anneke and Beppie are already scurrying around, snatching *pepernoten* off the floor.

Suddenly there's another loud cracking sound, and this time I look up and actually *see* the cookies crash through the ceiling.

"Holy smokes!" I say again as they bounce all over the hardwood floor like some kind of weird cookie hailstorm.

Stan and Troy appear out of nowhere and slide toward us like they're scoring a run in baseball, crying, "Out of the way!" and "They're mine!"

"Troy! Stan! This is Billy and Casey!" Dot calls as her brothers snatch cookies off the floor and drop them in cloth bags strapped tight across their chests.

They stop for a second, look at Billy and Casey, and cry, "This is no place for sissies!" then get back to snatching cookies off the floor.

Well, I guess there's no quicker way to lure boys into battle than to call them sissies, because just like that, Casey and Billy are down on the floor tumbling and tackling and diving for cookies.

CRACK! Another batch of cookies pelts us from above.

"Good grief!" Marissa squeals, covering her head with her arm. "They're little rocks!"

Now, they weren't exactly *rocks,* but they sure weren't soft-batch cookies, either. They were little tan ovals, about half an inch across, and when I bit down on one, I discovered it was hard, but not in a crunchy way. More in a really *solid* way.

I also discovered that it was . . . *good.*

Like a dense little spice cookie.

"I can't believe you just *ate* that!" Marissa hisses. "They look like reindeer plops!"

CRACK! A new batch bursts through the ceiling, and this time I dive after them. "Sinterklaas doesn't use reindeer. He rides a horse! And if you don't watch it, his helpers will stick you in the sack!"

Holly's already on the move, and she and I start slip-sliding across the floor, grabbing at cookies like crazy. Then—*CRACK*—another batch pounds us from above.

Holly laughs, "This is wild!" and dives after the scattering cookies while—*CRACK*—another batch nails us.

"I love this!" I call over to Dot.

"*Ja,* me too!" Billy shouts.

Now, while they're all scampering around, I take a minute to watch the ceiling. I mean, I know cookies can't come through the ceiling.

It's impossible!

Holly notices me watching and starts doing the same. "How *do* they do it?" she whispers.

We wait and wait and wait, but nothing happens.

And the instant we look away—*CRACK*—another batch bombards us.

So we give up trying to figure it out and just dart around collecting cookies. And after we've all had the chance to build up a bit of a stash, I notice Stan and Troy eyeing Casey's and Billy's paper sacks.

Dot sees it, too. "Billy! Casey! Watch out!" she calls, but her brothers are already all over them, trying to wrestle their sacks away.

"Bombs away! Pghhhh!" Anneke cries, piling on top of Stan.

"I'm king of the mountain!" Beppie squeals, climbing on top of Troy.

"You're a girl!" Anneke yells at her sister. "You can't be king!"

"Okay, I'm *queen* of the mountain!" Beppie shouts back, and starts bouncing on top of her brother.

"Uncle!" Billy chokes out from somewhere at the bottom of the pileup.

CRACK! The room thunders with more cookies, which makes everyone abandon the pileup and scurry after *pepernoten.*

CRACK! Another batch scatters all around us.

16

And that's when the actual combat warfare begins.

Stan throws a handful of cookies at Billy.

Billy throws a handful back.

Pretty soon all four boys plus Holly and me are running and sliding around the house, hurling cookies at each other, trying to raid each other's stashes, laughing our heads off while cookies keep crashing through the ceiling.

"You guys are crazy!" Marissa shouts from the sidelines, and, really, there's no other way to describe it.

Well, this goes on for another fifteen minutes, and finally I'm just wiped out. So I sit down on the floor and try to catch my breath, and pretty soon everyone else is doing the same thing. "Truce?" Casey asks Stan.

"No way, dude. I'm getting your stash."

But then, *BAM-BAM-BAM-BAM-BAM,* someone's pounding on the front door.

"Sinterklaas!" Anneke squeals, and right away Stan and Troy jump up, then do a fakey stumble and fall, blocking Anneke and Beppie from reaching the door.

"Out of the way!" Anneke cries, and Beppie squeals, "I want to see him! I want to see him! Hurry! Before he flies away!"

"What's he doing at the door?" I ask Dot. "Isn't he on the roof?"

"He leaves gifts on the doorstep when he's done with the cookies." She looks around, and when she spots her mom giving her a thumbs-up from across the house, she grabs her sisters' hands, steps over her brothers, and says, "Out of the way, boys! We want to see Sinterklaas!" She nods us over. "Come on!"

So we all gather by the door, but when Dot swings it open, I don't see any presents.

All I see is a very strange-looking man.

And I may not be Dutch, but right away I know—
It's definitely not Sinterklaas.

THREE

The man on the porch *does* have long hair like Dot described Sinterklaas, but it's black, not white. And he *is* wearing red and gold like Sinterklaas, but I'm pretty sure *what* he's wearing is not something Sinterklaas would be caught dead in.

It's *spandex*.

Or, you know, some other stretchy, Morphsuit-ish fabric.

And over his stretchy-looking red-and-gold bodysuit, he's wearing tall black boots that have buckles everywhere, red knee and arm pads, and a gold chest plate that looks like a cross between a hot-rod grille and a catcher's chest protector. And in the middle of the chest plate there's a big red *J* with a black lightning bolt behind it.

Topping all that off are heavy gold gloves, a Roman centurion helmet, and a black mask across his eyes. And around his waist is a *utility* belt.

You know—like Batman wears?

Only instead of high-tech Bat-gadgets in his utility belt, this weirdo's got a hammer, a flashlight, and a slingshot.

I almost say, Hey, Halloween was over a month ago! But even though he'd need to do some serious lifting to be mistaken for a real superhero, from the way he's standing and from the jut of his jaw, I'm getting the feeling that he actually *believes* he's a superhero.

What's messing with his stance, though, is that he's carrying a peacock.

A peacock that's squirming and squawking and trying to peck his arm off.

"I don't think that's Sinterklaas," Beppie says in a scared little voice as she hides behind Dot.

Without a word, Anneke hides behind Dot, too.

"Who *are* you?" Stan asks, stepping forward.

"Why, I'm Justice Jack!" the weirdo says in a big, booming voice. Then he cocks his helmeted head backward and says, "And that's my assistant, the King of Clubs."

We look past him, and there on the path in front of the house is an old dirt bike.

With a sidecar.

And a red pennant flag with a big gold *J* in the middle of it.

And sitting in the sidecar is another guy wearing a mask, who shakes a wooden club in the air and calls, "Greetings, citizens!"

Troy's face screws up sideways. "Justice Jack and the King of Clubs?"

"At your service, young sir!" Justice Jack says, holding out the peacock. "We'll get back to work rounding up the rest of your brood."

"What are you *talking* about?" Troy asks, not taking the bird.

"Yeah," Stan says, stepping forward. "And why are you trying to give us a peacock?"

Surprise seems to pop right through Justice Jack's mask. "We've got the wrong place?"

"Apparently!" Troy says, rolling his eyes.

"Clubs!" Justice Jack calls over his shoulder. "We've got the wrong place!"

Suddenly Mr. DeVries is there, working his way through us to the open doorway. "Hey, vat is this?"

"Our apologies, sir!" Justice Jack says. "We're trying to do a civic good deed! Someone in this vicinity had their borders violated by an evildoer! We are simply trying to restore order to your fair community!"

Mr. DeVries squints at him. *"Vat?"*

From the sidecar, ol' Clubs calls out, "Someone cut open a fence and let a bunch of prize peacocks out. We thought this was the place, but we don't got a GPS in this thing and we musta took a wrong turn."

Mr. DeVries steps out onto the porch and points toward Meadow Lane. "Try up the road, *ja*? Go out, turn left to the main road, then left again, and a quick right onto Shady Lane, *ja*?"

"Shady Lane?" the weirdo asks.

"*Ja*—it's a little road like this one here. You'll see a red barn, *ja*? Can't miss it. That's the Stamos place. They have peacocks."

"Thank you, good sir!" Justice Jack says, then cries, "To the High Roller!" and charges off the porch. But as he passes the peacock to the King of Clubs and roars away on his dirt bike, me and my friends are all looking at each other with bug eyes, going, "The *Stamos* place?" because there's a girl we go to school with named Sasha Stamos who's . . . well . . . *different*. And even though we knew she lived in a farmhouse in Sisquane with six brothers and twelve cats, all of a sudden knowing exactly where felt kinda . . . weird.

Almost creepy.

Then Beppie whimpers, "Daddy? Was that Sinter-klaas?"

"Nay, *schatje*," Mr. DeVries says, scooping her up in one arm and Anneke in the other. "That was Justice Jack."

Now, the way he says this is all matter-of-fact and cheer-ful. Like a weirdo running around in red-and-gold spandex carrying a peacock is a perfectly reasonable thing to find at your door, and Justice Jack is a perfectly normal name for someone to have.

Then I remember—I'm in the Land of Blue, where treats appear in shoes, cookies come through the roof, and a man in red robes riding a white horse is expected to leave presents at the door.

Mr. DeVries' eyes pop wide as he looks across the porch. "Vat is this?" he says, and suddenly Anneke and Beppie have forgotten all about Justice Jack and are squirming out of his arms. "Presents!" they squeal, and before you know it, they're dragging a burlap sack inside.

Well, apparently Sinterklaas is a fan of books, because Dot and her brothers and sisters each get one.

They also each get scarves and mittens.

And it's a little awkward being in the middle of this family tradition, just sitting there while all the DeVries open presents, but then at the bottom of the sack Mrs. DeVries finds gifts for "the Honorary Dutch."

We all go, "Really?" and I don't know—there's something totally cool about getting tissue-wrapped gifts out of a burlap sack.

"I got *stroopwafels*!" I cry, and I really am stupidly happy about it.

"I got *hopjes*!" Holly says, and she seems pretty happy, too.

Billy and Casey get packages of windmill cookies, and Marissa gets some kind of almond paste cookies that none of us Honorary Dutch can pronounce.

And when the burlap sack's empty and everything's been unwrapped, Mrs. DeVries winks at her husband and says, "What do we say to Sinterklaas?"

All the DeVries kids—even Troy and Stan—look up at the ceiling and call, "*Dank u wel*, Sinterklaas!"

"You too," Mr. DeVries says, leveling a look at the rest of us.

So we do the best *"Dank u wel"* that we can—which in Billy's case sounds like "Donkey well!"—and before too long Dot stands up and says, "I better let Nibbles out of the basement."

"Good idea!" Mr. DeVries says. "Make sure you close

it up tight, *ja*? It's supposed to rain tomorrow." Then he adds, "Say, maybe your friends can help you take him for a walk, *ja*? He's been cooped up all day."

Mrs. DeVries nods. "Yes, please."

Well, we're all for that except for maybe Marissa. "Do you have flashlights?" she asks in a timid little voice. "It's really dark out there."

"*Ja*, sure!"

So before you know it, we've got Nibbles out of the basement and on a leash, and the six of us are going for a walk.

"Did you know Sasha lived so close?" I ask Dot as Nibbles drags her left down Meadow Lane.

Dot shakes her head. "Dad's the friendly neighbor, you know? He helps out everybody around here. He's never mentioned them before, but that's probably because I've never talked about Sasha at home." She laughs. "You guys, yes! Sasha, no."

Marissa moves in closer. "She was out all week, did you notice that?"

"I'm sure Lars did," Holly says with a snicker. "Those two are gross."

We all nod, 'cause Lars and Sasha like to sneak off behind the buildings around school and give each other splotchy purple necks.

"He's that tall guy?" Casey asks.

I nod. "The one with the whooshy hair."

Billy does an extreme hair whoosh, then says, "I'm so smart you be whooshin' you were me!"

We all laugh, and then Holly says, "What I hate is

that he acts like everyone else is dumb, but he's not even that smart."

Marissa nods. "Sasha is, though. That girl is scary smart."

We're all quiet a minute, and then Dot says, "Why would they raise *peacocks*?"

Holly shrugs. "Maybe they sell the feathers?"

We walk along a little more, and finally Casey asks what everyone else is thinking. "So is that where we're heading? To the peacock farm?"

"Let's do it!" Billy cries. "Maybe we can still catch Justice Jack!" Then he adds, "And maybe I can take down the King of Clubs and ride shotgun in the High Roller!"

Casey snorts. "And be what—the Billy Club?"

Billy leaps into the air. "Yeah! I'd be an awesome sidekick!"

Marissa rolls her eyes like, Oh, don't I know!

"So wait a minute," I say. "Are we walking up to Sasha's, or sneaking up?"

"Sneaking?" Dot says over her shoulder. "With this beast?"

I laugh. "Good point." Because the whole time we've been walking, Nibbles has been zigging and zagging, sniffing at the ground like a hound, dragging Dot along.

We're at the main road now, so we hang a left, then cross over when we see a signpost that's near a group of three mailboxes.

"This is Shady Lane," Marissa says, looking up at the sign. "Are we sure about this? Even the name sounds iffy."

The road is dirt and dark. It goes downhill, then

disappears off to the right, but there are six of us, two flashlights, and a *dog*, so what's to worry about?

"Stamos is at one-eleven," Casey says, shining a light on one of the mailboxes. "The others are two-fifty and three-fifteen, so theirs'll be the first property."

"Let's do it!" Billy says.

So off we go down Shady Lane.

FOUR

We've barely taken the first turn on Shady Lane when an eerie cry cuts through the darkness. *Errr-eeeeerw!*

"What's that?" Marissa gasps.

Then we hear it again, but from another direction.

Errr-eeeeerw!

And again from right behind us.

Errr-eeeeerw!

"That sounds like a cat caught in barbed wire," Billy says. "Here, kitty, kitty!"

Errr-eeeeerw!

"That's no cat!" Marissa squeals.

Errr-eeeeerw!

"We're surrounded!"

"By peacocks," Casey says, shining his flashlight on a big bird that's under an oak tree to our left. But this bird doesn't have long, gorgeous feathers and a blue neck like the one Justice Jack was carrying.

It's . . . brown.

"I think that's a pea*hen*," Holly says.

Now, instead of lunging toward it like you'd expect a dog to do, Nibbles hightails it behind Dot and buries his furry face in her legs. Then he just stands there quivering like a big ol' scaredy-cat haystack.

We spend a minute staring at the bird, and finally Dot says, "Do you think we should try to catch it?"

"Let's do it!" Billy says. "Peace offering to the Sasha-nator!"

"We need a peace offering?" Casey asks.

I eye him. "Wouldn't hurt."

So Billy takes off his jacket and hands it to me. "Go for it, Sammy-keyesta!"

"Me?"

"You don't want me to do it—I'll blow it."

"No, you won't!"

"Aw, just do it."

Casey offers to give it a try, but at this point I would have felt stupid letting him take over, so I creep up and blanket the bird with Billy's jacket.

"You did it!" Billy cries when I have the thing wrapped up and in my arms. "A good deed, indeed!"

"You sound like Justice Jack," I tell him as we head out again.

"Justice Jack is awesome!" Billy cries.

"Justice Jack is a nutcase," I mutter.

Now, it turns out that Dot's dad was right—there's no missing the Stamos place. But that's not because of the big red barn or the tall chain-link fencing or the line of large metal containers. It's because Justice Jack and his goofy dirt bike contraption are in the middle of the long dirt driveway surrounded by a swarm of men with nets.

Big nets.

On long wooden poles.

The men are obviously mad. Like, one wrong move and—*presto*—those nets'll become pitchforks. But what makes me go "Uh-oh" is the *policeman* standing next to a squad car parked near the dirt bike.

"Is that Officer Borsch?" Marissa asks.

I nod. "You'd think getting married would have given him a life."

Billy laughs. "He's too old to have a life, Sammy."

"Hey, when I'm his age, I plan to have a life!"

Casey gives me a smarty-pants grin. "We're here, too. Are you saying we don't have a life now?"

I blink at him, then march forward. "Let's just deliver the bird and find Sasha."

"Wait—now you *want* to find Sasha?" Marissa asks, chasing after me.

"Uh . . . I think I'll stay back here with Nibbles," Dot calls, and Holly decides to keep her company.

So Marissa, Billy, Casey, and I head toward the congregation, and when Officer Borsch sees us, he does a double take. "*Sammy?* What in the world are *you* doing here?"

"Uh . . . we caught one of the birds, and—"

Justice Jack leaps forward and his head whips back and forth between Officer Borsch and me. "Commissioner, did you say *Sammy?*"

You know those people who are gum chewers, and when they hear or see something shocking, the only way you know they're actually shocked is that they stop chewing? Their eyes don't bug, they don't jump back like, *Whoa*, they don't gasp or faint or even say, What?

They just stop chewing their gum.

Well, that's exactly what Officer Borsch is like, only he's not a gum chewer.

He's a tooth sucker.

So now instead of freezing mid-chew, he freezes mid-suck.

Which, let me tell you, is not a pretty sight. His left cheek is pinched up, his already squinty left eye is stuck in super-squint, half of his lip is arched up, and you can see a sliver—just a little sliver—of his coffee-stained teeth.

"Commissioner!" Justice Jack cries again. "Is this or is this not"—he turns his masked weirdness on me—"Sammy Keyes?"

I take a step back with my blanketed bird, and before I can stop my mouth from being stupid, it tells the truth. "Yeah, I'm Sammy, but—"

He turns to Officer Borsch, who's still frozen in mid-suck. "*This* is the person who's been giving evildoers a nonstop tour of Fist City? BAM! POW! ZAP!" he cries, punching his fists through the air. He looks at me again. "That's been *you*?"

"I didn't *hit* anyone," I tell him, taking another step back.

"But you black-eyed the Mob! Uncovered a meth lab! Busted up a dogfighting ring! Cuffed those counterfeiters! Brought down a blackmailer! Cemented a gangster in a wheelbarrow!"

"Stop it!" I cry, because even though I *had* done all those things, it's not like I'd done them in one *day*. And hearing him list them like that was really . . . embarrassing.

Then finally, *finally,* Officer Borsch snaps out of it and steps between us. "Who she is is none of your concern," he tells Justice Jack, then faces me and lowers his voice. "I didn't tell him any of this. He's got a police scanner and no life." He rolls his eyes. "Unless you call *that* having a life." Then he adds, "Probably a good idea for you to get out of here."

But Justice Jack has already moved around Officer Borsch. "All this time I thought you were a man!" he says to me. "Who'd expect Sammy to be a woman, let alone a *girl*? Not me! But it doesn't matter! You've inspired me, man! I mean ma'am! I mean miss! Justice Jack exists because of you!"

Well, this is all a little much. So I take *another* step back and go, "Uh . . . we're just here to return a bird?"

"Just like Justice Jack!" the nutcase cries. "See?" he calls to the army of Big Nets. "Crime fighters to your rescue!" He swoops in on me again and drops his voice. "I can't believe you don't wear hero gear—at least a mask! What if someone recognizes you? What if the evildoers of the world return for revenge? What if—"

"Here," I tell him, shoving the bird into his arms and snatching back Billy's jacket. "This is the only thing that's getting returned."

"A pea*hen*?" he exclaims, like I've just handed him a pot of gold. He turns to the Big Nets and cries, "Your supply problem is over!"

"We don't have a supply problem," one of the Big Nets growls. "We have an *escape* problem."

Suddenly Justice Jack snatches a buzzing cell phone

31

from the back of his tool belt. "A security breach on McEl-len!" he cries as he reads the text. Then he gasps, "Scoun-drels!" and turns to Officer Borsch. "Urgent situation at City Hall, Commissioner—some hooligans have made off with the statue!"

"What stat—" Officer Borsch squints at him. "The *soft-ball* statue?" Then he puts his hand up and says, "Never mind!" and you can tell there's no way Officer Borsch is going to get his news from a wannabe superhero.

Justice Jack seems to take no offense. He just re-holsters his phone, then forces a business card on me:

JUSTICE JACK
It's a Good World. Let's Take It Back!

It lists three different ways to reach him to report "crimes in motion that need to be stopped!"

"To the High Roller!" he cries, then charges to his tricked-out dirt bike, where his sidekick is sneaking swigs from a flask. "Farewell, citizens!" Justice Jack shouts as he fires up his rig and roars off with his flag flapping through the air.

"That dude is *awesome*," Billy squeals after he's gone. "I finally know what I want to be when I grow up!"

Marissa looks at him like he's a Nibbles nugget gooshed on the bottom of her shoe. "Are you *serious*?"

He gives her puppy dog eyes. "I'd let you be my sidekick . . . ?"

"This is not a joke!" one of the Big Nets calls. "Now, are you going to take a report, or what?"

"Please," Officer Borsch says to me, "take your friends and go," and I'm happy to do just that.

Now, the whole time we've been there, eerie peacock cries have been meowing through the air. And when we join up with Holly and Dot, Holly kind of shivers and says, "I would not want to live out here. Those cries are creepy!"

Casey nods. "Maybe that's why somebody cut them loose."

"Well, it sure didn't shut them up!"

"I'm glad we can finally go," Dot says, yanking hard on Nibbles' leash. "He's after something in those bushes, and I can't get him to quit."

"Couldn't be a bird," I tell her with a laugh.

She laughs, too. "Or a cat or a mouse or any other animal." She yanks hard, dragging Nibbles along. "The only thing he goes after is—"

She stops short, then turns to look at the bushes that Nibbles is trying to get to.

"Is what?" I ask her.

Slowly she turns to face me, and her eyes are huge.

"People."

FIVE

Casey shines a light at the bushes and takes a few steps toward them.

"No!" Marissa says, grabbing his sleeve. "For once, just once, can we go somewhere without *looking* in, or *hiding* in, or *falling* in bushes?"

"I'm just going to shine a light," Casey tells her. "It'd be pretty hard to fall in."

"No!" she says, pulling him back. "Someone will fall in. Someone always falls in!"

The rest of us stare at her.

"Why?" she squeals. "Why do *we* have to go investigate when Officer Borsch is right there!"

"What if it's just a lizard?" Casey asks. "You want the Borschman to investigate a lizard?"

"It is not just a lizard! It is never just a lizard! It's whoever cut the fence and let the peacocks out!"

Now, this whole time, Marissa's been talking in a fierce whisper. And while she's been yanking on Casey's sleeve, Nibbles has been yanking on his leash, trying to get to the bushes.

"I'm with Marissa," Dot whispers.

I look over my shoulder. "Officer Borsch has kinda got his hands full . . . ?"

Marissa starts storming toward the Big Nets. "Fine! If you won't tell him, I will!"

"No, wait!"

For a minute we all look at each other like, Hello? Who said that?

And then something comes *out* of the bushes.

It's a boy.

Tall.

Gangly.

And the first thing he does is whoosh his hair.

We all go, "Lars?" and he says, "Shhh!" and then tells Casey, "Turn off that light! They'll kill me if they find me here!"

So Casey clicks off the flashlight, and Nibbles finally gets his nose on Lars and sniffs him like crazy.

"So what are you doing here?" Holly asks. "And why'd you cut the fencing?"

"I didn't cut the fencing!" He looks at her like she's an idiot. "And what do you *think* I'm doing here? It's the only way I can see her!"

"Because . . . ?" I ask.

Now he looks at *me* like I'm an idiot. "Because her parents are making her be homeschooled again."

"They are?"

"Where have *you* been?"

Now, Sasha had said she thought our school was a big

waste of time, but I didn't think that was the reason she was suddenly back at home. "Maybe her parents are just trying to protect her from vampires?"

He stares at me. "What?"

Marissa eyes him. "Uh, your necks?"

Even in the darkness I can see him blush. "Look, can you just let me get out of here? I didn't cut the fence, Sasha did. But if they find me here, we're both dead!"

We girls all go, "*Sasha* did?" and Casey and Billy go, "Why?"

"Because I accidentally left the gate open when I met up with her, and the birds got out! And she knew her dad would go ballistic, so she cut the fence."

I shake my head. "That doesn't make any sense."

"It doesn't *have* to make sense to you, okay? *You're* not the one dealing with them! And I would have been out of here already, but by the time I got back to the road, her brothers were swarming the place with nets. Then the cops showed up. Then that *freak* showed up. Then *you* showed up. And then your stupid dog wouldn't quit sniffing!"

Holly snorts. "You're calling the *dog* stupid?"

Lars pinches his eyes closed. "Look. Can you *please* just let me leave? Things are hard enough on Sasha without them finding out I was here."

I shrug like, Who's stopping you? And Lars Teppler zips up the road and out of sight.

"I see what you mean about him," Casey says as we start hiking out of there.

Now, what I'm thinking is, Yeah, that was classic Lars.

But what pops out of my mouth is, "Actually, I feel kind of sorry for him."

Everybody looks at me. "What?"

"Well, first off, he fell for Sasha, which is scary enough right there. But now he's all sneaking around in the dark in the boonies because that's the only way he can see her." I look at Casey. "Sort of like having to meet up with someone in the graveyard."

Casey gives me a wry smile, and Billy goes all ghosty on us, saying, "A frighteningly similar situation!" because with Casey's psycho mom and sister determined to keep us apart, the graveyard's been our secret meeting place for the past month or so.

Still. This parallel between Casey and me and Sasha and Lars bugged me. I didn't *want* to feel sympathy for them. I'd rather think they were disgusting and hateable.

Because they are.

But I also hate having to sneak around with Casey. It doesn't make me feel clever or smart or superior. . . . I'd way rather have an aboveboard life where I'm *not* hiding things from other people. It would be so much more . . . carefree.

And on the drive back into town in Mr. DeVries' truck, it hit me what a ridiculously sneaky life I live. I mean, besides having to hide my relationship with Casey from his mom and sister, there's the whole business of living in a seniors-only building. I have to sneak up the fire escape, then sneak inside and make sure the coast is clear, then sneak down the hall to my apartment. And because it would be a huge mess if someone—say, the manager or a neighbor or the *police*—stopped by unexpectedly and I got caught living there, everything I own has to be hidden away.

So believe me—I don't own much.

And if someone *does* come by when I'm home, I've got to sneak into Grams' bedroom and hide in the closet. And every morning when I leave for school, I've got to sneak back *out* of the building and down the fire escape.

Plus, I've got the whole sneaky Mom Issue. The school thinks I'm living with my mom, so when something happens and they demand to see her, it's always this huge juggle of lies because she's nowhere near Santa Martina.

So yeah. My life is just sneaky, sneaky, sneaky. But what was churning my stomach on the drive home from Dot's wasn't just realizing how *good* I'd become at being sneaky, but also realizing that if I had to choose just one thing I hate about my mother—which, believe me, would be hard—it wouldn't be that she dumped me in a building full of old people so that she could go to Hollywood and become a soap star. And it wouldn't be that she decided she was in love with the only person on the planet I wouldn't want her to be in love with—Casey's dad.

It would be that she's sneaky.

Incredibly and successfully sneaky.

And I was so busy getting nauseous over the fact that the thing I hate most about her is the thing we have in common that I didn't even realize we'd pulled up to Holly's place.

"You okay?" Casey asks, because Holly lives in an apartment across the street from the Senior Highrise and

I'm supposed to get out, too, but I'm just sitting there, spaced.

"Huh? Oh, right! Sorry!" I give Casey a quick hug, thank Mr. DeVries for letting us invade his celebration, grab my *stroopwafels,* and scoot out. Then I wait until Mr. DeVries' truck is out of sight, because I can't risk more people knowing where I live, which in this case includes Mr. DeVries and Billy.

When the truck is gone, I say bye to Holly, then hurry across the street and slip into the shadows of a hedge on the Senior Highrise property. And after I'm sure that the coast is clear, I make my way up the fire escape to the fifth-floor landing.

The only person who's ever caught me sneaking in through the fire escape was our old neighbor Daisy Gray-bill. She was waiting for me in her dirty pink bathrobe, and when she saw the door inch open, she pounced and shrieked, "Ah-ha! I knew it! I knew it!" while she pointed a shaky finger at the bubble gum I'd crammed into the doorjamb to keep it from latching.

It was a close call, but I made up some excuse about taking the trash down for Grams, and since she couldn't exactly *prove* anything, I squeaked out of that one.

Barely.

Then she died and Mrs. Wedgewood moved in.

Mrs. Wedgewood.

Wow.

Imagine a tuskless walrus wearing a crooked wig and a muumuu and you'll have a pretty good picture of Mrs. Wedgewood.

And although pouncing may not be part of the Big W's repertoire, eavesdropping and blackmail sure are. Actually, what she does is more like *wall*dropping. The rest of her may be a wreck, but that woman has bionic hearing and isn't afraid to use it.

So my worries with the Wedgie Woman are usually because of what happens *inside* the apartment, not *outside,* but this time when I peek down the hallway, I see a congregation of at least a dozen old people right outside Mrs. Wedgewood's door.

Now, I *know* the building's full of old people, all right? But it's not like I ever see them. I mean, if *I* can see *them,* chances are *they* can see *me.* Besides, they mostly hole up in their apartments with their TVs blaring.

Well, unless it's Monte Carlo night down in the rec room.

Anyway, the *point* is, witnessing a whole *mob* of them outside of Mrs. Wedgewood's apartment—seeing all those walkers and canes, and hearing the clack of angry dentures— is surprising and kinda . . . *scary.* So I pull back quick and crouch down, then take a deep breath and wrap an eyeball around the corner to try to figure out what's going on.

Right away I notice two things: One, Mrs. Wedgewood is not in the crowd.

Believe me—there's no hiding the Big W.

And two, Grams is.

Now, my grams stands out because she looks like a teenager compared to most of the rest of the mob. For one thing, she bothers to get dressed in the morning. And I'm not talking some stretch pants and Velcro shoes—I'm talking a skirt, nylons, *pumps*. . . . Grams is a very classy dresser.

But she's also the only person in the group who's trying to calm things down. "Give him a chance," she's telling the clacking mob. "He said he'd be right out."

"I don't consider this to be right out!" one old lady snaps at her.

"I tell you, she's skipped town!" another one says.

"How much did you *give* her?" Grams asks.

"Enough!" the first old lady huffs, and then the other one says, "She said she could double my money, maybe triple it!"

"So you just *gave* it to her?" Grams asks.

"I live in this dump, don't I? What have I got to lose?"

Grams blinks at her. "The money you gave her?"

"Stop it, Rita," an old guy barks. "You're not making us feel any better." He bangs on the door with the handle of his cane and shouts, "Garnucci! Get out here! We want to know what's going on!"

Mr. Garnucci is the building manager, so whatever's going on, they've called in the building's only big gun to solve it. And obviously they're not happy with how long he's taking, because they *all* start banging, either on the door with their canes or on the wall with their walkers and fists.

And it *is* scary.

It's like the Attack of the Osteo Army!

And just as I'm thinking that there's no way I ever want an angry mob of old people after *me,* Mr. Garnucci opens the door.

"Calm down, all of you!" he barks at them.

"Maybe if you'd tell us what you found, we would!" an old guy barks back.

Mr. Garnucci steps out and locks Mrs. Wedgewood's door. "Well, it does *not* look like she's skipped town."

Now, I'm thinking, Skipped? *Skipped?* Who would ever use that word to describe Rose Wedgewood? Maybe she *lumbered* out of town, or *quaked* out of town, but . . . *skipped?*

And then one of the old ladies warbles, "All you need to skip town is money!"

"Yeah!" another one cries. "And she took plenty of that from us!"

Mr. Garnucci looks around at the crowd. "You people are all supposed to be broke! How much did you *give* her?"

There's a moment of complete silence, because what Mr. Garnucci said is true—only people who qualify financially are allowed to live in the Senior Highrise. But then they all start talking at once. "She took everything in my mattress!" "I pinched pennies for years!" "She told me not to tell anyone else!" "She said it was a once-in-a-lifetime tip!" "Yeah! She musta figured we don't have that much lifetime left!"

Mr. Garnucci puts up both hands. "Did you get receipts?"

The Prune-Faced Posse goes quiet again.

Mr. G shakes his head. "Well. She's not in there dead. Her things all look in order. And since you don't even know how long she's been gone, what do you expect me to do? She coulda gone across town for a burger!"

"More like the whole cow!" someone yells.

"Not nice, Mrs. Orren," Mr. G scolds.

"But true!" she snaps.

"The point is, you don't know where she is. Maybe she's gone to a movie! Maybe—"

"Maybe she's skipped town!"

Mr. Garnucci heaves a sigh. "The police are not going to do anything if this is all you've got."

"So that's it?" someone demands. "You're not going to do *anything*?"

Before Mr. Garnucci's even done shaking his head, a woman with her hair in a salt-and-pepper bun on the very top of her head steps forward and huffs, "Well, *I* know someone who will help us."

The Polident Patrol turns to face her. "You do?"

"He's a fine young man," Bun-Top says as she opens her purse with shaky hands and produces a business card. She holds it out for the others to see, and one of the old ladies cries, "With a name like that, you know he'll help us!"

"What's his name?" Mr. Garnucci asks.

The mob turns to face him like they're ready to take on the world.

"Justice Jack!"

SIX

When the hallway was finally completely clear, I slipped into our apartment with my *stroopwafels* and whispered, "Sounds like the Wedgie's got a big scam going."

"You heard all of that?"

I nod. "Did *you* give her any money?"

"Heavens no! Although she certainly tried to persuade me. She claimed to have a top-secret tip that could make me rich."

"What kind of tip?"

"She was very mysterious about it, but she acted like handing her a bunch of money would be doing *me* a big favor. She even tried some baloney about you needing a college fund. A college fund! As if she cares."

For an itsy-bitsy fraction of a second, I get the very strange urge to hug Mrs. Wedgewood. I mean, the counselors at school really talk up college, but my own mother has sure never mentioned it, and I'd bet my high-tops she's never even *thought* of starting a fund.

But then I remind myself that Mrs. Wedgewood is a sweet-talking blackmailer and that Grams is right—what does she care?

Grams gives one of her classic *hrmph*s. "I can't believe any of them lent her even a dime."

"So do you think she left town?"

"Where would she go? People live here because they have no place else to go."

"What about all the money they gave her?"

"How much could it be? Not enough to live on for any length of time, that's for sure."

"So where do you think she is?"

Grams shakes her head. "I have no idea, and frankly, I don't care."

I actually believed her, but the next morning I woke up to the sound of her making a phone call in the kitchen. She was trying to sneak it, but since the apartment's about as big as a cracker box and I sleep on the couch, I heard anyway.

"Who are you calling at seven-thirty in the morning?" I groaned, moving my cat Dorito off the top of my head, where he's been sleeping lately.

She turned her back quick to hide the wall phone—like somehow that would change what she was doing.

"Grams, it's Saturday! Whoever it is is going to hate you!" And then it hits me. "You're calling the Wedge?"

"Shhhh!" she says, turning to face me.

"She can't hear me, Grams. She's not home."

Grams hangs up the phone. "So where is she, then?"

I laugh and flop back down. "I thought you didn't care."

"But it's raining cats and dogs outside!"

"It is?"

"Yes! And I just cannot picture her managing in this weather."

"What's to manage if you're holed up in a cushy hotel with room service?" Then I add, "Besides, whales love water."

"Samantha! Be nice!"

I sit up a little. "Why do I have to be nice when she blackmails me into doing her chores and errands?"

Grams frowns, but what can she say, really? I'm right.

Anyway, around nine o'clock the Prune Patrol started calling *us*. And Grams had a little chat-fest with people I'd never even heard of, saying stuff like, "No, Teri, I'm sorry. There's no sign of her yet." "No, Eunice, no sign. . . . Sure, I'll let you know." "No, Gwenith, there hasn't been a peep, but I'll call you if she comes home." Every fifteen minutes the phone would ring, which seemed to electrify Grams but annoyed the heck out of me.

"Can't you set up a phone tree or something?" I finally asked.

"A phone tree?"

"You know, where you call two people with any news and then *they* call two people, and pretty soon everyone's got the message?"

"That sounds so complicated. Who would set it up? And someone would surely drop the ball."

So the phone kept ringing and Grams kept promising and I kept being annoyed.

And then Marissa called.

"It's for you," Grams says, sort of taken aback.

Right away I can tell Marissa's desperate about something. "Can you meet me at the mall?" she asks in a sort of panic-whisper.

"What's wrong?"

"It's complicated."

"Your parents?" I ask, because her family's been in crisis mode for months now.

"No," she whimpers.

"Then what?"

There's a pause where I can tell she's holding her breath, and finally she blurts out, "Danny called."

Every cell in my body stops moving. There's no oxygen being turned into CO_2. There's no transfer of ions across cell walls. There's no beating or breathing or blinking. I can't even gasp.

See, Danny Urbanski is a smooth-talking liar and Marissa had had a crush on him for *years*. But when he was arrested for being a bona fide criminal, I was sure she was finally over him. Plus, Billy had stepped into the picture and she seemed to be happy with him.

"Please, Sammy?" she begs, and her voice is just a squeak. "I know it's raining, but is there *any* way you can get to the mall?"

She's obviously desperate, so I tell her I will. But when I get off the phone, Grams is horrified. "You're going out in this weather?"

"I have to, Grams. She's a wreck." I head for her closet to borrow a jacket. "I'll be fine."

"You'll take my umbrella is what you'll do," she says, and I can tell that her granny foot has just come down.

I pull it out of the closet. "Fine." And even though it's

huge and black and ugly, when you whoosh it up, it becomes the Awesome Dome of Dryness, which is nice when it's raining cats and dogs.

Or even cats and mice.

Anyway, I'm all set and ready to go, only when I peek out the front door to make sure the coast is clear, what do I see?

Two old ladies trying to break into the Wedge's apartment.

One's wearing a thick black sweater and has a nose as big as a beak, and while she's prying at the doorframe with a long, fat screwdriver, the other one—who's got hair so white it looks blue—is wiggling a credit card into the gap beside the lock.

I ease the door closed and whisper over to Grams, "You're gonna want to see this."

Grams takes one look and marches right over to Mrs. Wedgewood's, going, "Sally! Fran! What are you doing?"

Now, Grams left our door wide open, and since I don't want to risk one of the hobbling housebreakers noticing me close it, the first thing I do is grab Dorito and lock him in the bathroom so he can't escape. Then I hurry back to the front door, and even though I *can* peek out, it's kind of a dangerous thing to do. Especially standing up. It's like if someone sees an eyeball at eye level, they know it's a person.

But if there's an eyeball down near the ground, they either don't notice it or they think it must have been a dog or a cat or something. And, really, I can't stand not knowing what's going on. I mean, come on—there's two old biddies out there breaking and entering!

So I get down and sort of crocodile my way to the door, and when I peek around the corner, there's Grams wrestling the screwdriver away. "Stop it, Sally! You cannot just break into someone's apartment!"

"This is none of your concern!" Screwdriver Sally snaps.

"That's right, Rita," the one with blue hair says as she jiggles the credit card. "We just want what's ours."

"What makes you think it's in there? I thought you said she skipped town!"

"Then we want something of equal value," Screwdriver Sally tells her.

Grams stops wrestling. "So you're going to *steal* from her?"

Blue gives a calm little hunched-back shrug. "She stole from us, didn't she?" She wiggles the card some more, then stops and looks over at Grams. "I have no idea how to do this. Do you?"

Grams shakes her head.

"They make it look so easy in the movies."

Sally says, "Come on, Fran. Let's go. I have a better idea."

"What's your better idea?" Grams asks as they start down the hallway.

"None of your beeswax, Rita. We don't need you tattling!"

I scoot back quick, and after they hobble by, Grams comes in and closes the door. "Could you hear all that?"

I nod. "They're nuts. And I know this is big excitement around here, but I really need to get to Marissa. Can you check and make sure they're gone?"

So she does, and when her head pops back inside, she says, "Better make it quick!"

I start to, but then I remember. "Dorito's locked in the bathroom!"

She scoots me along. "I'll let him out. Now hurry!"

So I zip down the hall and out to the fire escape before some angry old bird comes after me with a screwdriver.

Marissa was waiting for me by the tower clock in the middle of the escalators. We used to meet at the arcade, but her gaming habit got annihilated by her dad's gambling habit, and since she's now always broke just like me, our new go-to area is the clock. It's actually a cool place to hang out because on one side you can watch people go up the escalator, and on the other you can watch them come down. And if you look up in any direction, there's a whole circle of railing where you can see people hanging out or walking by on the second level. It's a prime people-watching spot.

Anyway, on my splish-splashy walk over to the mall, I'd told myself that I needed to be a good friend and *listen* to Marissa even though the thought of her slipping back under Danny's spell made me want to slap her silly. I mean, if you take the evil of Heather Acosta, dip it in Teflon, and wrap it in a dazzling smile, you'd pretty much have Danny Urbanski. I was sure Danny had done a righteous job of gouging the Teflon for good, but when I got to the mall and saw the look on Marissa's face, I knew it hadn't, uh, *stuck*.

I sat down next to her. "Talk to me."

"Don't you love how they decorate the mall for Christmas?" she says, looking around at all the tinsel and lights and holly wreaths. "And the music. I love Christmas music."

I fasten the band around Grams' dripping umbrella. "You better not have made me come out here in the pouring rain to talk about Christmas decorations."

She heaves a sigh. "Danny called this morning."

"And . . . ?"

She gives me a look somewhere between fear and hope. "I was suspicious at first, but, Sammy, he's changed!"

I bite back a *Sure he has*, 'cause there's nothing new about Danny Urbanski totally snowing Marissa. "Okaaaaay . . . how has he changed?"

"He's humble and remorseful, and . . . and . . . Sammy, he was *crying*."

I mutter, "Alligator tears, maybe."

"No! He was really sincere!"

And that was the end of me trying to listen. "Humble, remorseful, and sincere? Those are big words for a little liar with a long history of *working* you."

"I knew you'd be mad, but, Sammy, people *do* change. He's been going to counseling and to church. He says he hates the person he used to be."

We sit there, quiet, for what seems like a week. And finally I take a deep breath and go, "So, what does this mean?"

"I don't know," she whimpers.

"Well, what does he *want*?"

She pulls a squinty little face. "For me to give him another chance?"

Now, it's not like Danny was ever Marissa's boyfriend. He was just her über-crush. He knew it, too, and would string her along by being all charming and flirty and sunny while behind her back he was sucking face in dark corners with Heather Acosta.

"We're talking as a friend?" I ask her.

She pulls another squinty face. "I think as more than that."

"You think."

"Sammy, it was one conversation. He wanted me to forgive him. But he said how much he liked me and missed having me in his life."

"But he didn't come out and say he wanted to go out?"

"He *implied* it. And he invited me to meet him at church tomorrow."

"So, what did you say?"

"That I had to think about it."

I cover my face with my hands and lean my head back. "What about Billy?"

"I know," she whimpers. "I know."

I drop my hands and give her an angry look.

"I know," she says again. "I *know*." Then she adds, "And I *do* like Billy, and he *is* fun, but, Sammy, he acts so . . . immature."

I look her in the eye. "Billy is the same Billy he was when I warned you not to break his heart."

"I know," she whimpers again.

She's acting totally pitiful and ashamed and sorry, but still—I can tell that nothing I say will stop her from giving Danny another chance.

And I'm just about to tell her that for a person who's so good at school and good at sports, she sure is bad at boys, when someone on the level above shouts, "Stop, you scoundrel!"

Even without looking up, I know exactly who it is.

SEVEN

"It's Justice Jack!" Marissa gasps, looking up.

"You won't get away with this!" he bellows from above us. "I will hunt you down like the cutpurse you are!"

Apparently, Justice Jack doesn't have a grappling hook or a lasso on his utility belt, because the guy running away from him is already halfway down the escalator and Justice Jack is just hollering over the railing at him.

And maybe a real superhero could vault the railing and land like a cat on the moving steps, but this is Justice Jack— a guy in a mask and motorcycle boots.

"Look!" Marissa cries, pointing to the man charging down the escalator. "He *does* have a woman's purse!" She looks around. "Someone has to stop him!"

Now, it's pretty obvious that that someone isn't going to be Justice Jack. And it sure doesn't look like it's going to be any of the people the purse snatcher is shoving past. Or any of the people who are just standing around staring. And since the purse snatcher is wearing shades and a sweatshirt with the hood up, it's not like anyone's going to be able to ID him later, either.

So Marissa's right—someone's got to stop him. But when I get up, Marissa pulls me back. "I didn't mean you! Why *you*?"

I grip Grams' umbrella. "Because I've got *this*." Then I charge forward.

It's actually only been a few seconds from the time Justice Jack first shouted, but the purse snatcher has been *flying* down the escalator and he manages to get off before I can reach it. So since I can't block him with the umbrella like I was planning, or jab him in the stomach with the big, fat point, I lunge after him with the crook of the umbrella handle.

What's funny is, the umbrella seems to know exactly what to do. It loops around the guy's ankle, and before you can say, Holy flying felons, Batman! he's splat-flat on the ground and the purse is skidding across the floor.

Behind me I can hear motorcycle boots pounding down the escalator, and in no time Justice Jack is towering over the purse snatcher with one boot on his back.

"Nice work, citizen!" he booms so the whole mall can hear, then says to me through his teeth, "I can't believe you don't wear a mask! Aren't you worried people will come after you?"

I unhook the umbrella and tell *him* through *my* teeth, "I'd feel like a dork in a mask!"

His eyes go all mushy and hurt.

"Look, *I'm* not a superhero. I don't need a mask!"

Now his chest totally puffs up, and he stretches a gloved hand into the air with his finger pointed. "Villains, I give you fair warning!" he announces. "Justice Jack is fighting back!"

In the movies this would probably have gotten big cheers and a round of applause, but in the Santa Martina mall?

There was one handclap.

One.

And then the purse snatcher starts squirming.

"Down, you despicable thief!" Jack bellows at him. "Unless you want a tour of Stomp City!"

Over by the big glass entry doors, I notice a man and a woman in uniform hustling into the mall. It's sort of my survival policy to leave when cops arrive, so I start to, only then I see it's these two bumbling cops Marissa and I know all too well. So instead of just leaving, I *hightail* it back to Marissa. "Let's get out of here!"

"Is that Squeaky and the Chick?"

"Yes!"

Now, the fastest, easiest way for us to escape is to go up the escalator. So while Justice Jack bellows, "At your service, fair citizen!" to a lady in a fuzzy orange scarf who's retrieving the purse, we hurry up the steps.

"I feel like I'm in a really bad cartoon," Marissa whispers, glancing back at what's going on below. She chases after me as I hurry down the main corridor. "So where do you want to go?" Then she adds, "I'm sorry I dragged you out here in the rain. I'm sorry about everything!"

And just like that, it all comes back about Billy. "I don't know," I tell her, and, really, all of a sudden I want to get away from her as much as I want to escape being interrogated by Squeaky and the Chick.

Marissa hustles to keep up. "You hate me, don't you?" she says, all dejected-like.

"I don't *hate* you," I tell her. "But I am mad."

"I knew you would be," she says, and she's obviously feeling really sorry for herself.

"Come on, Marissa! Billy's a sweetheart! I know he's goofy, but I think he acts like that to cover up other stuff." I look at her. "Has he ever talked to you about his dad?"

She shakes her head.

"Have you ever *asked*?"

"I don't want to ask him about his dad!"

"Why not?"

"If I ask him about his dad, he could ask me about mine!" She drops her voice waaaay down. "And there's no way I want people to know my dad's got a gambling problem." She moves in closer. "Or that he's joined Gamblers Anonymous!"

"Gamblers Anonymous?"

She backs away. "See? Even you're shocked. And you knew he had a gambling problem!"

"I'm not *shocked*, but . . ." I look at her. "There's such a thing as Gamblers Anonymous?"

She snorts. "Of course there is. They've got Anonymouses for everything."

We walk along for a minute without really knowing where we're going, and finally I say, "So what *do* you and Billy talk about?"

"Sometimes school. Sometimes TV shows." She shakes her head. "But mostly he just acts silly. You know—trying too hard to make me laugh."

I think about this, then shake my head. "Wow."

"Well, what do you and Casey talk about?"

I laugh. "Mostly our problems! His mom and sister, my mom, his dad being *with* my mom . . . There's never a shortage of things to say." I look at her. "I actually think it's why we're so close."

Marissa looks down. "I feel terrible saying this, but I think I liked Billy more before we started going out."

"So why didn't you mention any of this before?"

"I don't know. I think hearing from Danny . . . it just made me realize what I *didn't* feel for Billy."

"So that's it?" I ask. "You're breaking up with Billy?"

Her face crinkles. "I have to, don't you think?"

Now, I've been walking really fast, so we're already about at the end of the corridor, which means we're either going to have to go inside the gaping entrance of a big department store or loop around and head down the other side of the mall.

Well, unless we do a sharp U-turn and go back the way we came, but that would feel really stupid.

And since I like department stores about as much as overcooked broccoli, I automatically start to loop around.

And that's when I spot the mall cop.

He's not strolling, let me tell you. He's waddling toward us as fast as he can, and he's looking all amped, talking sideways into the walkie-talkie on his shoulder like he's about to take down a serial shoplifter.

I nudge Marissa. "Mall cop, ten o'clock."

Marissa automatically looks ahead and a little to the left. "He's looking at *us*? How could he—" She turns to me. "The umbrella!"

The guy's definitely acting like a hound dog after squirrels. And even though we haven't done anything wrong, I sure don't feel like being cornered and caught—or even barked at. So I tell Marissa, "Follow me," and ditch it into the department store.

"Where are we going?" Marissa whispers.

Now, when you're thirteen and broke and living in a town like Santa Martina, you sometimes wind up snooping around places that maybe you shouldn't—like the crazy maze of hallways and stairs that happens to be behind the mall's Employees Only doors.

So knowing we could escape that way, I grabbed Marissa and zigzagged her through the men's department, over to appliances—where the refrigerators made for great cover—then past the photo studio, around the corner to the gift wrap counter, and straight for an Employees Only door.

"Not the roof!" Marissa whispers as we slip through.

I laugh because it's true—usually when I drag Marissa through an Employees Only door, we wind up on the roof. "Don't worry, I wouldn't go up there in the rain. Even with the Awesome Dome of Dryness."

"Then where?"

"*Out* of here!" I head down the corridor. "You know, *down*."

She chases after me. "Why are we even doing this? I hate acting guilty when I'm not!"

"Look, there's no way that mall cop is after us so he can pin a Good Samaritan medal on me. He probably wants to give me a mall-cop ticket for interfering with mall-cop business!"

"Aw, c'mon, Sammy. . . ."

"I'm serious! You saw the way he was coming at us!" I start down a set of cement steps. "Or what if that purse snatcher is saying he'll sue because he broke something when he went splat? And if the mall can't find me so he can sue me, he'll sue them for letting me get away!"

"What? Wait—could he really do that?"

"Hudson says people are sue-crazy. He says burglars will sue for getting hurt in the house they broke into."

"That's ridiculous!"

"Exactly! But Hudson says sometimes they *win*. Or they get the charges against them dropped because they're causing so much trouble."

"So you think that's why the mall cop's after you? Because a purse snatcher wants to sue you?"

"How should I know? But even if it's as simple as Squeaky and the Chick having an APB out for the girl with the umbrella because they want to get to the bottom of what happened, I do not want to deal with all their nosy questions. The first thing cops always want to know is your name and address."

"Oh, right. I forgot about that little problem. Sorry."

We're at the bottom of the steps now, and I take a left down another corridor. "Yeah, well, I can't afford to forget about it."

"Sammy, I'm sorry. I'm sorry about all of this. Making

you come to the mall in the rain, not listening to you when you warned me not to hurt Billy . . ."

I stop and turn to face her. "Look, it's not just hurting Billy. It's Danny hurting *you*. I don't trust him, and I don't want you to get sucked back into the Danny Vortex." I point the umbrella at her. "Are you going to meet him at church tomorrow?"

She pulls a face like she's worried I'll skewer her. "Yes?"

I start marching again. "Then I'm going with you."

EIGHT

Getting out of the mall's back-corridor maze reminded me a little of sneaking into the Highrise. A lot of zigging and zagging, and when we finally found a door, we were really careful to peek around it before making a move.

"Where is this?" Marissa asked, because the walkway outside went straight to a hedge, then turned left. And with the rain pouring down the way it was, we couldn't see much.

I opened the door a little wider, but I still couldn't figure out where we were. "I'm not sure. Do you want to stay here and wait for the rain to let up?"

"There's no way I want to get caught back here!"

"So where do you want to go?"

"Hudson's? The library?"

"The library's way closer."

Which was true. Once we found Cook Street, all we had to do was cross over and go half a block down McEllen. "Okay! The library it is."

So I whoosh open Grams' umbrella and Marissa puts up her little collapsible jobbie, and off we go, through the pounding rain.

62

"The library's over that way!" I call after we get out of the mini hedge maze. Then I notice that two of the metal arms of Marissa's umbrella are sticking out like small skewers. "That thing's a joke!" I tell her. "Get under here!"

So she ducks inside the Awesome Dome of Dryness and collapses her broken-armed umbrella. "Oh, thank you!"

"I can't believe you walked all the way from your house with that thing!"

"It wasn't broken like this when I left. And it wasn't raining this hard! This is crazy!"

We hurry along a walkway to a little road that cuts between the mall and the parking structure. And we're getting near Cook Street when all of a sudden a cop car pulls up and cruises right beside us with its lights flashing.

"I cannot believe this!" I moan.

"Just talk to them!" Marissa says. "It's not like we can escape!"

But I keep right on walking because I don't *want* to talk to them. Besides, what kind of idiot tries to pull over pedestrians in the pouring rain? The whole thing is stupid! And what if I ignore them? Or ditch them? What are they going to do? Get out and cuff me?

But then the siren chirps, and even though it makes me jump and makes me *mad,* I know Marissa's right—there's really no escaping this.

So I stomp my foot and go, "Maaaaaan!" and turn to face the police car. And that's when I see that it's *not* Squeaky and the Chick.

It's Officer Borsch.

"I was afraid it was you!" he hollers through the open passenger window. "Get in!"

"We didn't do anything wrong!" I holler back at him.

The passenger door swings open. "Just get in!"

So we dive into the front seat, and after I've collapsed the umbrella and closed the door, he stares at the Dripping Dome of Dryness. "Where did you *get* that thing?"

"It's my grandmother's," I tell him.

"Ah," he says—like that explains everything.

He powers up the window, and then we just sit there with the wipers flapping back and forth while he looks straight ahead, not saying a word.

Marissa eyes me like, Now what? and I give her a shrug like, I have no clue!

"So," he finally says. "Where to?"

"Where to?"

"Where were you going?"

This kind of throws me because it's not at all like Officer Borsch. Usually, he jumps right in telling me what he wants me to do or where he wants me to go or how much trouble I'm in for what I've supposedly done. So at first I just blink at him, but finally I blurt out, "We were on our way to the library."

"Ah," he says again, and looks straight ahead like he's driving.

Only he's not.

He just sits there.

Going nowhere.

Finally I say, "Walking would definitely be faster than this."

This seems to snap him out of his little body freeze. "I don't know how you did it," he mutters as we start moving, "but you sure gave them the slip."

I slouch a little. "Look, I didn't want to waste all afternoon answering nosy questions. Especially not from Squeaky and the Chick."

His eyebrows go flying. "Squeaky and the Chick?"

"They're idiots, Officer Borsch. I can't believe you let them on the force."

He sighs. "I had nothing to do with it." He eyes me. "They transferred from Reno."

"From *Reno*?"

"They came highly recommended." He frowns. "And now we're stuck with them."

I hesitate, then ask, "So you understand why we ditched them, right?"

"No comment. I'm more concerned about you teaming up with that madman."

"With Justice Jack?" I ask.

"*Please* don't call him that. It just feeds into his whole superhero fantasy."

"Well . . . what do *you* call him?"

"Besides the Masked Moron? His name—Jack Wesley." He eyes me. "Something I shouldn't have told you, but there you go."

"Why are you so down on him?" Marissa asks. "I mean, he's trying to help out, right? Isn't that a good thing? And he did stop a purse snatcher today!"

Officer Borsch sucks on a tooth, then says, "According to radio traffic, a mysterious girl with a big black umbrella did that."

"I didn't really do anything," I tell him. "The guy was getting away and I just tried to help out. I probably wouldn't have noticed him at all if it wasn't for Justice Jack."

"Don't call him that!"

"Wow, Officer Borsch. Why *are* you so down on him? The guy may be kinda cartoonish, but he wants to fight crime, not commit it, right?"

"That may be so," Officer Borsch says with a sigh, "but petty crime has gone way up since he's decided to 'help out.' " He looks at me. "Up, not down!"

"Like what kind of petty crimes?"

"Missing dogs. Stolen bicycles." He shakes his head. "There have been ten stolen bicycles in the last two weeks! And everywhere I turn, there's Jack!"

"And you think it's *his* fault?"

"Maybe the petty thieves are goading him. Maybe they want to see the guy appear out of a phone booth or rappel down a building. Maybe they're baiting him so they can have a good laugh." He shakes his head. "Why else would someone break into City Hall and steal the softball statue?"

"They really did?" I ask, because it seems so . . . *stupid*. I mean, if you're going to break into City Hall, there's got to be better stuff to steal than a bronze statue of a bunch of people down on one knee, gazing up at a softball. The statue is probably supposed to be inspiring, but when you first see it, you go, What the heck? And *then* when you get

66

closer, you kind of shake your head and go, Wow, really? And then you start to notice the little mounds of supposed dirt around the people and you think, Is that bronzed barf?

Plus, the eyeballs of the people are creepy. Like the artist used marbles for the pupils, then popped them out.

So even though Santa Martina is nuts for softball, having a statue like that inside City Hall is so over-the-top that everyone's kind of embarrassed by it.

Well, everyone except Mayor Hibbs. Rumor is, he thinks it's the most amazing statue ever.

Which is probably why it's in the foyer of City Hall.

Anyway, Officer Borsch sucks on a tooth, making a big ol' tisking sound, then says, "They unbolted it from the base and dragged it through a side door. What we can't figure out is why the alarm didn't go off. It should have when they broke the window to get in."

"Why would anyone *want* that thing?" Marissa asks.

"That's my point," Officer Borsch says. "It's worth nothing but aggravation."

I shift around in my seat a little to face him better. "Except to Mayor Hibbs, right? I've heard he, like, *worships* it."

The Borschman eyes me. "That's common knowledge?"

Marissa and I both laugh. "Oh yeah."

Then something hits me. "What if you worked at City Hall and you had to walk past it every day, and every day you thought it was stupid and embarrassing and that there should be some other, you know, more *traditional* statue there! What if the whole city council wanted it gone! What if they've been trying to get it changed for years but the mayor's been vetoing them! What if—"

"Sammy, Sammy, stop! You're suggesting the *city council* stole the statue?"

"Okay, no. But *everybody* thinks the statue is embarrassing. How can you say it has anything to do with Justice Jack?"

"Well, maybe it didn't have anything to do with Jack originally," Officer Borsch says, "but it does now." He eyes me. "He's vowed to 'bring the perpetrator to justice!' As if the mayor being all over us to find it isn't bad enough."

"Maybe he'll actually help," I tell him as we zoom past City Hall. "Maybe he'll track them down and give them a tour of Stomp City."

"Stop it!" the Borschman cries. He takes a deep breath, holds it for a minute, then blurts out, "Whatever you do, do *not* become that lunatic's sidekick, do you hear me?"

"Whoa—his *sidekick*?" I laugh. "I've seen his sidekick, Officer Borsch. I'm not interested."

"You wait," Officer Borsch warns. "He's going to try to recruit you. And he talks a good game, Sammy, but trust me—the man's a loser."

I frown at him. "Wow. That's pretty cold."

"But it's true! His 'secret hideaway' is a pink trailer on his mother's property. And his 'laboratory' where he fabricates his 'crime-fighting arsenal' is a shed. And you've seen what he drives!"

"The High Roller?"

"Don't! It's a dirt bike with a sidecar."

I grin. "A sidecar for his sidekick."

Officer Borsch nose-dives to a halt at the library drop-off curb. "Which I'm begging you to *please* never get into."

"Officer Borsch, you worry too much. I'm not crazy, you know."

"No, but *he* is. Or at least he might be." He frowns, then adds, "And he's a little too fascinated by you, so can you please do me a favor and steer clear of him?"

Well, the last thing I want is for the Borschman to have a heart attack over some harmless guy in tights and a mask, so I tell him, "Sure. And thanks for the ride." And I start to get out of the car, but at the last minute Marissa stops scooting and asks Officer Borsch, "Uh . . . is there any way I can maybe get a ride up to East Jasmine instead? My umbrella's kinda thrashed and it's a long walk."

Officer Borsch grumbles, "Now I'm a taxi service?"

I've already stepped out and whooshed open the Awesome Dome of Dryness, and since Marissa's house would make for a long walk back to the Senior Highrise, I tell them, "Not for me. I'm good here!" Then I lean forward and say to Marissa, "Call me. I want to hear what happens with Billy."

So they take off, and I go inside the library, where it's warm and dry, and while I browse around, the back of my mind sort of rattles with the things Officer Borsch had said. And it's funny—I'd thought Justice Jack was a wacko, too, but Officer Borsch putting him down made me want to stick up for him. I mean, how could it hurt to have someone like him patrolling the corridors of the mall?

Plus, I hate it when people call someone a loser.

Maybe I'm overly sensitive about it, but I do.

Then I started thinking that maybe Officer Borsch had become a cop because *he'd* always wanted to be a super-hero. Maybe he was *jealous* of Justice Jack! Maybe instead of a uniform and badge, he'd always secretly wanted tights and a mask and his very own crime-fighting lab.

A picture of Officer Borsch in his clandestine crime lab with a Borschman costume at the ready and surveillance cameras mounted all around popped into my head. And that led me to wondering what Justice Jack's secret hide-away and crime lab were really like. I mean, Officer Borsch can be pretty critical when he doesn't like someone.

Believe me—I've been there.

And *that's* when I got a brainstorm.

One that I promised myself would *not* get me into trouble.

NINE

I hurried over to one of the library's computers, got on the internet, and did a white pages search for "Jack Wesley" in Santa Martina. There were only two of them, and since one was seventy-eight and the other was twenty-seven, I went to Google Earth and put in the address of the twenty-seven-year-old.

And then there it was.

Justice Jack's secret hideaway.

The picture wasn't razor sharp or anything, and there were lots of trees all around getting in the way. And even though it was mostly an aerial view of the property, I could make out a building, plus something pink that was pretty large, and what looked like big messy piles of rusted junk.

I zoomed in and rotated the image, but all that really did was make things fuzzier and squashed. So I pulled back out and just sat there staring at the monitor for a while. Even with only this fuzzy view, it was pretty clear that Justice Jack lived out in some chicken-pickin' area and wasn't exactly rolling in dough.

For some reason this made me kinda sad. Obviously,

Justice Jack wanted to be a superhero, but if *this* was his secret hideaway? Maybe Officer Borsch was right. I mean, from this picture he sure didn't seem like a winner.

And then right behind me a voice goes, "Hey, loser."

Now, I don't need to turn around to know who it is.

It's the Twisted Sister.

The Dirty Disser.

The Hateful Hisser!

The one and only Heather Acosta.

I do turn around, though, because it's never a good idea to let your archenemy anywhere near your back.

Unless you enjoy knives sticking out of it, that is.

Sure enough, it's Heather, along with her half-witted sidekick Monet Jarlsberg. Monet's carrying a sorry-looking umbrella that's dripping away, and while Heather seems pretty dry, Monet's left shoulder and half of her hair are soaked. Like she only got to use one little wedge of her own umbrella.

And, really, I have no idea why they'd weather a storm to come to the library. I mean, Heather coming into the library at all? And on a Saturday? It's like seeing a tiger walk into an igloo.

So I'm in the middle of trying to piece this little puzzle together when Heather says, "So who's at three-fifty-seven Sandydale Lane, and why are you spying on them?"

It's not often I feel stupid around Heather Acosta.

Mad, yes.

Defensive, yes.

But stupid?

I wanted to kick myself. And while part of my brain's

screaming, Why didn't you shrink the window? another part's going, Don't do it now! You can't do it now! and then my mouth takes over, telling her, "It's research for a historical perspectives project."

So *now* my brain goes, Historical perspectives project? What's that supposed to be? And you have history with her, you dope! She knows there's no project!

But Heather doesn't call me out on it, and my hand just calmly clicks Google Earth closed as I tell her, "It's not like you to come into the House of Knowledge." I log out and stand up. "Here, you can have it. I'm sure it'll help you find your way back to Stupid Street."

But as I grab my umbrella, Monet points to it and gasps, "Heather, look!"

This is not an oh-look-at-the-awesome-umbrella gasp.

And it's not a now-*that*-would-have-kept-us-dry gasp.

It's a *she*-was-the-girl-with-the-umbrella! gasp.

Which meant they must've heard about the purse snatcher at the mall.

Which meant that I was now busted.

And I'm thinking, Maaaaaaaan! How can trying to help get a person in so much trouble? Only then it hits me that Heather's not looking at me like she's going to run off and tell the police that she caught the getaway girl with the big black umbrella.

She's looking stunned.

Almost *hurt*.

And then a woman wearing a fuzzy orange scarf hurries up to me, saying, "It's you! You stopped that man and saved my purse!"

Why didn't I just go home?

But I didn't and I'm stuck and there's obviously no getting out of the mess I'm in.

Only then something *else* very strange happens.

The woman puts a hand on Monet's shoulder and says, "Aren't you going to introduce me to your friend?"

Monet goes all shifty-eyed and then eeks out, "Ummm . . . this is Sammy."

The woman gives her a curious look. "And I am . . . ?"

Monet forces a smile, and without really looking at me, she says, "And this is my mom."

And just like that, *poof,* I'm in a great mood because there is nothing more fun than being your archenemy's dopey sidekick's mother's hero of the day.

I put out my hand and say a real friendly "Nice to meet you, Mrs. Jarlsberg!"

She shakes it and says, "Thank you so much for stopping that man! I'd just been to the ATM, and he would have gotten away with three hundred dollars if it wasn't for you!"

"I'm sure someone else would have caught him," I tell her. "It was no big deal."

"Well, I'm *not* so sure. And it was a big deal to me! It would have put a huge dent in our Christmas." She opens her purse and rummages around a little, and Heather's and Monet's eyeballs totally bug out as she hands me a twenty.

Now, as much as I could use the twenty, I don't feel right about taking it. "Oh, that's okay," I tell her. "Really. I'm just happy you got your purse back."

But she stuffs it in my jacket pocket and says, "You're taking it." Then she looks at me like I'm some strange animal in a terrarium. "Not only are you brave, you're polite and humble." She glances at Heather and Monet, and you can practically see a lightbulb come on over her head. "Say . . . we're here to check out a few rainy-day movies. . . ." She smiles at me. "How would you like to come over and watch them with us?"

Well, there's no way in the world I want to spend the day—rainy or otherwise—with Heather and Monet. And there's also no way I feel right about keeping the twenty. So I hold out the money to her and I'm planning to say Thanks but no thanks to the movie invite, but then I see the horrified looks on Monet's and Heather's faces, and I get a wicked idea.

"Sure!" I tell her, then smile at Heather and Monet. "That would be great!"

Mrs. Jarlsberg pushes the twenty back and says, "Wonderful!" but Monet jumps in with, "Mom, I've been trying to tell you—I have a headache! I don't want to watch a movie!"

Mrs. Jarlsberg blinks at her. "But—"

"And I really need to get home," Heather says.

"But—"

Now, the more awkward Heather and Monet act, the more fun this is for me. But it's not like I need Heather to hate me more than she already does, so I tell Mrs. Jarlsberg, "That's okay. I have homework I should be doing anyway."

"Well, put your money away," she says, because I'm still holding it out. "You've earned it." Then she snorts and says, "That Justice Jack guy would have taken it, believe me. Talk about needing attention." She cocks her head a little. "Who is he anyway, do you know?"

I shrug. Like, Beats me!

"Do you think he was hired by the mall? Like a mascot to break up the loiterers?"

I shrug again. "Maybe."

"Mom," Monet says in her whiny little voice, "I told you I have a massive headache. Why are we still here?"

"Okay, fine, sweetheart, let's go." She smiles at me. "It was *so* nice to meet you. Thank you again."

"Glad I could help," I tell her. "And thank you for the reward."

As they walk away, Heather looks over her shoulder and mouths, "Loser!" and flips me off behind her back.

Mrs. Jarlsberg had been so nice that it actually flashed through my mind to tell her that her daughter was spinning deeper and deeper into Heather's Black Hole of Hatred and that she needed to dispatch a rescue mission ASAP. I mean, if the person who saved her purse laid out the truth, maybe she'd listen.

Then again, probably not.

So I just watched them go, then headed for home and tried to shove Heather out of my mind.

On my way back to the Senior Highrise, I found myself going right by City Hall. And since I wasn't in a hurry or anything, I decided to take a little detour and check out the foyer.

It was the weekend, so the place was locked up tight, but I could still peek in and see the big base where the statue had been. And even though the foyer had been sort of a joke with the statue there, now that it was gone, the place looked . . . worse.

It wasn't because there was a big ol' base and no statue. Or that the room seemed empty.

It was because you now noticed all the pictures of politicians and plaques and stuff that were hanging on the walls.

It was boring.

Generic.

I shook off the thought that the statue actually *belonged* there and looked around for a broken window. I couldn't find one, but figured that with all the rain, they'd probably replaced it right away. I did notice a long scrape mark on the tile floor that led to a side door, though. And when I walked around the building, I discovered that the side door led to a small parking lot—one that was bordered by walls on two sides and a pretty big hedge on the third.

I didn't see any floodlights or mounted cameras in that area, so I started to understand how someone could have backed up to the side door at night and loaded in the statue without being seen.

The whole way back to the Highrise, I couldn't help thinking about the statue. I mean, seeing the empty base made it hit home—the most ridiculous statue in the world really had been stolen.

But why?

Did somebody actually want it?

Or did they just want it *gone*?

"There you are!" Grams whispered as I slipped through the door.

"Is Mrs. Wedgewood home?" I whispered back, figuring the reason we were whispering was that the Whale had returned to breach another day.

"Rose? No. No sign of her. I wish I could say the same for the people she swindled. I am getting very tired of them knocking on my door." She handed me a tuna sandwich and a glass of juice. "I'm afraid you may be spending some time in the closet this evening."

Well, she was right about that. Three separate times I had to collect any evidence that I was there and dive for the closet, and one of those times it was Mr. Garnucci at the door.

Now, usually when I dive for the closet, I leave Grams' bedroom door at least partly open and the closet door cracked so I can kinda hear what's going on. But when I heard it was Mr. Garnucci, I closed everything up tight and just held my breath until Grams finally let me out.

"He's gone," she whispered.

"What did he want?"

"He'd heard I might have a key to Rose's apartment."

Which was true.

She does.

Wedgie Woman had given it to her so we could rescue her when she fell off the toilet and couldn't get up—something she does more often than I want to think about.

But it's also convenient for her when she pulls her little blackmail stunts—having a key makes it so we can hurry over to do her bidding and she doesn't even have to go through the trouble of answering the door.

Anyway, I crawl out of the closet and ask, "So, what did you tell him?"

Grams gives me a prim look and whispers, "I denied it."

"But why?"

"Because he said it like he thought I might be involved in wrongdoing."

I follow her out of the bedroom. "Wrongdoing? Like, what kind of wrongdoing?" And then a crazy thought hits me. "He thinks you might have something to do with her being missing? Like *you* made her disappear? That's crazy! What would you have done with her?"

"Nobody thinks she's *dead*. But I didn't 'invest' with her and I do have her key. People are desperate and rumors are flying."

I think about this a minute. "Well, that's just crazy. If they knew why you have her key, they'd never think that!"

"But I can't tell them why I have it, so I just denied the whole thing. And I told Mr. Garnucci that Rose and I didn't get along well enough to warrant her giving me a key."

"At least *that's* true," I mutter. "So now what?"

"Now we wait for the next person to call or knock." She sits down on the couch and turns on the TV. "And I've been told that in another twenty-four hours they'll be able to report her as missing." She clicks around to the local news station and says, "And then you may want to spend the night at one of your friends' because I'm sure the police will be over for questioning."

And that's when the news guy on TV says, "A purse snatcher was stopped in his tracks today at the Santa Martina Town Center Mall, and the streets of Santa Martina may be a little safer tonight because of *this* man."

Suddenly there's Justice Jack, standing with his fists on his hips, filling up our TV screen.

"He goes by the name of Justice Jack," the newscaster announces, "and he says he's on a mission to save our town."

"Good citizens of Santa Martina!" the Masked Maniac booms into the camera. "I am Justice Jack and I'm at your service! I live for one goal—to bring our fair city a safer tomorrow!"

And with that he charges down the corridor of the mall and out of sight.

Grams gasps, "That's the man the others were talking about last night!" She blinks at me through her glasses. "Wow!"

Now, a "Wow!" out of Grams is quite an endorsement.

Actually, I don't know that I'd ever heard her "Wow!" anything before.

And maybe it was a good thing that she was so bowled over by Justice Jack, because she went straight to the kitchen to call all her Wedgie friends and missed the newscaster talking about "this real-life superhero's real-life side-kick . . . a mysterious person who vanished shortly after the altercation. Someone everyone's calling . . . Umbrella Girl."

I click off the TV quick and flop on the couch.

Umbrella Girl?

Oh, *great*.

TEN

Luckily, it wasn't raining the next day, so Umbrella Girl didn't need to bring her secret weapon to meet Marissa at Danny's church.

She turned into Skateboard Girl instead.

We didn't actually meet *at* the church, either.

We met at Hudson's.

Now, the first person I saw as I cruised up Hudson's walkway wasn't Marissa *or* Hudson. It was Marissa's little brother, Mikey—someone who used to be the world's most annoying fat kid and is now, thanks to Hudson's "boot camp," a whole lot happier and a whole lot smaller.

"Sammy!" he squeals from the porch, then jumps down the steps in a single bound.

I get off my skateboard and laugh. "Hey, Mikey! Man, you are looking great!"

"Dude, did you hear about Justice Jack?"

I laugh again. "Dude? Since when do you call me dude?"

"Since he calls everybody dude," Marissa says, coming through the front door. "And he's obsessed with Justice Jack. He's watched the news link over and over and over and *over*."

Mikey looks at me with his eyes cranked wide. "I can't believe you guys met him!"

Now, the new Mikey had become Spy Guy and had even been our ace in the hole once when dealing with Heather Acosta. He got so into it that on Halloween he went trick-or-treating as Spy Guy with a mask, a cape, and a big *S* on his chest. So him being excited about Justice Jack didn't surprise me. "Dude," I said back to him, "we met Justice Jack *twice*."

Marissa starts shaking her head and giving me the kill-it signal, but I'm not getting why.

"Twice?" Mikey asks, pogoing around.

I eye Marissa and try to pick up on why she's slightly spazzed about this. "No big deal," I tell Mikey. "The guy's everywhere."

"No big deal?" Mikey squeaks. "Dude, how can you say it's no big deal?"

"Spy Guy would love to be his sidekick," Marissa says, rolling her eyes.

I look at Mikey all hurt-like. "What? You're giving us the boot? Nice."

"But you guys aren't *real* superheroes," he says, bouncing up and down. "Justice Jack is!"

"Yup," I tell him. "Brought that purse snatcher down, *boom*."

Marissa grits her teeth and tells me, "Do not encourage him!"

"I was being sarcastic!"

But Mikey is too wrapped up in thinking about Justice Jack to pay any attention to us.

"He would've given that guy a tour of Stomp City, too!" he says, kicking his foot in the air. "Lucky for the Snatcher he didn't try to get away!"

I laugh. "The Snatcher?"

"Yeah! You know—like the Joker?"

Hudson's on the porch now, and after he tells me hello, he says to Mikey, "Hey, m'man—are we doing our laps? The girls need to get going or they'll be late."

"Thanks, Hudson," Marissa tells him, and after I park my skateboard on his porch, Marissa and I take off.

"So . . . ?" I ask her when we get to the sidewalk. "Did you get ahold of Billy?" 'Cause when she'd called me to set up our meeting at Hudson's, she hadn't talked to him yet.

"Yes," she says, kicking a pebble.

"And . . . ? How'd he take it?"

"I told him I thought we should go back to being just friends, and he seemed to take it okay." She kicks another pebble. "It's not like he was heartbroken or anything. He was just kind of quiet."

"How quiet?"

She shrugs. "Really quiet. Then he said, 'See you around,' like it was no big deal."

We walk along in silence for a minute, and finally I say, "I'm glad you broke up with him."

She looks at me. "You're serious?"

"Yes." I try to bite it back, but what I am is seriously upset, and it comes out anyway. "Because you just don't get him."

"What do you mean I don't get him?"

I look her in the eye. "Quiet *means* heartbroken." I

throw my hands in the air. "Good grief—I have to tell you that?"

"Look, I think you see something in Billy that isn't really there. I hung out with him for a month—more than a month! You think I can't see what's there?"

This time *I* go quiet.

"Stop that," Marissa finally says.

"Stop what?"

"Stop being quiet!" Then she snarls, "Or does this mean you're 'heartbroken,' too?"

I just shake my head a little. "How far is this stupid church, anyway?"

"You don't have to go, you know." She steps up the pace. "Actually, maybe you shouldn't go. Maybe you should hate me forever somewhere else."

"I don't hate you. I just can't believe we're back to dealing with Danny."

"*You* don't have to 'deal' with Danny. It's my business, not yours."

"What, so we're not going to be friends anymore?"

She doesn't say anything for, like, twenty steps. And finally she huffs out, "You need to give him another chance." Then she gets all buttery-faced and says, "I swear, Sammy, he's changed. You'll see."

The Community Church of Christ turned out to be nothing like St. Mary's Church, where Grams sometimes drags me. When you see St. Mary's, you know it's a church. It's got a pointy roof with a big cross, stained-glass windows, and a tall statue of Mary out front. And when you go inside, there are rows and rows of wooden pews, and up front there's an altar and an organ, and it smells like a combination of candles and wood polish.

This church was more like a rec hall, with a big, open room, a low ceiling, a lot of linoleum, and cheap Christmas decorations pinned to the walls. The kind of room where you could bring out Ping-Pong tables, or tumbling mats, or folding chairs, depending on what the activity of the hour was. And even though it seemed as if it should have smelled like either pancakes or sweat, it smelled like . . . nothing. Probably because it was just too cold for any odor molecules to be bouncing around.

"I wish I'd brought a jacket," Marissa whispers once we've stood inside for a minute. "And I don't see Danny anywhere, do you?"

There were people already seated in the folding chairs, but it wasn't *crowded* or anything, and, no, I didn't see Danny. And after we'd stood around for a few more minutes, the minister walked up to the podium and I could tell that the service was about to begin. So I whispered, "Are you sure this is the right place?"

"Yes."

"Did Danny know you were coming?"

"Well . . . no. But he said he comes every week!"

"Marissa, I am not sitting through a sermon if Danny's not here."

"He'll show up! Give him a chance!"

"Good morning!" the minister calls out. "If you could all take your seats, we'll begin."

"Let's go!" I say through my teeth.

"You can go," she says, moving toward the chairs. "I'm staying."

I roll my eyes and follow her, mumbling, "Oh, good grief."

"Just go!" she hisses.

"No way," I tell her. And for the next hour, while Marissa stares at the door, praying for Danny to show up, I pick at the old OUTCAST sticker on the back of the chair in front of me and wish I was somewhere, *anywhere,* else.

"I can't believe he didn't come," Marissa says when it's finally over.

"That's because you're back in a state of Dan-ial."

"He said he goes every week! And he *invited* me."

"Maybe if you'd told him you'd be here, he'd have backed up his lie by actually showing up."

"Don't call him a liar! It's just some misunderstanding! And I was still with Billy when he called!"

"Look, can we just go back to Hudson's and get something warm to drink?"

"I know," she whimpers. "I'm freezing."

So off we go to Hudson's, and since I don't want to sound like I'm harping on her for being such an idiot, and since she doesn't feel like talking to someone who obviously thinks she's an idiot, we don't say much to each other on the way back.

"How was church?" Hudson asks when he answers the door.

"Freezing," Marissa tells him, then gives him a desperate look. "Please tell me you have cocoa."

"Certainly!" he says, and leads us into the kitchen.

"Where's Mikey?" Marissa asks, pulling mugs out of a cupboard.

"He's in the study practicing his martial arts."

So I go to the study to see if Mikey wants cocoa, too, and I find him in front of a TV with a bathrobe on over his clothes, following along with a kung fu guru as he breaks down some fancy block-punch-twist-of-pain maneuver.

Mikey's got his back to me, so I just watch for a minute as he rewinds the lesson with a remote and goes through it again.

And again.

"Wow, Mikey," I finally say, which makes him whip around with his arms in a deadly attack position. His eyes are all intense, too. "Easy, boy! I was just about to say how you're going to be a black belt in no time . . . and see if you want any hot cocoa."

"Cocoa? Sure!" he says, and suddenly he's nine again.

So we head back into the kitchen, only before we get there, the doorbell rings.

"I'll get it," Mikey says, and charges for the front door.

"Is your mom picking you up already?" I ask Marissa.

She shakes her head. "Hudson's giving us a ride home."

"Probably another missionary," Hudson calls from over by the stove. "We get a lot of that around here. Especially on Sundays."

So I head to the door to help Mikey deal with whoever's peddling their version of God.

Trouble is, when we open the door, what's on the porch is definitely not a missionary.

ELEVEN

"It's Justice Jack!" Mikey squeals.

"Good day, citizen!" Jack exclaims in his booming voice. And then he realizes that it's me standing next to Mikey. "Have you no fear of retaliators?" he says to me in a low voice. "Evil yearns to crush you! Don't you realize the impending doom?"

So, okay, *now* he's sounding like a missionary.

Mikey's looking up at me with his eyes cranked and his jaw dropped, so I just give him a little wobble of the head and whisper, "You do *not* want to be his sidekick." Then I turn to Justice Jack and tell him, "I'm fine. We're fine. No one's in danger."

"If you wore a mask when battling crime," Justice Jack tells me, keeping his voice very low, "no one would recognize you when you answer the door of your abode."

"For one thing," I tell him back, keeping *my* voice very low, "I don't live here. For another thing, nobody *cares* who I am. I'm not a superhero. I'm thirteen, get it? I'm just a kid, invisible to the masses."

He stares at me through his mask a minute. "You underestimate your influence in this town."

Hudson's behind us now and cuts in with, "So how can we help you, Mr. Jack?"

And just like that, the Masked Maniac is back in superhero mode, booming, "It's Justice Jack, good citizen, and I am on a quest to bring warmth to the unfortunate."

"How's that?" Hudson asks.

"We're collecting jackets for the needy, as the nights have turned wicked cold and many in our fair city are without the means to keep themselves warm. Should you have a spare jacket you'd care to donate, that would be most appreciated!"

Hudson thinks a minute, then bobs his head. "Let me see what I can find."

So while he goes off to look for something to donate, Mikey, whose jaw has been unhinged this whole time, asks Justice Jack, "Have you stopped any bad guys today?"

"There's no escaping the Golden Gloves of Justice!" Jack says, holding up both hands and totally not answering the question. "And if the Gloves aren't enough"—he unholsters the hammer from his utility belt—"there's always the Jackhammer of Justice! Or"—he whips out the flashlight—"we'll teach them to see the light with the Justice Jack-o'-Lantern!" He slips the tools back on his belt and whips out a slingshot. "And if they refuse to see the light, they can say hello to the Pellets of Pain . . . *t*."

"Pellets of *Pain*? Or *Paint*?" Marissa asks.

"Both!" he cries, then produces a small handful of little plastic balls—one's gold, one's red, and one's glow-in-the-dark green. "Paintballs . . . And trust me, citizen, they hurt."

"Cool!" Mikey squeals. "Can I try one?"

"I'm afraid not, little shaver. We use these only in battle to mark our mark, should he try fleeing the scene."

Hudson's back now, carrying a heavy tan coat that looks like it came out of an old war movie. "Wow," I tell him. "That is *cool*."

"Thank you, kind citizen!" Jack says when Hudson hands it over, and even through his mask I can tell he thinks the coat is awesome, too. Like maybe he should change his whole costume so he could fight crime in it instead.

Hudson puts a hand on Mikey's shoulder and asks Jack, "How would you feel about posing for a picture with an aspiring crime fighter?"

Justice Jack turns his mask on me.

"Not me!" I tell him, and point to Mikey. "Him."

Justice Jack puffs up his chest. "Why certainly!" he booms in his superhero voice.

So Hudson grabs his camera and we all go out to the porch, and although Mikey is totally spazzing with happiness, he does manage to hold still long enough for Hudson to snap a picture of the two of them.

And Hudson's just put down the camera when Justice Jack suddenly whistles between his fingers. "Up here!" he calls out to a guy in a black mask and a blue cape. Then he turns to us and says, "The Ace of Hearts is helping me today."

"What happened to the King of Clubs?" I ask, checking out his new sidekick.

Justice Jack frowns. "He wasn't very reliable."

So up trots the Ace of Hearts. And now we can see that his cape is actually a threadbare towel, pinned to his

T-shirt, and that his face is really weathered and that some of his teeth are missing. "No luck," he pants.

Justice Jack looks him over. "We need to work on your hero gear," he says with a frown. "That's just not cuttin' it."

"*I* could be your helper!" Mikey cries. "I have a costume and everything!"

"No!" Marissa squawks, and Justice Jack sizes him up, saying, "Maybe in a few years, champ." And with that he bounds down the steps crying, "Onward!"

"I can't believe you gave him that cool coat," I grumble after he's gone.

Hudson shrugs. "I have to trust it will be put to good use." He smiles at us. "So . . . what about that cocoa?"

We all go, "Oh, right," then head back inside and make cocoa. And even though Mikey's on a superhero high that seems like it'll last the rest of his life, Marissa descends into Dannyville despair in no time.

"So what are you going to do?" I ask her when we get a minute alone on the porch.

"I don't *know*," she whimpers.

"If you call him, he'll just snow you with some story. Like he wasn't feeling well, or he overslept, or he's gone every single Sunday except today, or—"

"Stop it! What if it *was* something like that? It's not fair to judge him until we've heard what he has to say."

I roll my eyes. "Fine. Go call him. Get snowed."

But she doesn't call him. She just sits there looking out across the porch railing, until finally, very quietly, she says, "I don't think he could lie to my face."

"Since when?"

"Stop it, Sammy!"

I put my hands up. "Sorry. You're right. I should be helping you, not jabbing at you." I shake my head. "I just don't trust him, and I don't know what to *do*."

She looks me in the eye. "Go with me to his house."

"To his house? When?"

"Now."

"You're serious?"

She nods. "We'll go up, knock on the door, and see what his reaction is."

I think about the insanity of this a minute, then shrug. "Why not?"

So we announce that we're going for a girl-talk walk so Mikey won't ask to tag along, and then head out.

Now, Danny's house isn't exactly next door. From Hudson's, you've got to go past the mall, across Broadway, and then zigzag back into a neighborhood with old tract houses and thirsty yards. So it took us a good twenty minutes to get there, and when we did, Marissa chickened out.

"What? No! We didn't walk all this way for nothing!"

"But what if—"

I grab her by the sleeve. "You're going."

"But—"

She tugs back, but I drag her up to the front door and ring the bell.

"What am I going to say?" she whispers frantically. "It's like I'm checking up on him!"

But it's too late to turn back, because the door swings open and there's Danny.

"Marissa!" he says, his eyes popping wide. And then he looks at me and gets a little nervous. "Uh . . . what's up?"

I can tell Marissa's about to pee her pants, so I just shrug and tell him, "We missed you at church this morning."

He looks back and forth between me and Marissa. "You *went*?"

Marissa nods and gives him dopey little puppy eyes, which makes me want to slap her silly.

"Man, I'm so sorry," he says to her, oozing smooth as he steps out of the house and pulls the door mostly closed behind him. "I didn't feel good this morning so I just went back to bed! I've gone every single week until now, too!" He cocks his head a little. "I thought you said you *couldn't* go."

"I said I had to think about it," Marissa says weakly.

There's a moment of awkward silence where I'm just staring at Marissa, wondering if she noticed that he'd just used *all three* of the excuses I'd told her he'd try.

And then Danny says, "So you're checking up on me? Is that what this is?"

Marissa cries, "No!"

"So why didn't you just call?"

Marissa is about to quiver apart, so I jump in and tell him, "Look, Danny, you may be able to convince Marissa that you've changed, but you've got a credibility problem with me. You can understand that, right? I just thought it'd be a good idea to talk face to face."

He bristles. "So I've got to go through you to get to her?"

"The real question is, Why do you want to get to her?"

"Because I *like* her? Because she used to be my *friend*?"

Real calmly, I say, "See, I don't buy that."

"You don't *have* to buy that," he tells me, and from the glint of anger in his eyes I know I'm right—the new Danny is just a spit-shined version of the old Danny.

"So you've contacted Billy and Casey and all your other old friends, too?"

"Who I want to have back as friends is none of your business." Then he just can't help himself. He smirks and says, "I can tell you this, though—you're not on the list."

"But Marissa is, not because you actually *like* her, but because it's just been a shock to your system that she's not your groupie anymore."

Marissa gasps, "Sammy!" and she's looking horrified—like I just ripped the head off a bunny.

Danny looks at Marissa. "What is this?"

Marissa cries, "Sorry!"

"Well, what? Do I need her permission to talk to you?"

"No!"

"Good." He gives me a hard look, then turns to Marissa. "I'll call you," he says, in a just-me-and-you-baby way. But as he opens the door and goes inside, I get a glimpse of someone moving quickly out of view.

Someone I recognize.

TWELVE

Before I can even think about what I'm doing, I jab my foot forward and stop the door from closing.

From inside I hear Danny mutter, "What the—" as Marissa gasps, "What are you *doing*?"

I turn to her. "Heather's in there."

Marissa goes pale. "She's not!"

Danny body-blocks the opening in the doorway and looks down at my foot. "Come on. Really?"

I look him right in the eye. "So why's Heather here?"

"Heather's n—"

The door whips open and there she is, wearing way too much makeup and her usual sneer. "You got a problem with that, loser?"

Marissa stands there with her jaw on the ground while Danny pinches his eyes closed, then scrambles to explain. "Look, I've been through some really bad times and I'm trying to build my friendships back."

I snort. "By telling the truth and going to church and . . . what else? Oh, right, *changing*."

He looks at Marissa and points to me. "Why did you

bring her? I know you and Heather don't get along, but did you ever think that *she's* the reason?"

"Let's go," I tell Marissa, and as I start to turn around, Danny taps his chest twice and does a little sweep of his hand toward Marissa.

Like, My heart beats just for you, baby.

He's sly about it, too.

So Heather can't see.

I drag Marissa out of there, and when we're on the sidewalk, I say, "See? He hasn't changed a bit."

But instead of thanking me for exposing Danny for the snake he is, she snaps, "Why did you have to act like that?"

I stop dead in my tracks. "That was Heather back there. Heather! He was too busy to go to church because he was with *Heather.*"

"You don't know that!" she calls over her shoulder as she keeps marching along. "You're judging and jumping to conclusions!"

"I've got eyes! Open yours!"

"They are open!" she shouts back. "And I'm seeing a friend whose mind is closed!"

"Marissa, he *lied* to you. He said he didn't go to church because he wasn't feeling well and overslept. . . . Come on!"

"Maybe he did! You weren't there! How would you know?"

"And he was about to deny that Heather was there, but she blew it for him."

"You don't *know* that!" she shouts back. "Maybe he

was going to say, 'Heather's none of your concern' or 'Heather's not your business'!"

"Get real! He was about to say, 'Heather's not here!' "

"See? Judgmental!"

She's nearly half a block away and obviously not waiting for me. So I run to catch up with her. "Marissa, can't you see he's manipulating you?"

She gives me a detached look. "Or maybe *you're* the one manipulating me."

"Oh, and I'm the reason you and Heather aren't friends?" I throw my hands in the air. "Fine. Go ahead. Be her friend. Don't let me stop you." And, really, I just feel like taking off.

"Okay, I'm sorry. I know." She gives me a pleading look. "If he didn't like me—if he didn't want to be a better person—why would he call me and tell me all that stuff? And why would he act like he does?"

"*Act* like he does? You mean like giving you that phony little heart tap?"

"See? There you go again! Who says it was phony?"

"Marissa, he hid it from Heather. Can't you see he's just playing you?"

"*Why* would he play me? Why would he bother if he didn't like me?"

I think about this a minute, then say, "You know what? I think you telling him off last month really did get to him, but not because he's ever been in love with you, or cares about you as a friend."

"Then why?"

"Because you were the one person he'd always had

power over. If he gets you back, he'll feel like he's got his mojo back."

"His mojo," she says, like I'm the most ridiculous person she's ever met. "Sammy, why can't you ever just let things be what they are? Why do you have to pick them apart and talk about *mojo*?"

"How can you not want to understand what his game is?"

"Because it's *not* a game." She gives me a smarty-pants look. "Where's the box? Where's the board? Where's the rule book?"

"Well, obviously you could *use* a rule book, but Danny's not a board game kind of guy, and you know it. He's more looking to get to the next level."

"Whatever!" she snaps.

Which pretty much means she's done discussing it. So I don't say anything more, and our walk across town becomes a silent march. And after blocks, I really do want to give up and head for home, but it feels so wrong to leave things like this.

Plus, my skateboard's at Hudson's and I need to get it.

So we keep on marching along, and I know Marissa's probably thinking that I'm being completely unfair and judgmental and *mean*, which bothers me plenty enough, but what's bothering me a lot more is that a jerk like Danny could have any effect on a friendship as strong and long as Marissa's and mine. And I don't want to be combative about it, but, come on—how can she not see through him?

Apparently, Marissa can't think of anything to say to me, either, because she keeps walking faster and faster, and by the time we reach the mall, she's steaming along like a locomotive. But as we turn the corner and head down Cook Street, we both notice a crowd gathering across the street at the police station and start to slow down.

"What do you think's going on?" I say, nodding at the crowd.

"Something big . . ." Then she says, "Wait, it's Justice Jack!"

Sure enough, Justice Jack is making his way up the police station steps, carrying a big black Hefty sack over his shoulder.

Marissa shakes her head. "He looks like a comic book Santa or something."

"Yeah, huh?" I say back, and for some reason having those words come out of my mouth is a big relief.

Like, *Phew*. We can still agree.

"KSMY is there!" she says. "That's Zelda Quinn!"

There's no mistaking Zelda Quinn. She's KSMY's very own skunk reporter. She dyes her hair super-black, except for a fat white streak that's right up front. Grams likes to watch her, but I think she acts like everything is life-and-death. Even when she's covering something like an elementary school play, she's all *intense*. Like any second terrorists might infiltrate the multi-purpose room.

Anyway, the closer we get to the gathering, the more it looks like some weird news conference. Justice Jack stops about halfway up the steps, turns around, and swings off the sack while Zelda Quinn and her cameraman move around, trying to get good positions, and the rest of the people form sort of a wide horseshoe on the lower steps and sidewalk. It seems like a strange group that's gathered, too—a couple of them have shopping carts, a few have dogs. . . .

And then it hits me.

"I think he's giving away jackets to the homeless."

Marissa nods. "I think you're right!"

All of a sudden Justice Jack's voice booms through the air. "Downtrodden, you are not forgotten! The fair citizens of Santa Martina heard your shivers!" He opens the sack and produces a dark blue jacket. "Through their kindness I give you armor against the bitter cold! A shield against the chilling winds! And the strength that comes from knowing that people care." He pauses a moment, then raises the jacket high. "Consider these your Justice Jackets!" Then he starts handing them out, one by one, while the cameraman moves in for close-ups and Zelda Quinn puts her microphone in people's faces.

Marissa and I watch from across the street, because it's not like I want to be on the news at all, let alone with a bunch of homeless people.

Heather Acosta would have a field day.

And I'm torn between thinking the whole scene's cool, and thinking it's just really bizarre, when a voice behind us growls, "Since when does giving out six jackets rate news coverage?"

Well, there's no doubt that the voice belongs to Officer Borsch. But what I *am* doubting is the number of jackets. "It was more than that, wasn't it?"

He sucks on a tooth. "I can count to six."

And that's when something hits me. "Hey, he didn't give out Hudson's jacket. I wonder where that went."

"Hudson got suckered into giving up a jacket?" Officer Borsch asks.

"Well, I don't know about *suckered*. But it was a really cool jacket. Like something out of an old war movie."

Officer Borsch mutters, "Probably kept it." Then he adds, "And why'd he choose the station steps? Why not over at the Salvation Army or St. Mary's Church or somewhere that makes *sense*?" But before I can tell him, Beats me, he comes up with his own answer. "He thinks he can fool people into believing he's real law enforcement by being seen on the station steps, that's why."

I eye him and say, "Are you thinking about kicking him off?" because I can tell he's itching to.

"I'm going nowhere near him while cameras are rolling. It's lose-lose. Either I come off as the heavy, or I get sucked into lending him credibility." He gives his tooth a good slurp. "Looks like his little sideshow's about over anyway."

And it might have been, except right then Justice Jack spots Officer Borsch. "Commissioner!" he bellows across the street. "Join us!"

Officer Borsch groans, "Noooo."

Well, Officer Borsch isn't budging or even acknowledging him, so Justice Jack calls, "Commissioner!" again, and this time everyone on that side of the street turns around to see who Justice Jack is hollering at, including Zelda Quinn and her cameraman. And I'm sorry, but I do not want to be any part of a newscast where I'm standing by a *cop,* either.

Heather Acosta would have a field day.

And Danny Urbanski?

He'd start calling me a narc again, seeing how he accused Casey and me of being the ones who got him arrested.

Which, for the record, Casey had nothing to do with.

"Not good," Marissa says, reading my mind.

"Sorry, Officer Borsch, but we've gotta go. Good luck with the Jackman."

He snorts and grumbles, "He's a jack*ass,* if you ask me."

So Marissa and I hustle out of there, and as we make our escape onto Cypress Street, Marissa grins at me and says, "I kind of like that our town has its own superhero."

I grin back. "Only in Santa Martina."

So the good thing about running into Justice Jack was that it cooled things down between Marissa and me. Nothing had changed, really, but I felt a lot better, and I think she did, too. And since I didn't want to heat things up again, when we got to Hudson's, I just told her, "Be careful, okay? And call me whenever you want."

Then I got my skateboard and headed back to the Highrise.

THIRTEEN

I was so preoccupied with Marissa and Danny and poor Billy that I didn't think about Mrs. Wedgewood until I was sneaking down the hallway and into our apartment.

"Grams?" I whispered after I'd slipped my skateboard under the couch. "Grams?"

The bathroom door was closed, so I just tapped on it twice and said, "I'm home," figuring she'd give me the Wedgie Woman update when she got out. Then I went to the kitchen to find something to eat, because I was starving!

There was leftover tuna salad in a small bowl in the fridge and some Triscuits in the cupboard.

Good enough for me!

So I sat at the table and shook a ton of Tabasco on the tuna and ate straight out of the bowl.

"Meow!" Dorito said, rubbing against my leg.

"Sorry!" I mewed back. "It's spicy!" I rubbed him and whispered, "Don't tell Grams, okay?" because Grams hates it when I'm on the loose with hot sauce.

I ate fast, too, partly because I was so hungry, and partly because I didn't want to be scolded for eating right from the bowl, or for "ruining" the tuna with hot sauce . . . or for eating it all up!

But as it turns out, I didn't have to eat so fast because I'd practically licked the bowl clean and Grams still hadn't come out of the bathroom.

Now, okay. When I'm doing my business, I do not like people tapping on the bathroom door, telling me I'm running late or taking a long time.

You think I don't know that?

So I didn't exactly want to go up and rat-a-tat-tat Grams. But I started getting the feeling that something was off. Not *wrong*, but not *right*, either.

So I finally went and tapped on the door and said, "Grams?"

No answer.

So I tried the door, and when I discovered it was unlocked, I opened it.

No Grams.

And I'm standing there feeling pretty stupid when I hear a little thump come through the wall that our bathroom shares with Mrs. Wedgewood's bathroom. Then there's another thump.

And another.

It's a strange kind of thumping, too. A *small* sound. Like someone's knocking quietly.

And r-e-a-l-l-y slowly.

Now, if Mrs. Wedgewood had been a normal neighbor, I would have just thought, Hey! She's back! But the Mighty Wedge is not a normal neighbor. And the Mighty Wedge doesn't make small sounds. From falling off the toilet, to pounding on the wall for help, to lumbering across the floor with her walker, to *breathing,* everything Mrs. Wedgewood does is seismic.

Especially when she's in the bathroom.

And that's why a little lightbulb finally pops on over my head. "Holy smokes!"

I hurry to the front door and check the hallway to make sure the coast is clear, then I slip out of our apartment and tiptoe down to Mrs. Wedgewood's.

I try the knob, and when it turns, I look over both shoulders quick, then whoosh inside the Wedge's apartment, lock the door behind me, and beeline over to the bathroom.

And sure enough, there's my grandmother, nosing through the Wedge's drawers.

I just stand in the doorway with my hand on my hip, watching her, waiting for her to notice me. And after checking out the medicine cabinet, she finally does.

"Samantha!" she gasps, grabbing her heart.

I shake my head. "Unbelievable."

"I was just looking for clues as to her whereabouts!"

"In her bathroom?"

"I've heard you're supposed to look in the most unlikely spots! That if you can think of it in ten minutes, it won't be there. I thought maybe she—"

"Shhh!" I poke a finger in the air because something just went *click.*

"What?" Grams asks, but then we hear a woman's voice say, "Quick! Get in!"

I swoop inside the bathroom and close the door enough

so we can both hide behind it, but leave it open enough so I can still see through the crack between the hinges and the doorframe. And there, across the living room, go Screwdriver Sally and Blue—the same two old biddies who'd been trying to break into the apartment earlier.

Screwdriver Sally pulls two empty pillowcases from under her sweater. "Here," she says, handing one to Blue. "Anything that looks like we could pawn it."

Blue nods. "I'll start in the bedroom."

"You're going for the jewelry!" Screwdriver Sally says, like she's accusing her of something.

"So? We're splitting everything. Find what you can out here."

But Screwdriver Sally shakes her head. "I'm coming with you."

"What if Rita shows up? Someone needs to stay out here on watch!"

"Why would Rita show up?"

"She has a key!"

"She told Vinnie she doesn't!"

"Well, everyone still *thinks* she does, and that's the whole point! No one will suspect us—they'll think it was her!"

But Screwdriver Sally isn't about to let a little thing like getting busted stop her from keeping an eye on her partner in crime. She follows Blue into the bedroom, going, "Well, I'm coming with you."

The instant they've left the room, I scoot Grams along so I can get out from behind the door, then I grab her hand and put my finger in front of my lips. "We've got to move *fast*," I whisper. I pull her out of the bathroom, across the kitchen, and through the front door. Then I yank her back inside our apartment, flip around quick, and lock our door. "Good grief, Grams, what were you *thinking*?" She's shaking like mad, so I grab her hand again and drag her into the kitchen. "You have to call Mr. Garnucci. Now."

"Why?"

"Tell him you hear noises next door. Tell him you think Mrs. Wedgewood's apartment is being ransacked."

She just stands there, so I snatch the phone off the hook, dial, and stick the receiver up to her ear. "Yes, Vince?" she says when he answers. "This is Rita. I'm terribly frightened. It sounds like Rose's apartment is being ransacked! Yes . . . yes, I'm sure! Can you please hurry? Yes . . . yes . . . I'll stay right here."

"Perfect," I tell her when she hangs up the phone.

"How can you be so calm?" she asks. "We almost got caught!" Then she says, "I can't believe they walked right inside someone else's apartment! The nerve!"

I blink at her. "Hello? Like you didn't do the same thing?"

"I had a key!"

"They did, too! I locked the door after I came in!"

"You did?"

"Yes!"

"How did *they* get a key?"

"I have no idea!" I fly around grabbing my backpack and checking for anything that might give me away, then head for her bedroom. "I'd better hide."

Dorito's already in the closet when I duck inside it.

And I just sit there, in the dark, petting my cat for what seems like forever, until finally Grams peeks in and says, "He's here!"

"It's about time," I grumble.

After a few minutes she pops back and says, "I'm going over!" Then after that she comes hurrying back every now and then to give me an update. "He caught them red-handed!" "The pillowcases were stuffed full!" "They'd disconnected her DVD player!" "They emptied her freezer! Her *freezer*."

She was gone for a long time after that, and when she finally came back, she opened the door wide and said, "Everyone's gone."

"Everyone?"

"Well, I tipped off Gwenith and she took care that the rest of the building heard." She hrmphs. "And they thought they could frame me!"

My legs are super-stiff, so I kind of groan as I stand up and say, "They weren't going to frame you, Grams. They were just going to let everyone else *assume* it was you."

She hrmphs again. "Same thing."

I shake my head. "I thought you didn't *care* what happened to Mrs. Wedgewood. Why would you risk going over there?"

"I didn't think I was risking anything! How was I to know that Fran and Sally would trick Vince out of a key?"

"They tricked him? How's that?"

"I'm not sure, but that's what he was yelling at them. I've never seen him so mad! I hope he gives those two the boot!"

"But not you, right?"

"I wasn't cleaning out Rose's apartment! I didn't go in there with pillowcases!" She rolls her eyes. "You should have seen those two! They looked ridiculous!"

All of a sudden I'm picturing them, blue-haired and beak-nosed, hunched over with their pillow sacks flung over their shoulders, wearing masks and stretchy suits—one yellow and one red—with thick black rubbery old-lady shoes on their feet and black gloves on their hands.

They have big screwdrivers.

In holsters.

And then Justice Jack appears in between them with his big Hefty sack flung over his shoulder and—

"Samantha?"

"Huh?"

"Did you hear a word I just said?"

"What's that?"

"I was telling you about this."

She's holding a sheet of lined paper that had obviously been folded up quick because the creases are pretty crooked. It had also been ripped out of a spiral notebook, because there are little frayed ends poking out everywhere.

"What is it?"

She opens it better and hands it over. "I don't know, but there were pages and pages and pages like this. I couldn't make heads or tails of it."

I study the paper, and she's right—it is strange. It's like lab notes with rows and columns of numbers, and lots and lots of little fraction exponents. Which would seem to make it some kind of scientific notes, but (a) Mrs. Wedgewood doesn't seem like the scientific kind at *all*, and (b) there are also words. Words that have nothing to do with any kind of lab or science. Words like *Tripteaser* and *Over-n-Out* and *Dusk Before Dawn* and *Inevitable* and *Just Kidding* and *Sexy Librarian*.

I look at Grams. "*Sexy Librarian?* What *is* this?"

"Exactly." She shakes her head. "It seems that there's a whole side to Rose we know nothing about."

I snort, "Hard to believe," because after the number of times Grams and I have hoisted her back onto her toilet, after finding her upside down and backward and bare-bottom-up, I was sure we'd seen *all* sides of her.

But this *was* strange.

"Did you notice the numbers only go from one to six?" I ask her.

She looks over my shoulder and points to a bunch of big numbers in the margin. "What about this over here?"

"Yeah, I don't know."

The phone rings, and since we're standing right by it, we both jump. But when Grams picks it up and says hello, she's steady as can be. "Oh yes," she says, winking at me. "Isn't it scandalous? . . . Unbelievable. . . . You're right—I can't *imagine* doing something like that!"

I shake my head and roll my eyes.

My own grandmother.

Sneaky, sneaky, sneaky.

FOURTEEN

That night I had a dream that old biddies were rappelling down the side of the Highrise on fat ropes, wearing stretchy suits and masks and *capes*. They had empty pillowcases clamped between their teeth, and came to a stop outside our window and started trying to break in with a screw-driver and credit card.

Then all of a sudden Justice Jack appears inside the apartment and tells me to hide. So I squeeze under the couch, where I'm all hot and smooshed. Like a grilled cheese sammich being flattened with a spatula.

"Be gone!" Justice Jack cries through the window at the old biddies, and just like that, *poof*, they're gone.

"Beware, young one," he says, hanging upside down to look at me under the couch. "Evil is out to destroy you!" And then, *poof*, just like that, *he's* gone, too.

But I'm still stuck under the couch, and can't seem to move. And I get this total panic attack where I'm strug-gling like mad to get out from under the couch but I'm not getting anywhere and I can't *breathe*.

And then, just like that, *poof*, I'm sitting up, gasping for air.

Awake.

Grams is standing over me holding Dorito, shaking her head. "We really need to do something about this cat sleeping on your head." She looks up and down the length of the couch and tisks. "You can't even stretch out anymore, can you?"

"It's fine, Grams," I tell her, but she's right. The couch seems smaller every night.

And Dorito's sure not helping.

Anyway, maybe it was all the feeling boxed in, I don't know, but I was actually happy to be on my way to school. Happy to be free and *moving*.

The great thing about a skateboard is, you can pump hard, just cruise, or mix it up. Normally, I ride hard to school because I'm late, but I do like to mix it up. It feels good to really push yourself, and then go, *Ahhhhhh,* and enjoy it. And since for once I *wasn't* running late, I had a lot of fun riding to school.

All that feel-good goes away, though, when I shuffle up the school steps and run into Billy. "Hey, Sammy," he says, and it sounds really flat. Like he's been steamrollered and can't peel himself up.

I tell him hey back, and after standing there a minute, I blurt out, "Look, Marissa may be my best friend, but she's crazy and she's wrong and she's *stupid* when it comes to this."

"I just don't get it," he says as we walk along together. "I thought everything was fine." He looks at me. "I thought everything was *good.*"

And that's when it hits me.

He doesn't know about Danny.

And I realize I have to make a decision.

Am I Billy's friend, too?

Or just Marissa's.

Does this drag out until he finds out the hard way?

Or do I rip the Band-Aid off and just get it over with.

Holly's always telling me to listen to my gut, so that's what I do. "She got a call from Danny, Billy."

"What?"

He looks shocked, so I snort and say, "Yeah, exactly. But what's stupid is, she's falling for his smooth-talking apologies and she thinks he deserves a second chance."

He's quiet for a long time, and finally he says, "So they're going *out*?"

"No. He's just snowed her into thinking there's a *chance* they'll go out."

He shakes his head. "So we're back to the top of the slide."

"Yeah. We had a big argument about it. I think she's being an idiot." I give him a little shove. "*We* might have broken up over *you*."

He stops walking and squeezes me with a hug. And when he finally lets go, he seems to be more like his old self. "So why didn't you?"

I grin. "You can thank Justice Jack for that."

"Justice Jack," he chuckles. "That dude is awesome."

"Yeah, well, he was handing out 'Justice Jackets' to the homeless at the police station when Marissa and I were walking by fighting about you, and it sorta distracted us."

"Justice *Jackets*?" He full on laughs. "That dude is *righteously* awesome."

So I felt better about Billy's state of mind when we split up to go to our homerooms, but later when we converged outside of history, he was back to being bummed out.

"Aw, Billy."

He gives a little shrug and is about to say something, but then all of a sudden Lars is there whooshing his hair, hovering, making everything totally awkward. "Hey," he says, then just stands there.

"What's up?" I ask him.

Whoosh.

Then he looks down and says, "Sasha says thanks."

My eyebrows take a little stretch. And I want to say, Oh, *really*? because Sasha isn't exactly the thanking kind. But for some reason what comes out of my mouth is, "So everything's okay?"

He shakes his head. "I don't know what to do. She's trapped and her parents are, like, jail keepers. She cries all the time."

He's actually not being annoying or condescending. At that moment he just seems like a guy who's miserable and kinda desperate. So I ask, "How do you know? Do they let you talk on the phone?"

He pulls a mini-book of folded papers out of his back pocket. "We write notes." He unfolds the papers and shows us. The writing is scrawled, single-spaced, and double-sided. "This was just from this morning!"

"I wouldn't call that a *note*," Billy says. "And how did she get it to you?"

"We have a secret rock. I rode out there before school."

I look at Lars. "So, like, at six-thirty this morning you rode out to Sisquane?"

He nods. "My parents think I've joined the cycling team."

The bell rings, and as we start filing up the ramp, I ask, "Have you tried talking to her parents? Like maybe you could get, I don't know—supervised visits, or whatever?"

He snorts. "Just like jail." And suddenly he's back to being Lofty Lars, acting like he's smarter than everyone around.

"What could it hurt?" I ask, but he just shakes his head like it's the stupidest idea ever, and with another head whoosh he bolts up the ramp ahead of us.

"Rock of Loooove," Billy snickers like a lounge lizard, and for that instant he seems like the old Billy again.

And then Heather rushes by to beat the bell. There's still actual cigarette smoke coming out of her mouth as she turns and says to Billy, "Your girlfriend's two-timing, you know."

I wanted to shove her over the guardrail. What kind of person gloats about something like that? But she was already at the door, so I just called, "Your life's an ashtray, Heather."

Whatever *that* was supposed to mean.

Anyway, I was *really* glad that I'd followed my gut and told Billy about Marissa and Danny. It hadn't even crossed

116

my mind that Heather would knife him with the news, but of course she did.

That's just Heather.

During class I kept trying to catch Billy's eye and give him a smile or whatever, but Sad Billy was back and by the end of class he looked like Eeyore with a dark little cloud hanging over him.

I tried to give him a pep talk between classes but he didn't want to hear it. Then at lunch he didn't show up at our usual meeting place, and since Holly and Dot were in the dark about Marissa's little relapse, lunch was small-talky and awkward, with Marissa being a little too chatty and cheerful and me being quiet and glum.

Finally Holly asks, "What's going on?" because obviously something's not right.

I stand up and collect my garbage. "Ask Marissa." Then I take off. And since Billy's in both my classes after lunch, I got to see him sit through them all quiet and bummed.

Got to watch his little cloud get heavier and darker.

Unfortunately, Heather is also in those two classes, so I got to see her be all smug.

Got to watch her eye Billy and sneer.

And because *Marissa* is in sixth period, too, I got to watch *her* act like nothing was wrong.

"You're being just like your parents!" I finally hissed at her.

"What's that supposed to mean?" she hissed back.

"Their whole world is falling apart because your dad has an addiction, and they try to pretend like nothing's wrong!"

"I don't have an addiction, and the world isn't falling apart!"

"Yes, you do, and Billy's world sure is!"

Well, she didn't want to hear about *that*, so she huffed off and never came back. And after school she just cut out a side door.

So I ended school the way I'd started it—on the steps with Billy and my skateboard. "You meeting up with Casey?" he asked, but it sounded all choked. Like he was trying really hard not to break down.

"I'm thinking I'll hang with you for a while."

He stops moving and his head wobbles a little, and then he just sits down. Right there in the middle of the school steps, he just sits down. "She didn't even say hi."

So I sit down next to him, and, really, I don't know what to say.

She's a jerk?

She's an idiot?

You deserve way better?

Finally I say a real lame "I don't think she handled it very well, that's for sure."

He just gives a dejected shrug.

"Look, I don't understand it, but she's stuck on Danny, and I don't see her getting unstuck."

He shakes his head and stands up. "I need to go *do* something."

"Like what?"

"I don't know." He thumps down a few steps and says, "I wish I could find Justice Jack. I'd get in his sidecar and *ride*."

And that's when it hits me that I know something that'll totally take Billy's mind off of Marissa.

Something that'll have him jumping up and down with excitement.

Something I know I should absolutely *not* tell him.

But he's my friend.

And totally miserable.

So I do.

FIFTEEN

"You know where he *lives*?" Billy squeals. "Can we go?"

"I don't know, Billy," I tell him, trying to build up the suspense. "It's top-secret."

Billy drops his voice. "So how do *you* know?"

I drop mine, too. "I can't tell you."

He turns on the puppy-dog eyes. "Take me to the secret hideaway, please, please, pleeeeeeease?"

I frown at him. "You've got to *swear* to secrecy."

"Cross my heart and hope to die-aye-aye!" he says, making a great big X over his heart.

In the back of my mind I *am* having doubts, but I try to block those out. I mean, what can it hurt to take a peek, right?

After all, he's crossed his heart and hoped to die-aye-aye.

"Okay," I tell him, and then ask him to get a message to Casey to call Billy's cell when the high school's dismissed so I can let him know that I won't be meeting him at the graveyard. But also, since I'm on kind of a reckless roll, I'm thinking maybe he can meet us at Justice Jack's secret hideaway. For one thing, I want to see him, but I'm also thinking that it might be a good idea to hand Billy off to him afterward so Billy's not alone when he comes crashing down again about Marissa.

Getting ahold of Casey is really complicated because his mom decided she could keep us from talking to each other by taking away his phone. So now we have this elaborate relay system, which includes people Billy knows at the high school, code names, and pay phones.

Anyway, after a few minutes of texting, Billy closes his phone and says, "Done!" Then he looks at me with happy eyes. "Lead me to my leader!"

I cock my head. "Doesn't that make *me* your leader?"

Billy thinks a minute. "Very well, then. Leader, lead me to the *supreme* leader!"

"He's not *my* leader," I grumble. "And we're only going to his secret hideout, not him, got it?"

"Got it! Now lead on!"

So I set off, saying, "I'm trusting you, okay? No sharing this with anyone anywhere anytime."

He gives me a snappy salute. "Your wish is my command!"

"I don't know if you're going to like seeing it, Billy."

"Why?"

"Well . . . what do you think his secret hideaway's like? A cave? A hidden underground laboratory with a thick steel door? A penthouse suite?"

He squints at me. "In Santa Martina?"

I blink at him. "Okay. Good. Because it's none of those things."

"So? What is it?"

I pick up the pace. "A pink trailer."

"A pink trailer?" He does a little dance around me. "Are you serious?"

"That's what I've been told."

"A pink trailer would be *perfect*."

"It would?"

"Yes!"

"Why?"

He's still dancing. "He drives a dirt bike with a sidecar!"

"So?"

"He shoots paintballs with a slingshot!"

"So?"

"He has a *Jack*hammer and gives away Justice Jackets!"

"So?"

"*So?* Don't you get it? It's perfect!"

Well, I don't really, but if it makes Billy happy, then great.

Now, according to my little mental GPS, we've got about two miles to walk. And they *would* go a whole lot quicker on a skateboard, but since Billy's got nothing but his dancing feet, I just walk along holding my skateboard, listening to him, uh, *prattle* for at least fifteen minutes about the awesomeness of life as a superhero. And he's in the middle of saying something about Justice Jack being "pure of heart" when he interrupts himself to answer his phone. "Ya-lo?" He listens a second, then in a very nasally voice he says, "Please hold while I transfer your call," and hands the phone to me with a grin.

"Hey!" I say into the phone, and all of a sudden I feel stupidly happy.

"Hey," Casey says back. "Change in plans?"

"Billy needs a little post-breakup pick-me-up, so we're going to check out Justice Jack's secret hideaway."

"Whoa, wait, what? Marissa broke up with him?"

"Yup."

"Why?"

"I'll give you one guess."

There's a short pause. "Danny?"

"Bingo. And since the secret hideaway is a trailer way out in the sticks, it should be safe for you to meet us."

"Way out in which sticks?"

"It's right after the junkyard. You know where all those eucalyptus trees are? Turn in there, on Harmon. Sandydale Ts off of Harmon. It's at three-fifty-seven Sandydale."

"Three-fifty-seven Sandydale," he repeats. "See you there!"

When I hand the phone back to Billy, he takes it but he's looking at me kind of suspicious-like.

"What?"

"You're babysitting me?"

It flashes through my mind that I should deny it, but what comes flashing out of my *mouth* is, "No way . . . I'm Billysitting!"

He doesn't think that's too funny. "You don't have to, you know."

"Tough. You're stuck with me."

We walk along like that for a little while, and finally, in a really quiet voice, he says, "Thanks, Sammy-keyesta."

I grin at him. "Anytime, Billy-beasta."

* * *

In a way Justice Jack really did live in a secret hideaway. We had a terrible time finding it. I'd gone by the junkyard and that whole area before, but I'd never turned off the main road. And once we did, things started feeling really different. Really . . . *shady.*

The eucalyptus trees were huge. And everywhere. And everything was coated in a layer of eucalyptus leaves. It was like a giant blanket of long, flat, sage-colored paper spears that covered up anything that had stayed put too long.

The deeper down Harmon Street we went, the more it felt like we'd entered some strange sort of summer camp. For one thing, the pavement stopped after about twenty yards and the road became narrow and a sandy kind of dirt. And all the side roads were dirt, too, with tilting signposts that looked like they'd drifted over time.

But mostly it felt like a camp because instead of regular houses, there was a weird conglomeration of mobile homes. Some were on leveled ground with steps up and a skirting around them that looked like they'd planned to stay, but there were also a lot of broken-down motor homes and dilapidated camping trailers. Like people had rolled in for just the summer, but then the eucalyptus leaves had blanketed them in an enchanted sleep.

One that made them rust.

Or rot.

Or just collapse.

"I didn't even know this was back here," Billy whispers, and for some reason whispering seems like the right thing to do.

"Me either," I whisper back.

It was also hard to tell where we were. Or where 357 Sandydale was, anyway. The mailboxes were in big groups on posts at the bottom of the side streets, and once we turned up Sandydale, none of the trailers seemed to have numbers.

"Did *he* tell you he lived back here?"

"Justice Jack? No."

A big red truck is coming toward us along Sandydale, and it flashes through my mind that we could flag down the driver and ask, but I don't really want anyone to know where we're going, or who we're looking for.

The side of the truck says TONY'S TOWING in fancy white letters, and the back end is one of those flat steel beds that tilts down so cars can roll up. The driver's a big guy with dark curly hair, and let me tell you, he checks us over pretty good. But when we smile and wave, he does, too, and rolls down the window. "You kids lost?" He's got a Coke in his hand, and all of a sudden I realize I'm really, really thirsty.

"No, we're fine," I tell him. "Thanks, though!"

"It dead-ends. You know that, right?"

"Yeah," I tell him, like I'm an old pro at hiking up Sandydale Lane.

"Well, take it easy!" he says, and as he rolls down the road, my fantasy of being in a TV commercial where friendly people pass Cokes to strangers goes *poof*.

Billy's got his mind on other things. "Do you think Justice Jack'll be mad if he sees us?"

I shrug. "Maybe. Probably." But then I change my mind. "Actually, maybe not. He's been trying to recruit me."

125

"Really?" he squeaks. "What would you be? The Queen of Clubs? No, wait! The Attitude Ace!" And before I can say anything, he pogos up and down, going, "No, no, no! You could be the Dicey Dame!"

I laugh and shake my head. "Right now I happen to be Umbrella Girl."

He stops pogoing. "Umbrella Girl? Why would you be *Umbrella* Girl? That doesn't fit at all."

Well, obviously he doesn't watch the news and there's a lot to catch him up on, but right then a whistling sound cuts through the air. "That's Casey!" I put down my skateboard, wrap my hands around each other in one big sort of rounded fist, then blow into the hole between my thumb knuckles. And when a whistling sound comes out, I flap my left hand back and forth, matching the sound Casey had made.

"Whoa! How do you *do* that?" Billy asks, his eyes all wide.

Casey whistles again, so I do a return whistle and then break it down for Billy. "Lay your hands like this, curve them up, and blow!"

Billy tries it and nothing comes out. "How?" he asks. And since Casey's whistled back, trying to figure out where we are, I have Billy watch as I make the fist, then blow and flap my hand, warbling out another whistle.

He tries again, but only whooshes air. "You've got to teach me! And what you're whistling sounds like the theme song from *The Good, the Bad and the Ugly*."

"Huh?"

"You know! That old movie? It sounds just like that!" He shakes his head when I give another whistle. "Where'd you learn how to do that?"

I grin at him. "From Hudson, of course."

He tries, but gets nothing.

"It takes practice," I tell him. And I'm about to blow once more when I spot Casey. "Over here!" I call with a wave, and hurry back down Sandydale to give him a great big hug and a smooch. Then we just grin at each other like a couple of fools as we walk back to Billy.

"Hey, man," Billy says when we meet up. "You've got to help me master that whistle. It's awesome."

"Sure thing," Casey tells him. "Maybe on the way back." He looks around. "So where's this secret hideaway?"

"We haven't found it yet," Billy says. "We're lookin' for a hot-pink trailer."

"I don't think it's *hot* pink," I explain. "Just pink."

"How do you know it's pink at all?" Casey asks. "And how do you know it's back here? Did Justice Jack tell you?"

"No," I mumble, and, really, I don't want to get into the whole backstory of my little chitchat with Officer Borsch. Luckily, it turns out I don't have to, because just then a familiar sound roars through the air. "Hide!" I say, dragging Billy behind a big tree.

"The High Roller!" Billy cries, 'cause he recognizes the sound, too.

Sure enough, a minute later Justice Jack is tearing up the road on his dirt bike, and there's someone in his sidecar.

Someone who's wearing a big bulky blindfold.

"Out, you impostor!" Billy cries after they've roared up the road a ways. "That sidecar is mine!" Casey and I grin at each other and shake our heads, but Billy's already started running. "Come on!" he cries. "What are you waiting for? To the Jack Cave!"

SIXTEEN

We'd lost sight of the High Roller, but the road was dirt and still sort of wet from all the rain, so following the tracks was easy.

So was finding Justice Jack's hideaway.

"I think that's it," I say, pointing past some trees.

"That has to be it!" Billy cries.

Casey eyes me. "Really?"

It wasn't hot pink—more a chalky pink. And it had faded black trim, so even though it was long and boxy and ugly, it was ugly in a rare, funky-cool kind of way.

"That is the raddest thing I have ever seen!" Billy whispers.

The High Roller's parked between the trailer and a big metal shed that has palm trees and toucans and a sunset painted on it. And above the shed door there's a big, bright orange-and-blue sign that says WELCOME TO PAIR-A-DICE.

Next to the Pair-a-Dice shed there's a frayed hammock strung between two eucalyptus trees, and a sorry-looking round table and chairs. And poking up through the table is a patio umbrella with dried palm fronds strapped onto the top.

Only some of the fronds are missing.

And one of the umbrella arms is broken.

Just beyond the hammock and table there's a huge pile of junk. Half a truck, rolls of fencing, a stack of wheels, barrels . . . big junk with loads of little junk all around it. It's like someone did a claw-grab of the junkyard, swung the load over, and dropped it on the outskirts of Pair-a-Dice. And splattered all over the junk are splotches of red, gold, and glow-in-the-dark green paint. And we're just soaking all this in when a voice over to our left hollers, "JACK!"

We duck quick behind the trees we're near, and when we peek out at where the hollering's coming from, what we see is a middle-aged woman in slacks and a blazer, flying out of a mobile home about a hundred feet away.

"JACK!" she calls again, holding a scrap of paper in the air as she runs toward the pink trailer.

The Pair-a-Dice shed opens, and Justice Jack jumps out, ready for action.

"Three o'clock tomorrow!" the woman cries, wagging the paper. "Buckley's Coffee Shop!"

"You're serious?" he calls, running toward her, and even though he's still in all his hero gear, his voice isn't Justice Jackish . . . it's just Jackish.

They're right next to each other now, talking at a regular volume so we can't really hear what they're saying anymore, but they're obviously happy and excited about something.

And then a guy wearing a long tan coat and big aviator goggles strapped to his forehead steps out of the shed.

"Wassup?" he calls, and even from that one word it's easy to tell that he's been drinking.

The woman takes a step back and her voice goes way up. "What's *he* doing here?"

"It's okay," Justice Jack tells her. "I blindfolded him."

"I'm here for training!" the goggle guy tells her. "I'm the Royal Flush!"

"More like the Royal *Lush*," she shouts at him, then turns to Jack. "Can't you see he's been drinking? Or don't you care?"

Billy's not paying much attention to what they're saying. He's more into what the Lush is wearing. "Wow," Billy gasps, "that is the most *awesome* coat ever!"

"It was Hudson's," I say through my teeth, and I'm actually pretty ticked off about it. "It was supposed to be a Justice Jacket."

The woman has grabbed Justice Jack and is dragging him away from the Lush and over toward us. "Must be his mom," Casey whispers. "Who else could manhandle a superhero like that, huh?"

"You need to stop taking in strays, you hear me?" the woman's telling Jack. "You will get nowhere if you associate yourself with the likes of *that*."

"Aw, come on, Mom," Justice Jack says, "he's got nowhere to go."

"Exactly! That's his direction and destination, and there's no way I'm going to let you wind up there, too!"

"What are you talking about?"

"Get rid of him, Jack. Get rid of him now! And don't bring any more of your 'assistants' to the property!"

"How am I going to teach them the ropes? We need to practice our moves! He needs to learn how to wield a weapon! How to take down a perpetrator!"

The woman sucks in a deep breath, closes her eyes, and very calmly says, "Jack, that would be fine if your 'assistants' weren't such losers."

"Mom!" Justice Jack looks over his shoulder quick to make sure the Lush didn't hear. "Don't be so heartless! He just needs a chance."

She snorts. "And a bottle of whiskey."

"Mom!" But he looks down and shakes his head. "Look, I'm having trouble finding someone reliable, all right?"

"So just don't have an 'assistant'!"

"Superheroes always have an assistant!"

She tosses a glare over her shoulder. "You've *got* to be able to do better than that!"

He's quiet a minute, then says, "There is this girl. . . ."

His mom's ears practically perk right off her head. "A girl? Is she . . . Does she . . . ?" Her eyes narrow down on him. "Is she another stray?"

"No!"

She studies him a minute. "Does she have a job?"

He shakes his head. "She's still in school."

"School? Good! So she's smart?"

"She's really smart."

"So? Have you asked her?" And before he can answer, she goes, "You need to get out there and *ask*. I've told you this your whole life. Don't be afraid of girls. You'll get nowhere by not asking." She wags a finger at him. "This could be good. This could be really good. Broaden the appeal. More people will relate."

"Yeah, but—"

Now, the thing with eucalyptus trees is they have these pods. *Hard* pods. They're like brown wooden rocks dangling up among the leaves. And since these trees were *big*, they had pods to match. They were, like, an inch across, and were all over the carpet of leaves we were standing on. No woodland creature plucked them and placed them there, either.

They *fell* there.

And you know that old expression, The bigger they are, the harder they fall?

Well, right as Justice Jack is about to answer his mother, one of those big rocky pods goes *bombs away* and pelts Billy on the head.

"Yow!" he yelps, then looks at me like, Uh-oh!

We pull back quick and hold our breath while everything goes dead quiet.

"Who was that?" Mama Jack says, and before you know it, Justice Jack has pounced around the trees and is standing there like he's ready to wrestle down a bear.

But then he realizes it's me.

"Sammy?" he says, blinking at me through his mask. "How did you—"

"Oh, great," his mom says, because she's there now, too. "You let kids *follow* you?"

Billy steps forward and gives Justice Jack a snappy salute. "I would be honored to take on the role of your

133

assistant, sir! I would be trustworthy and reliable and proudly wear the Mask of Justice."

"The Mask of Justice!" Jack says, and you can tell he's warming up to Billy fast.

"No!" the mom says. "He's just a *kid*. You won't be taken seriously if you—"

"Batman had Robin!" Justice Jack exclaims. "And . . . and . . ."

"And Captain America had Bucky!" Billy cries.

Casey and I look at him. "Bucky?"

"Yeah! He was an orphan and he was awesome!"

"Go," Mama Jack says, pointing down the road. "You kids go and don't come back!"

"Yeah, go!" the Lush says. "And quit trying to steal my gig!"

"Get *him* out of here, too!" the mom demands, pointing at Lushy. "And don't bring him or any other strays here again. They'll ruin everything!" She turns to go, then turns back. "And do it now! I have to get back to work!"

Well, she storms off, and you can tell Jack is torn. And embarrassed. I mean, what kind of superhero gets bossed around by their mother?

Jack snaps the goggles off the Lush and tugs off Hudson's coat. "Come on," he says to the guy—who now definitely looks like a bum. "Maybe you can train on your own."

"You're firing me?" the guy says.

"We need to regroup. Find a better strategy." Then he moves in closer to us and drops his voice. "I don't know how you found me, but I could use some decent help."

He ends this little plea by looking right at me. So I put

my hands up and shake my head, but Billy squeals, "Me! Pick me! I'm telling you, I'd be an awesome sidekick!"

I put my arm out like I'm keeping Billy back. "Your mom's right—we're just kids."

But Jack's not giving up. "There's nothing more noble than the cause of justice. You're never too young to help make the world a better place."

Then he whips out a card and hands it to Billy.

"No!" I cry, but Billy snatches the card anyway.

"I need someone twenty-four-seven," Jack says. "Crime waits for no one."

"That's *time*," Casey says.

"Well, neither does crime," Jack says. Then he looks over his shoulder at his demoted sidekick, who's got his back turned to hide that he's swigging from a bottle. "And if you booze, you lose," he grumbles.

I step forward. "Look, we're not available twenty-four-seven. We go to school. We do homework." I eye Billy. "And we have *parents* who wouldn't want us riding shot-gun on a dirt bike!"

"Why are you here, then? Why track me down, if not to join forces?" He crosses his arms and puffs out his chest. "The lure of justice is strong, young one. Don't deny it!"

"Look, I—"

"And don't think you can infiltrate my secret hideaway without obligation!"

I blink at him. "You're saying we owe you something because we figured out where you live?"

His chin juts up slightly. "You have, at a minimum, a moral obligation to keep the location secret."

I shrug like, Sure, whatever, no problem.

"And should you—"

"JACK!" his mother yells from her mobile home. "GET RID OF THEM! NOW!"

Jack's mouth screws around to one side, then he suddenly whooshes off toward Pair-a-Dice. "Schoolboy," he calls over his shoulder to Billy, "we'll talk."

"No!" I call back at him. "You won't!"

But it's easy to see that no matter how hard I try, I won't be stopping this runaway train.

SEVENTEEN

Justice Jack waved and his flag flapped and Billy shouted, "You're awesome!" as the High Roller roared past us along Sandydale. The Lush was in the sidecar, blindfolded.

"I wouldn't ride in that thing blindfolded," Casey said. "Why doesn't he just take it off?"

"I wouldn't need one," Billy cries. "I know exactly where he lives!"

"And you're sworn to secrecy, remember? You crossed your heart and hoped to die-aye-aye?"

"Aye, aye!" Billy says, giving me another snappy salute.

I eye Casey. "You too."

He eyes me back. "Aye, aye!"

"So how come you're Umbrella Girl?" Billy asks, and he's kind of pouting. Like it's not fair that I've got a stupid name and he doesn't.

"Umbrella Girl?" Casey asks. "Do tell!"

So I wind up explaining what happened at the mall, and since Billy had been in such a great mood the whole time we'd been traipsing through the eucalyptus forest, I forget for a minute why I'd taken him there in the first place and find myself motormouthing about Marissa—which I notice makes Billy's bubbling go a little flat. So I try to cover up *that* by telling them about going to the library, which, of course, puts me in Heather territory. And even though I've been trying really hard not to bag on her around Casey, how can I talk about her and not?

So basically I squirt stupid sauce all over myself, and then squirt some more. And since we're now at the pavement and I'm totally feeling like I need a shower, and since I don't want to risk anyone on the main road spotting Casey and me together, I say, "Well, I'd better go!"

"Wait!" Casey calls, and catches up to me. "Is everything okay?"

"I'm an idiot. Why'd I have to bring up Marissa? Or Heather? Sorry."

"I don't care about Heather. And Billy's fine."

"No, he's not!" I whisper. "He's just distracted. Please hang out with him as long as you can. Marissa totally blindsided him."

He nods. "So what about tomorrow?"

"Let's pay-phone after school."

Which is code for him calling my school's pay phone from his school's pay phone when the high school lets out.

He nods and gives me a quick hug and a kiss. "I miss you!"

"I miss you, too!" But Billy's there now and I don't want to get too mushy. "Oh!" I say to Billy. "Speaking of missing people, tell him about Lars!"

"Rock of Looooove!" Billy says, and since that seems to, you know, re-carbonate him, I tell them, "See you tomorrow!" and take off on my skateboard.

* * *

There was no one rappelling down the Highrise or trying to break into the Wedge's apartment when I got home. It was . . . quiet. And Grams wasn't rifling through anybody's drawers. She was just sitting on the couch reading a book.

"Dinner smells awesome!" I tell her as I slip my skateboard under the couch and swing off my backpack.

"Roasted chicken and potatoes," she says with a smile.

And then I notice that the table is set for three.

Now, the only other person to ever eat dinner in the apartment with us had been my mother. And I can't think of a better way to tie my stomach in knots than to have a meal with the attention-wrangling Lady Lana. She's like a bolt of pink lightning zapping through a meadow. Not that I'm saying life with Grams is peaceful. Meadows do have bees and cows and birds milling about. Probably snakes. Definitely mosquitoes. And once in a while a big ol' bear ambles through.

But pink lightning?

You're like, *Whoa!* What was that? because you can't quite believe that pink lightning just streaked through your meadow, destroying the whole balance of things, and then vanished. And even after it's long gone, you're wiped out and nervous, worried that it might strike again.

So, anyway, when I see the third setting, I moan, "Oh no."

Grams give me a playful little look. "Not in the mood to see Hudson?"

"Hudson?"

She looks at the wall clock. "He'll be here in fifteen minutes." And her book must've been pretty good, because all of a sudden she jumps up and says, "Fifteen minutes!" and hurries toward the bathroom. "Maybe you can toss the salad? Everything's chopped and ready. It's on the second shelf. In the refrigerator!"

I kind of chuckle, 'cause where else would it be?

In the closet?

She leaves the bathroom door open, so while she's in there fixing her face and I'm in the kitchen fixing the salad, I ask her, "Any news on the Wedge?"

Her head pops out. "The police were here today taking a missing person report. Finally!" Then she disappears.

"Was it Officer Borsch?"

"No," she calls. "It was a man and a woman." Her head pops out again. "They didn't seem too bright."

"Did the woman have a long blond braid?"

"Yes!"

"Did the guy use big words to say small-word stuff?"

"Yes!"

"That was Squeaky and the Chick."

I can hear her spraying her hair as she says, "Those two will never in a million years find Rose. And that Justice Jack fella seems to be a dead end, too."

"They really called him?"

"Cynthia Orren did."

"Is she the one who had his card? The one with the salt-and-pepper bun way up on her head."

Grams steps out of the bathroom looking pretty much like she did when she stepped in, only with more colorful lips. "Isn't that an *awful* hairstyle? Lord knows what she's thinking."

I toss the salad and kind of shake my head, because the longer I live in the Senior Highrise, the more it seems like *junior* high. "But she called Justice Jack and . . . ?"

"And a group of them met with him in the lobby. Gave him a picture of Rose and told him their woes. He vowed to find her, but obviously he hasn't." She pulls the salad dressing out of the fridge and gives it a good shake. "Vince Garnucci told me he thought he was ridiculous, but Hudson seems to think he's a decent fellow, and I've got to admire a man who's willing to step up and defend the rights of the citizenry."

"The citizenry? Is that actually a word?"

She hrmphs. "Of course it's a word."

The doorbell rings, and even though we're expecting Hudson, we can't be a hundred percent sure. So I duck into Grams' bedroom just to be safe, and after Hudson's inside and the front door's shut tight, I come out and put the flowers he's brought in a vase while Grams takes his coat and flutters about.

And, really, the two of them are so cute with the way they're kind of awkward and ridiculously formal and sort of *twinkling* around each other like a couple of happy fireflies. And I was starting to feel like I shouldn't even be there when Hudson comes into the kitchen and asks, "Did you hear the latest about Justice Jack?"

I'm tempted to say, What, that he gave the most awesome coat in the universe to a drunk guy in goggles? but I manage to clamp my mouth shut after "What."

"He rescued preschool kids from a snake."

"A snake?" I ask. "Wait—in December?"

His bushy eyebrows go up a little. "You raise a good point. Maybe it was flushed out of its hibernation den by the rains?" He gives a little shrug. "Regardless, apparently Justice Jack heard the screams and came to the rescue, much to the little ones' delight." He chuckles. "Can you imagine?"

I pull the chicken and potatoes out of the oven, picturing a bunch of little kids rushing around Justice Jack as he hefts a monster boa and cries, "You are safe, little citizens!"

"A day they won't soon forget, I'm sure," Grams says. And I'm taking off the hot mitts when I hear her ask him, "Do you have any idea what this might be about?" and when I turn to look, she's handing him the folded page that she'd ripped out of the Wedgie's notebook.

He studies it a minute. "Looks like a bookie's notes to me."

"A *bookie's* notes?" Grams gasps. "Like gambling?"

He nods. "*Tripteaser, Over-n-Out, Dusk Before Dawn* . . . these sound like racehorse names."

I pull a face. "*Sexy Librarian* is a racehorse name?"

He gives a little one-shoulder shrug and a grin.

Like, Yeah.

Grams' eyes are totally bugged out as she looks at me and exclaims, "She's betting on the ponies?"

"Who is?" Hudson asks.

"Wedgie Woman," I tell him.

"Rose Wedgewood," Grams says, and the look she gives me is definitely saying, Mind your manners!

"Is that your"—he hesitates—"your well-rounded neighbor?"

Grams nods. "She hasn't been home in days." She looks at me. "She must have gone to a racetrack!"

"But . . . I believe horse-racing season starts between Christmas and New Year's," Hudson says.

"Is there a preseason?" Grams asks.

Hudson shakes his head. "I don't know that much about it, but I wouldn't be surprised."

Grams takes the paper back and murmurs, "So Rose plays the ponies. . . ."

It *was* pretty surprising.

Although, thinking about it, the Wedge *was* pretty cagey.

And a master blackmailer.

In a weird way, it did sort of make sense. And for the first time since she'd gone missing, it hit me that maybe she really wasn't coming back.

I just stood there a minute, letting it sink in.

I don't know why, but it was strangely upsetting.

EIGHTEEN

Billy was not sulking by himself on the school steps the next morning. When I got on campus, I saw him over by Mrs. Ambler's classroom, but he just waved and called, "Sammy-keyesta!" and kept on trucking to class.

Now, maybe that was because the bell was about to ring, or maybe that was because Marissa and I usually meet up before school and he didn't want to have to deal with her, but if it was the Marissa part, he had nothing to worry about.

I didn't see her anywhere.

I also didn't see her at break, but when I spotted Billy going into history, I ran up to him and said, "Hey! How are things?"

"Things are super-cool!"

I eye him. "I haven't seen Marissa today, have you?"

"Who?" he asks like a funny-faced hoot owl.

But then we step inside the classroom and overhear Anastasia Vickers saying, "They *eloped*?" to Heather.

"That's right!"

Anastasia shakes her head. "You can't elope when you're thirteen!"

Heather shrugs. "Well, they ran off together. Whatever."

I hate gossip. It's catty and destructive, and half the time it's not even true. Or only partly true. I also hate it because people like Heather live for it. She loves to hear it, loves to spread it, loves to *start* it.

Especially if it's smack about me.

So hearing her gossip about someone was nothing new. What *was* new was me wanting to ask her about it. Because right away I noticed that Lars Teppler was absent, and the only person I knew—or *people,* actually—who were desperate enough to run off together were Lars and Sasha.

But where would they go? How would they live? Neither of them could pull off pretending to be eighteen.

He still had peach fuzz!

So I couldn't help wondering—were Lars and Sasha who Heather was gossiping about? And the more I wondered, the more I really wanted to know!

Not bad enough to ask Heather, of course. She'd just laugh and call me a nosy loser. But since Anastasia and I get along fine and since she sits between me and the pencil sharpener, I slipped her a note that said, *Was Heather talking about Lars and Sasha?* the first chance I got to go use the thing.

Sure enough, on my way back to my seat she gives me a little nod.

For the rest of class I just sat there thinking, Wow. And even though I tried to convince myself that it was probably all rumors and exaggerations and maybe even lies, Lars *was* absent and he *had* seemed desperate, and I couldn't help believing that it was probably true.

I also couldn't help feeling sorry for him.

Sorry for both of them.

I could just see him dashing over on his bike to rescue the fair maiden who was imprisoned in a barn on the outskirts of town. I could picture them frantically escaping in the moonlight, checking over their shoulders, not believing that they were actually getting away.

But there were big nets out there—not just her family, the police. And no matter how hard they pedaled, they'd get caught. Caught and hauled back home.

And then what?

Things would be worse than ever.

By lunch the whole school was talking about it, including Marissa. I guess she was happy to have something to talk about besides her and Billy—or her and Danny—because she was motoring at the mouth about how exciting and *romantic* it was.

Holly was the one to finally hand her a reality check. "You think it's romantic? It's December! It's cold! Where are they going to stay? They're going to run out of money! They can't get jobs! What are they going to live on? It's miserable being on the run with no place to go and nothing to eat!"

And instead of going, Wow. Yeah. I suppose you would know, Marissa says, "They're in *love*, Holly. It's not the same as what you went through. Love will get you through anything."

"Not if you're hungry and cold," Holly says, shaking her head.

"Or pregnant," Dot says.

We all look at her, horrified: For one thing, this is *Dot*, who's always just sweet and cute and, well, innocent. But also just the thought of it maybe happening was scary. What a mess that would be.

"Well, what do you think?" Dot says, looking us over. "That they're out there roasting marshmallows?"

Marissa starts packing up her stuff. "You guys are such downers."

"Where are you going?" I ask her.

"Somewhere happy," she says with a haughty little sniff, and takes off.

Now, I hadn't seen Billy since history, but I didn't think much of it because I figured he was just avoiding Marissa. But when he was absent in science and drama, I started to get a little worried. I could see him ditching drama, but science? That class is hard.

So during drama I went up and asked Marissa if she'd seen him, but she just said no and then went back to talking with her new, happy friends.

After school I tried calling Billy from the pay phone, and when it rolled over to voice mail, all I said was, "Hey, it's Sammy. Just a little worried about you because you weren't in science or drama. Call Casey's house and tell him you're okay, okay?"

But when I was pay-phoning Casey after school, he didn't seem too worried. "Marissa was definitely not on his mind on our way home yesterday. All he talked about was Justice Jack."

"But that's just some fantasy world. Today he was back in junior high."

"You know," Casey says, "the place I'd look for him would be Buckley's. Justice Jack had some meeting there at three o'clock, remember?"

"But . . . why would Billy ditch school for something that starts *after* school?"

"I have no idea, but if he didn't go home sick, I bet that's where he'll be." He snickers. "Any chance to see Justice Jack."

"You want to meet me there? It should be safe, don't you think? It's seems like an old-guy hang—not someplace Heather or your mom would ever go."

"Yeah, I sure don't know anyone that goes there."

"Me either." I look around, 'cause all of a sudden I'm worried that Heather may be lurking nearby. "I'll make sure I'm not followed."

"Sounds good. See you there!"

So I head out on my skateboard, and to make sure nobody's following me, I take a few detours, turning down streets I don't need to take, zigzagging the long way over to Buckley's.

By the time I turn onto West Main, I'm positive nobody's following me, and I'm also sure Casey's right—if Billy's not sick, he'll be there.

I ride until the coffee shop is right across the street, then I pop up my board and wait for a break in traffic so I can cut over.

Only there *is* no break in traffic.

So I'm finally deciding that maybe it would be a smart idea to head up to the light instead of jaywalking when a bright red sports car goes flying by.

There's no missing Candi Acosta in her Hot Mobile. It's not just that the car is bright red, or that her hair is red, it's the *way* she drives, zooming around other cars, acting like she's in the Indy 500 instead of downtown Santa Martina.

The good thing about her being a speed demon is that she has to concentrate on cutting off other cars and flooring it through yellow lights, so she doesn't really have time to notice people on the sidewalk who are considering jaywalking.

Or, with *her* on the road, suicide.

Still, I was kinda worried that maybe she'd seen me.

Or that maybe Heather was in the car and *she'd* seen me.

And what if they'd already passed by Casey coming from the other direction and realized he and I were going *toward* each other? What if they were flipping an illegal U-turn right now, racing back so they could bust us and throw Casey out of the house?

I told myself I was being dumb, but since all the traffic made jaywalking seem even dumber, I went clear down to the corner, waited for the light to finally change, and kept my eyeballs peeled for red sports cars as I crossed the street and made my way back down to Buckley's.

Buckley's Coffee Shop seems like a place that's been around since the beginning of time. Or at least since before the mall was built. It's got big windows on each side of the door, with dark green booths and shellacked pine tables shoved up against them. There's also a long breakfast counter with tall stools, but I've only ever gotten a glimpse of it, because there are always old people sitting at the booths by the window. And since old people in restaurants never seem to have anything to say to each other, there's a lot of staring out the window going on, which makes peeking inside even more awkward than just walking by.

Sure enough, there are a couple of old guys staring out the window from a booth as I walk by. The High Roller isn't parked out front, but I'm not surprised by that, either. There's not much parking on Main Street, so most businesses have parking in back. And since I'm so sure that Billy will be there spying on Justice Jack, and since I'd taken about ten miles of detours and am sure Casey will already be there, I just yank open the door and go inside.

Right away a really awkward vibe fills the air.

It's like the building itself gasped.

And then every old neck in the place slowly creaks around to face me.

The big guy wiping down the breakfast counter comes to a halt and just stands there looking at me.

The cook behind the order carousel freezes in the middle of putting two plates on the pass-through counter.

Even the bobcat that's mounted above the back door is staring at me.

And that's when it hits me that I'm the only female in the place.

"Pssst!" I hear from my left, and believe me, I'm more than a little relieved to turn and see Casey.

He's sitting in a booth, alone, and when I slide in across from him, he says, "Billy's not here, and neither is Jack, but I've been watching that guy over there." He nods across the diner. "He doesn't fit in here at all."

Right away I know exactly what he means. Instead of a T-shirt and flannel like everyone else in the place is wearing, this guy's got on a black button-down shirt and black slacks that are obviously high-end. He's by himself, scrolling through his phone. There's no food or coffee on his table, just a pair of shades that pushes his look toward Secret Service, only he's kinda too scrawny for that. Plus, his hair's shaggy, in a very un–Secret Service sort of way.

Casey's watching him, too. "I think he may be the one Jack's supposed to be meeting."

"He's not from Santa Martina, that's for sure." I look around. "But what about Billy? I really thought he'd be here."

"Maybe he did go home sick?"

"He seemed fine this morning."

All of a sudden the big guy from behind the counter is standing at our booth. "You kids ready to order?" His big, broad belly is at eye level, and even him just standing there is really intimidating.

"Uh . . . is there a menu?" Casey asks.

Old guys at the booths near us snicker, and Big Boy just sorta grins. "We make anything. Just tell us what you want."

I look up at him. "But how do we know how much it is?" I glance at Casey and then back up at Big Boy. "We're kinda on a budget."

Big Boy nods. "Don't worry. We're reasonable."

"But—"

"And there's always dishes!" an old guy at another booth calls, which makes all his friends cackle and snort.

"Okay," Big Boy says, "how about we go at it the other way around. What do you like, and how much you got to spend? We'll rustle up something for you based on that."

But all of a sudden there's a little commotion by the back door and a chorus of voices calls out, "It's Justice Jack!"

"Greetings, good citizens!" Jack bellows, making his grand entry.

And that's when we see that Justice Jack has a sidekick with him. Only his sidekick isn't wearing a torn cloth mask or a frayed towel cape.

He's got on a black leather mask, a black bomber helmet, a tight red shirt, bright red gloves, black jeans, and . . .

Hudson's awesome coat.

And even as covered up as he is, there's no doubt about it.

Jack's new sidekick is Billy Pratt.

NINETEEN

"Quite a character," Big Boy says, watching us stare at Justice Jack and Billy. "You kids knew he was coming? Is that why you're here?"

I give him a guilty little shrug.

"So it's not an after-school snack you're looking for."

It feels like he's about to kick us out, so Casey starts scrounging through his pockets and manages to scrape up about three dollars, while I put in thirty-seven cents.

"Uh-huh," he says, eyeing our measly pile of cash. Then he takes a good hard look at each of us and nods. "Seeing how it's your first time here, why don't we say the Cokes are on the house. And let's get you a better table, maybe a little closer to the action."

We both just stare at him a minute, not really believing our ears. Finally I choke out, "You're serious?"

He cocks his head, telling us to follow him. "Welcome to Buckley's."

We wound up in a small booth right across the aisle from where Jack and Billy were sitting with the Man in Black. Billy had given us an impish grin and slipped a finger in front of his lips, so he knew we were there. Jack did, too, although he seemed more worried than happy to see us.

"So, Jack—" the Man in Black is saying, but Jack cuts him off.

"With all due respect, good sir, the name is Justice Jack."

"He's no ordinary Jack!" an old guy in the booth next to him says, and everyone else in the place follows up, shouting, "He's *Justice* Jack!"

"And this," Justice Jack takes the opportunity to announce, "is my faithful assistant, the Deuce!"

"All hail the Deuce!" the same old guy shouts.

"Hear! Hear! Long live the Deuce!" the rest of them call.

Casey and I look at each other like, The Deuce? but Billy's obviously loving it. He stands up and lifts his arms high like he has legions of adoring fans. "Thank you, good people!"

Now, the Man in Black is looking a little uncertain. Like, Where am I, and who *are* these people? He leans forward across the table and says something that we sure can't hear, and apparently Justice Jack and Billy can't hear, either, because they lean in, too. And then the three of them have a hush-hush powwow while Casey and I sip our Cokes, hoping their huddle will break up already so we can hear again.

Finally the Man in Black leans back and raises his voice. "What do you mean, you have to blindfold me?"

Justice Jack crosses his arms and puffs out his chest. "It's the way it has to be!"

154

Just then a rocking ringtone cuts through the air, and the peanut gallery of old guys calls out, "The Justice Jingle!" as Jack snatches the phone from his belt.

Casey grins and whispers, "Did you recognize that?"

"What?" I whisper back.

"His ringtone." I shake my head, so he says, " 'Jumpin' Jack Flash' by the Stones."

We go back to watching Jack, whose eyes are wide behind his mask as he checks out the display and shows it to Billy.

"City Hall?" Billy cries.

Jack makes a show of putting the phone on speaker mode. "Justice Jack. It's a good world. Let's take it back!"

"Jack, it's Mayor Hibbs," comes the voice from the other end.

"Yes, Mayor!" Jack says in his booming Justice Jack voice. "How may I be of service?"

"The statue's still missing and my police force is apparently dumbfounded," Mayor Hibbs announces, sounding like a junior version of Justice Jack. "I want it back before it's sold for scrap! I'm willing to make a proclamation! A commendation! A dedication! What's your pleasure?"

"My pleasure?" Justice Jack asks.

"Would you like a Justice Jack Day? Keys to the city? Your own float in the Christmas parade? Any of those! Just find my statue!"

"Consider it done, Mayor!" Jack booms, and the entire restaurant starts chanting, "Justice Jack! Justice Jack!" as he hangs up.

"Is it always like this?" the Man in Black shouts over the chanting.

"Some days are busier than others," Jack shouts back.

The Man in Black just stares at him a minute, then stands. "Let's go."

"To the hideaway?" Jack asks. "The blindfold requirement still—"

"Fine. Let's go."

Justice Jack gets out of the booth, waves to all the old guys in the place, and calls out, "Farewell, wise men!"

"Go get 'em, Justice Jack!" they holler as he and Billy and the Man in Black go out the back door.

Casey and I slurp down our Cokes, and after Casey slips a dollar under our empty glasses, we head out the back door, too, waving a quiet thanks to Big Boy as we go.

The Man in Black is already blindfolded and in the sidecar, and Justice Jack is revving up the High Roller. Billy's squeezed onto the seat behind him with his hands clamped on Jack's shoulders.

"Man, what have I *done*?" I moan as they pull away.

"Well, we know Billy's nuts," Casey says, "but I can't believe that guy agreed to be blindfolded. I wonder who he is."

And that's when I notice the shiny black car over to our right with a personalized plate that reads SKT AGNT.

I work it out in my head. "Secret agent?"

"Maybe a skirt agent?"

"A skirt agent? What's a skirt agent?"

He shrugs. "Got me. But what kind of secret agent would advertise that he's a secret agent?"

I pause. "Good point."

"So?" Casey asks after a minute. "You ready to go?"

"Go? You want to follow them?"

"Sure, why not?" He grins. "Better'n homework."

"But—" And all of a sudden I feel really sad. I mean, it would be a lot of fun to ride out to Pair-a-Dice with Casey, only we can't.

"What?"

"I saw your mom roaring down the road right before I crossed the street."

"Oh."

I can tell he'd completely forgotten how we're not supposed to be seeing each other, and for some reason what pops out of my mouth is, "Lars and Sasha ran off together."

His head snaps up. "Seriously?"

"Crazy, huh?"

He looks a little worried. "You're not thinking . . ."

"No!" I shrug and look down. "It's just sad."

"Because they're doomed?"

I nod.

He lifts my chin. "Well, don't worry. We're not doomed. We'll just be smart and work around my crazy mother, okay?"

I nod. "At least Grams is on our side. And Hudson and Billy and Holly and Dot and even Marissa."

"See?" he says. "Not so bad." He gives me a mischievous

grin. "So how about you go one way and I go another, and we meet in paradise?"

I laugh. "Pair-a-Dice is not my idea of paradise."

He gives a cute little shrug. "As long as I'm with you . . ."

I throw my arms around him. I mean, what kind of guy says stuff like that? Then I pull back and give *him* a mischievous grin. "Race ya!"

"You're on!" he laughs. "I'll meet you where the road turns to dust!"

Then we throw our boards down and hurry off in opposite directions.

I took the same route I'd taken with Billy, only this time I had no one to talk to as I rode by the junkyard, so I actually noticed some things.

Like that the junkyard doesn't call itself a junkyard.

It's a *salvage* yard.

Sorta like Mrs. Wedgewood is well rounded.

Really. The place is *acres* of junk—zillions of cars, tons of old farm equipment, stacks of pipe and rebar, big heaps of tires . . . and then there's what looks like the demolition section. Smashed metal of all shapes and sizes . . . and makes and models.

And popping up here and there among all the *junk* are corrugated metal buildings. The one closest to the street has big sprayed-on letters that say OFFICE. One farther back says WAREHOUSE. Another says HUBCAPS.

Can you believe that?

A whole building for hubcaps.

And all this junky mess is surrounded by chain-link fencing that's topped with coils of razor wire.

Razor wire.

Like someone's going to go, Hey, Fred, let's break into the salvage yard and steal some junk!

Anyway, I'm checking all this out, passing by the big open gate, when a little hiccup happens in my brain. It's just a tiny glitch in my mental breathing, but something about it kind of throws me. And pretty soon I'm not pumping like I'm in a race with Casey. Pretty soon I'm looking over my shoulder, hearing Mayor Hibbs' voice in my head: *I want it back before it's sold for scrap!*

So I skid to a halt, turn around, and power back to the office building. It's not far inside the gate, and besides, Casey had to go the long way, which wasn't fair.

A quick little detour would, you know, even things up.

There's a pack of dogs snoozing together in a corner of the office, and they perk up when they hear me walk in, but they don't *get* up. Two of them have one blue eye and one brown eye, which is kind of scary-looking, especially since the blue is so blue it's almost white.

But after they check me over, they just go back to snoozing. So I walk past them and up to a counter where a guy in dark blue coveralls is typing at a computer while talking into the phone that's cradled at his shoulder. ". . . Yeah, we got one. It'll fit an eighty-eight or eighty-nine. . . . No problem. . . . Seven-thirty to four-thirty, closed Sundays. . . . That's right. . . . Good enough."

When he hangs up, he looks at me and says, "What can I do ya for?"

"Uh . . . has anyone come in here trying to pawn a life-size statue?"

"Uh . . . ," he says back, "we're not exactly a pawn-shop."

"But if someone had something that was big and metal, would you buy it from them? You know, like for scrap or salvage or whatever?"

"Hmm. Depends on the metal."

"It's bronze."

His eyebrows go up. "Solid bronze, or coated? And what kind of bronze?"

Well, I had no idea. I didn't even really know it *was* bronze. It's just what people who talked about the statue always said it was. And since the clock was ticking, I just decided to cut to the chase.

"You know the statue in City Hall? The one that was stolen?"

"No . . ."

"You haven't heard about that?"

He gives a little laugh. "I try to avoid City Hall."

"Well, you've seen the softball statue, right?"

He shakes his head, and I can tell that he really has no idea what I'm talking about.

"Well, look. If someone comes in here trying to sell you a statue—or pieces of a statue that might add up to softball players—call the police, okay?"

He shrugs. "Sure."

"Actually . . ." I scrounge through my jeans and dig up Justice Jack's card, which at this point is pretty bent and rumpled. I smooth it down and pass it over the counter. "Call this guy."

"Justice Jack?" he says with a sideways grin. Then he laughs and adds, "I never in a million years thought he'd catch on."

"So you've heard of *him*?"

"Oh yeah."

Then the phone rings, and that's the end of our conversation.

TWENTY

Casey was already waiting at the end of the pavement, and after I told him about my junkyard detour and he got done teasing me about being Sidetrack Sammy, we hurried up to Pair-a-Dice, crunching through a bed of eucalyptus leaves as we cut off the road to get in close.

The High Roller was parked in front of the pink trailer, and there was a bicycle that hadn't been there before leaning against big metal barrels that were standing between the trailer and Pair-a-Dice.

The door to Pair-a-Dice was open, and although we could hear noise coming from inside, we couldn't really tell what people were saying or doing, and there was no way to peek in without being seen.

Finally Casey whispers, "That sounds like Pac-Man."

It did, too. "Want to check for windows around back?"

He says, "Sure," so we tiptoe through the leaves, making our way between the side of the shed and the heaping mound of paint-splatted junk. And when we get behind the shed, what do we see?

More junk and no rear windows.

There *is* a big dent and a split in a seam where two sections of corrugated metal sheets come together, though. So I peek through that while Casey puts an eye up to a hole where a large screw that had held two other sections together was missing.

Now, I don't know *what* I was expecting to see. Maybe a few plastic chairs? Some rakes and shovels? Stacks of, you know, *junk*?

But instead, I find myself looking at a cross between a cabana, a casino, and an arcade. There's a Pac-Man machine, which Billy is playing, a pinball machine, a refrigerator, a microwave, an orange velvet couch, a roulette table, a poker table, a slot machine, Lava lamps, a television, and cool tropical decorations everywhere.

There's also a floor-to-ceiling curtain that's pulled across the whole left wall. And I guess I'm not the only one wondering what's behind it because the Man in Black is pointing over at it.

Now, I can hear that Justice Jack and the Man in Black are talking, but the Pac-Man noise is making it hard to understand what they're saying. I try putting my ear up to the split in the seam, but all that does is make the Pac-Man noise louder, so I switch back to looking in time to see Justice Jack whoosh aside the curtain and reveal . . .

A big, boring sheet of plywood.

And in my head I'm going, *Huh?* but then Jack flies into action, flipping down wooden legs, pulling levers, yanking down the plywood, and snapping things upright. In less than thirty seconds, we're looking at a fully loaded workshop.

"Whoa!" Casey whispers. "It's like a Murphy bench!"

Billy's abandoned the Pac-Man machine, and we can hear Justice Jack announce, "From the Justice Jackknife to the Jack-Attack Smacker, this is where the Painful Punch of Justice begins!"

Now, while Justice Jack is showing Secret Agent Man around the workbench, I'm noticing something about this mysterious visitor—he's had his arms crossed the whole time and his phone is at kind of a weird angle in his hand.

I turn to Casey. "I think that guy's recording stuff on his phone!"

"I think you're right!"

The Justice Jingle sounds and Jack snatches up his phone, and before he's even said anything into it, he booms, "I'll be back in a flash!" and dashes out the door.

Billy takes a seat on the orange couch, but Secret Agent Man ambles over to the door and looks around, then steps out.

"Okay," Casey whispers. "This is just weird. Who is that guy and why is Jack showing him everything? And why would a guy with a high-end sports car even care about some poor schmuck's fantasy hideout?"

"Do you think we should bust him for taking pictures?"

"You mean let them know we're here?"

I nod. "Maybe get the phone and delete the pictures?"

"Are you saying we should *tackle* him?"

"Well, no, but—"

Just then I hear the crunching of leaves from around the building, so I put a finger up to my lips quick and motion Casey to hide with me behind a pile of junk. Good thing we moved quick, too, because about three crunches later Secret Agent Man comes into view. He's talking on his cell in kind of a hoarse whisper and he's obviously all hyped up. ". . . It's unbelievable! You couldn't make this stuff up! Picture *Hancock* meets *Dog the Bounty Hunter*. . . . No, he's not homeless. He's just this side of it, though. He lives in a pink trailer out in the boonies. . . . Yes, pink! And he's . . . Did those pictures land yet? Look at the pictures! And those news clips his manager sent? Those are all for real." There's a short pause and then, "No, I'm supposed to meet with her this afternoon. . . . I have no idea. . . . Look, I'm telling you, this is solid gold. It'll start a bidding war. It's fresh and unique and . . . it's real, but it's *un*real! The *mayor* called him today while we were at this coffee shop full of old geezers—offered to give him his own float in the Christmas parade if he can get back some statue that's been stolen." There's a long pause and then, "Right, right, I know, but he has this young sidekick. Calls him the Deuce. Cute kid, very marketable. . . . Yeah, I know. . . . Okay, no problem. . . . Fine. . . . Fine. . . . Hey, I gotta go. He's looking for me." Then he hangs up and goes back the way he came.

"*Hancock* meets *Dog the Bounty Hunter*?" I whisper to Casey.

"*Hancock* is an old Will Smith movie about a homeless superhero, and I think *Dog the Bounty Hunter* was a reality show."

"So . . . that guy's a *Hollywood* agent?"

Casey nods. "That would be my guess."

"And he's here because he wants to turn all of *this*"—I wave my arms around at the assorted junk—"into . . . what? A reality show?"

"You couldn't script this stuff," Casey says with a little laugh. "The High Roller, the pink trailer, Pair-a-Dice . . ."

"And a very marketable sidekick." I blink at him. "Wow. Do you think Billy knows what's going on?"

"He almost has to."

I let everything soak in for a minute and then sort of shake my head. "This all feels really . . . *big*."

And it *does,* but something feels off about it, too. Sort of *un*real. Not because there's suddenly some guy running around Santa Martina in tights and a mask.

It's Santa Martina.

Weird stuff happens.

It's more a feeling that it all started happening out of nowhere. Like, *poof,* a superhero appeared.

Well, superhero-slash-clown.

You know.

But obviously Pair-a-Dice wasn't built yesterday, and you don't just throw together a mad-scientist workbench or the whole Justice Jack persona or get a fan club like the one he had at Buckley's overnight.

Still.

A Hollywood agent?

It suddenly all seemed . . . *fake*.

"Pssst!"

Casey's by the right side of the building now, looking down the breezeway between the pink trailer and Pair-a-Dice, waving me over.

So I follow him around the corner, stooping low as we scurry in behind the big metal barrels. "Everyone's outside," he whispers. "What do you want to do?"

"Lay low," I whisper back.

A small white car turns onto the property as Casey and I get settled behind the barrels, and when the driver steps out and we see that it's Justice Jack's *mom,* Casey and I eye each other like, Now what?

Only, like a couple of magnets clicking together, I suddenly get it.

"She must be his 'manager'!" I whisper.

Sure enough, she steps forward and shakes Agent Man's hand like he's a long-lost friend. "I'm Sheri. It's a pleasure to meet you in person."

"Likewise."

"So what do we think?" she asks him. "He's everything I said and more, isn't he?"

Agent Man nods and says, "This has potential." But the way he says it is nothing like the way he was talking on the phone. It's much more ho-hum than that. "I'll need to check in with some of my contacts—get their reaction." He turns to Jack. "It was nice meeting you." He smiles at Billy. "And you." Then he eyes the High Roller and says, "Can we head back to town? I've got to get going."

Justice Jack's mom looks pretty deflated, but Jack seems oblivious. "Certainly!" He turns to Billy. "Deuce! You're taking the Rushin' Roulette back into town, right?"

"Yes, sir!"

"Can you lock down the lair?"

"Consider it done!" Billy says, sounding like Junior Jack.

"Then we're off!" Justice Jack cries. Only, after charging forward two steps, he stops, turns, and hurries toward the pink trailer. "Got to hit the Jackpot first!"

Casey and I look at each other and mouth, "The Jackpot?!" and have the hardest time not busting up.

A minute later we hear the toilet flush in the pink trailer and Jack comes bounding down the steps. "Anyone else?" And when Billy and Agent Man shake their heads, Jack cries, "To the High Roller!"

The minute they've roared off, Mama Jack gets in her little car and drives it up to the mobile home, parking it around back. So when we're sure the coast is clear, Casey and I scoot around the barrels and the bike and zip inside Pair-a-Dice, where Billy's putting up the workbench.

"Dude!" he says, jumping. "Where'd you come from?"

"Uh, school?" I tell him. "By way of Buckley's?"

"Yeah, yeah, right, whatever," he grumbles.

I cock my head a little. "Billy!"

"It's the Deuce, Sammy-keyesta, and I have had the most awesome day of my life, so, no, I don't want to get a lecture about ditching school."

"Who's lecturing?"

"I know you think this is stupid. You probably think it's *dangerous,* but—"

"I think this place is awesome," Casey tells him. "And I think you look pretty superhero-ish in that getup."

And just like that, Billy's eyes light up. "There's something about wearing a mask—dude, it transforms you."

Casey nods. "I can see that."

"So is it a secret that you're the Deuce?" I ask. "And what's the plan?"

Billy scowls at me. "Of course it's a secret. And why does there have to be a plan?"

I shrug and just shut up, because I'm obviously being brilliant at pushing the wrong buttons.

And that's when we hear someone coming.

"Hide!" Billy whispers frantically, but it's too late.

Mama Jack has just entered the building.

TWENTY-ONE

"What *is* this?" Mama Jack demands.

Now, if I had a job that I really, really liked and my friends showed up and got me in trouble, I'd be ticked off. And from the look on Mama Jack's face, Billy's in danger of getting fired whether Justice Jack likes it or not. Her cheeks are flushing, her finger's coming up like a gun, and I just know she's about to yell, Get out! All of you! Get out and don't come back!

I mean, that's what all adults yell when they catch kids where they're not supposed to be, right?

And since I don't want Billy to be mad at me forever, I blurt out, "Wait! We overheard that agent say he thought Jack and all of this"—I wave my hands around—"were solid gold."

Her hand freezes. It's still pointing like a gun, but at least she's not firing. She gives me a hard look, then Casey, then Billy, then me again. "Are you sure?"

"Positive."

She's still suspicious. "How'd you hear that?"

"We were, uh . . ." I look at Casey, who shrugs like, Go

ahead. So I tell her, "We were worried about our friend becoming your son's sidekick, so we came up here and were, you know, kind of hanging around outside."

"Spying, you mean."

I pull a face. "Yeah. But if we hadn't been, we wouldn't have overheard that agent guy make his sneaky phone call out back, and you'd never know what he *really* thinks."

Her pistol finger starts coming down. "So what exactly did you hear?"

"Well, overall he was really excited. He didn't act that way around you, I know, but when he thought no one was listening, he was totally amped. He said it was solid gold and that he thought they could start a bidding war."

Her little finger pistol is down and her mouth is wide open. "He said that?"

I tell her, "Yup," and Casey wiggles his eyebrows at Billy and says, "He also said you're cute and very marketable."

I backhand Casey and look at him like, Why'd you tell him that? but it sure turns Billy's mood around. "Dude, you're serious?" He grins. "I'm gonna be a reality star!"

Mama Jack is shaking her head, muttering, "That little sneak. He acted like he barely cared." She looks at Casey and me and seems to make up her mind. "You two are welcome here anytime. And I think it's nice that you're worried about your friend." She rolls her eyes a little. "I'm worried about my son! But there's no talking him out of his fantasy, so we're trying to turn it into something real." She sticks her hand out. "I'm Sheri, by the way."

I shake it. "I'm Sammy, and this is Casey."

"And I'm a little cute Deuce!" Billy singsongs. "You don't know what I got."

I look at him like, Huh? but Mama Jack seems to get him. "Well, Little Cute Deuce," she laughs, "if this moves forward, we're going to have to meet with your parents."

Billy's merry little mood vanishes. "No! They will totally not get this!"

Mama Jack crosses her arms. "We'll persuade them." She points a finger at him. "And no more cutting school. Today was important, but from now on, you and Jack'll have to work around it."

"How do you work around it?" Billy cries. "Crime doesn't stop because school is in session!"

"You sound like Jack," she grumbles. "That's his excuse for not getting a real job." She wobbles her head a little. "He *has* to be available to save the world twenty-four-seven."

"It's true!" Billy cries.

She raises an eyebrow at him. "You want to turn out like his other assistants?"

Billy just stares at her.

"They were once young and cute, too. Get what I'm saying? If you're gonna do this, you need to work it in around school."

Billy finally looks down. "Yes, ma'am."

She snorts, "Ma'am," but you can tell she likes the way it sounded respectful. "Leave the hero gear here," she tells him. "It wasn't free."

"The mask is awesome," Billy says, snapping it off.

"Something about it makes you feel like you really can take on the world."

Mama Jack heaves a sigh. "That's what Jack says. When he started this whole thing, I did my best to talk him out of it. But then he came up with the costume, and that was it. The costume seemed to have this *power* over him."

"Without it," Billy says, stripping off his gloves, "you're just a small-caliber do-gooder."

Casey and I bug our eyes at him, while Mama Jack shakes her head. "I've heard *that* before, too, and if I had any sense at all, I'd call your mama right now and get you out of that costume for good. But I like you a whole lot better than those bums he's been trying to get to fly right, and call me selfish, but if Hollywood thinks you're cute and marketable, I'm stayin' out of it."

"Speakin' of mamas," Billy says, heading for the door, "I'd better get home."

"Speakin' of mamas," Casey says, "I'd better, too."

"And I'd better three," I laugh.

"Wish Jack had had some friends like you when he was your age," Mama Jack says, closing the door to Pair-a-Dice as she follows us out. "He was a little different to begin with, but after his dad died, he went into a bit of a fantasy world." She frowns. "And kids can be merciless."

So there I am, standing in the wide open, thinking about what she'd just said, when I hear something roaring up the road. I know it's not the High Roller, 'cause it's a smoother roar than that, but still it does sound familiar, and when I turn to look, what do I see?

A streak of red flashing between eucalyptus trees.

At first I'm going, *No . . . it can't be. . . .*

But who else drives like that?

"Casey, look!" I gasp.

The second he sees it, he cries, "Hide!"

Mama Jack says, "What's wrong?"

Billy's by the bike, so Casey and I dive for him, yanking him with us behind the barrels. "Don't let her know we're here!" I call to Mama Jack.

"Who?"

"The woman in that car!"

"Who is she?"

"Just tell us when she's gone!"

But we can see fine from behind the barrels, and we watch as the car slows waaaaaaaay down.

"What's your *mom* doing here?" Billy whispers.

Casey keeps his eyes glued to the road. "Good question."

"I feel like Pongo and Perdita in *One Hundred and One Dalmatians,*" I whisper.

"How sad that my mother's Cruella De Vil," Casey mutters.

I cringe. "Sorry."

"No, you're right. This is totally like that."

"So who am I?" Billy asks.

"Patch," Casey and I say at the same time, then grin at each other.

"That's the hyper puppy? The one who barks at the TV?"

"That would be the one," Casey says.

Billy sighs, "Awesome."

The car's straight ahead now, crawling past the property.

And then . . . it . . . stops.

The window powers down, and when we see that the car has a passenger, Billy says what we're all thinking. "Uh-oh."

"Where's three-fifty-seven?" Heather shouts at Mama Jack.

"Right here," Mama Jack calls back. "Who you lookin' for?"

There's a little hesitation and then, "My friends. They said they'd be here!"

I snort. "Friends? More like juicy prey."

"But why are they here?" Casey whispers. "You gave me the address over a pay phone!" He turns to Billy, but before he can accuse him of anything, I say, "Heather saw me looking up the address on the internet at the library."

Billy and Casey both stare at me, and finally Billy says, "This is bad, Sammy-keyesta. This is very bad."

Mama Jack has hollered back, "What do they look like?" and Heather's now describing us. "A guy and a girl . . . my age . . . probably got skateboards . . ."

Mama Jack laughs. "Good luck riding a skateboard up here!" Then she shakes her head and says, "You must have the wrong address. We don't get that kind of traffic."

The window goes up, and as the car prowls along, Mama Jack edges closer to the barrels and tells us, "Stay put. She'll be back." Then she adds, "Probably a good idea if I don't hover around, but before I go, who are they, and who gave up Jack's hideaway?"

"They're not looking for Jack," I tell her. "They're looking for Casey and me. It's his mom and sister, and they hate me."

"Ah," she says, tossing a grin at me over the barrels. "Sounds like a surefire way to make him like you even more." Then she heads for her mobile home.

Now, it's not as if I haven't worried that the reason Casey likes me is because he's not supposed to. And even though he's done and said lots of things that make me believe that it's not true, I find myself slipping back into the Land of Doubt.

Casey can tell what I'm thinking and kisses my temple. "Don't be stupid."

"Yeah, Sammy-keyesta, don't be stupid," Billy says, kissing my other temple.

I heave a sigh. "Thanks."

A short minute later Candi's car comes cruising back down the road, and it's going a lot faster than it was before.

"So now what?" Billy asks when they're gone. "There's only one way out of here, and the Deuce can't dawdle."

I grin at him. "Dawdle? Is that what deuces do?"

"That's what they *can't* do. I'm serious. I've got to get home before my dad!" And he does seem a bit panicked, but he puts that aside long enough to eye me and say, "You're just jealous because the Deuce is such a better name than Umbrella Girl."

I laugh. "Oh, right. That's it."

"Look," Casey says, "just go. My mom'll be long gone

by the time you hit the main road, and even if they see you, what are they going to do?"

"Run me over?" Billy says.

Casey and I both laugh, because his forehead's all wrinkly with worry. "Well, besides that," Casey says, "you'll be fine."

So Billy grabs his bike, and says, "What about you guys?"

Casey nods. "I'm thinking maybe we'll go up to the end of the road and see if there's a shortcut out of here."

I grin at him. "A shortcut?"

He grins back. "Got something against shortcuts?"

"You are such a bad influence."

"Me?"

And I guess we were being kind of googly-eyed because Billy hops on his bike and says, "I'd be ready to puke right now, only I've joined the Justice Force and have better things going than loooooove." He pushes off and calls, "Like ridin' the Rushin' Roulette!" then tears out of there.

"The Rushin' Roulette," Casey says with a little snort. Then he grabs my hand. "Come on. Let's see if there's another way out of here."

And off we go, in search of a shortcut.

TWENTY-TWO

Sandydale continued for another hundred yards or so, then stopped at a long metal guardrail attached to wide wooden posts. There was an official yellow road sign with big black letters that said END bolted to the middle of the guardrail, so it was pretty clear that we were supposed to stop and turn around.

The thing about shortcuts is, there's never a sign that says RIGHT THIS WAY! According to Marissa, *shortcut* is code for dark, scary, or dangerous . . . usually all three. And even though I always tell her she's just being a scaredy-cat, I have to admit that shortcutting usually involves at least a little heart thumping. I mean, even if where you're going isn't marked NO TRESPASSING, it's a *shortcut,* not an "alternate route" or something, you know, *official,* so chances are you *will* be trespassing. And even if no one cares that you're cutting through a blocked-off alley, or climbing a fence, or diagonaling across a construction site, it always *feels* like you're about to get busted, or mugged, or, you know, killed.

Anyway, a shortcut isn't so scary after the first time you've taken it, *or* if you know other people have taken it.

You're not on the shortcut frontier anymore. It's been scouted. Broken in. *Survived*.

So even though the sign on the guardrail said END, and even though it looked like if we went past it, we'd get lost in a shadowy eucalyptus forest that for sure sheltered wolves and snakes and bloodsucking bugs, I saw something that told me we were actually *not* on a shortcut frontier.

Tire tracks.

Fat ones.

"Hey, check it out," I tell Casey, and we follow the tracks around the guardrail until they disappear onto a bed of eucalyptus leaves. And after we've crunched along the leaves for a while, Casey says, "You look like a bloodhound."

I stop and stare at him. "A bloodhound?"

"Yeah, with the way your head's down and going back and forth. . . . What are you doing?"

"Following the broken leaves."

He notices that, yeah, there's a wide trail of crushed leaves. "Oh." He laughs. "Sorry."

"Bloodhound," I grumble.

"I said sorry!" So he starts looking, too, and every once in a while we come to a section of dirt where we can see actual tire tracks. It's like finding small islands in a river of leaves where we can sort of mentally catch our breath and go, Okay, I'm not imagining things.

"Those look like dually tracks," Casey says.

"Dually tracks? What's a dually?"

"Double tires, usually in back, singles up front." He shrugs. "That's what it looks like to me."

It doesn't take long for us to wander out of sight of the guardrail. I try to keep my bearings straight, and I *think* we're heading east, but it's pretty late in the afternoon and with all the trees it's not easy to tell from the sun which direction we're going. And I'm starting to worry that this is one of *those* shortcuts—you know, the kind that makes you later than you would have been if you'd taken the long way home? But then the broken leaves make a hard right, and after a few more tire-track islands, we find ourselves looking at a chain-link fence with razor wire along the top. There are no trees whatsoever on the other side of it. Just acres of old cars.

"So we're at the junkyard," I say, looking around. "But why would someone drive out here when there's no gate?"

"Sometimes people dump stuff out in the boonies, but I don't see anything like that around here, either."

I laugh. "Maybe they were trying to take a shortcut and ran into a dead end!"

Casey laughs, too. "Maybe!"

Then I notice something on the ground near the fence. It's about the size of a glove, and it's sort of reddish brown with big black specks on it. "What *is* that?"

When we move in closer, the big black specks levitate.

I go, "Ew!" because I've seen flies on dead stuff before, and let me tell you, it's gross.

"It's just an old piece of meat," Casey tells me.

So, okay, maybe it's not a *carcass,* but it's still giving me the heebie-jeebies. And since it's already getting dark, I just want to *go.* So I look to the left and right, but there's fencing and eucalyptus trees as far as I can see in both directions. And I'm about to ask Casey if he wants to follow the fence to the left or the right or just go back the way we'd come when he says, "Hey, check this out."

He's over by what looks like a long scar running straight up two rows of chain link, and when I get closer, I see that there's a long twisty metal thing holding the rows together.

Which is odd enough, but there are also weird markings in the dirt. There's a wide gouge with what look like half hoofprints running along either side of it. Like a dying horse had dragged itself along going, Water! Water!

Or, you know, Neigh! Neigh!

Or something.

Anyway, what's extra-strange is that the markings start on our side of the fence and go right under it and into the junkyard without stopping.

"This is *weird*," Casey says after we've studied it for a minute. He puts down his skateboard. "Unless this opens up." He grabs the long twisty metal thing between his fingertips and turns. And in just a few twists, the rows of chain link begin to separate at the bottom like stage curtains at a play. He grins at me. "Shortcut!"

Now, it's not like me to stop and, you know, *think* in the middle of taking a shortcut, but going through the junkyard seems like a bad idea. So I ask him, "*Why* are we shortcutting through the junkyard?"

Casey looks at me. "Uh . . . to avoid my mother?"

"But what if there's no little twisty thing to let us out the other side? What if we get *stuck*?"

Casey thinks a minute, then says, "What time is it?"

I look at my watch. "Almost five."

"You're right. Let's just follow the fence around." And I can tell he's worried now because he's supposed to be *home* by five.

So we twist the sections back together as fast as we can and hurry along the fence until it finally turns a corner at the dead end of a narrow alleyway.

And even though the alley is shadowy and dirty and has a junkyard on one side and the back side of slummy apartments on the other, both of us are hugely relieved. "Let's go!" Casey says, grabbing my hand.

The alley's just gravel and dirt, so we have to run instead of ride, but when we get to the first real side street, we toss down our boards and take off. And since it's pretty obvious from the graffiti and the people hanging around that we're in gang territory, we ride *fast*.

Finally I recognize where we are. "I think that's Broadway!" I call up to him, and when I'm sure it is, I tell him, "I better turn off! Pay-phone me tomorrow!"

He comes skidding to a halt and stops me before I can cross the street. "You," he says, giving me a kiss, "are amazing."

He takes off and I call, "So are you!" then watch him until he turns and rides out of sight.

Now, I was way more worried about Casey getting home late than I was about being late myself.

Grams is someone I can *explain* things to.

Candi is someone who just explodes.

That doesn't mean I take it easy as I'm riding toward the Senior Highrise. I'm pushing so hard that the bottom of my shoe feels like it's smoking. And with all the rush-hour traffic and people out Christmas shopping, I'm having to really focus on where I'm going.

Still, there are some things that will break your concentration no matter how focused you are.

Like a walrus on wheels.

I actually fall off my skateboard when I see her. And even though she's in a wheelchair, there's no mistaking the Whopping Wedge.

Especially since she's being pushed toward the front door of the Senior Highrise.

By Justice Jack.

"He *found* her?" I choke out. Then I grab my skateboard and tear across the street shouting, "Mrs. Wedgewood! Mrs. Wedgewood!" and manage to catch up to them right before they reach the door.

"Samantha!" she says when she realizes it's me, and gives me the sweetest, gentlest smile you've ever seen on a blackmailer.

I look at Justice Jack. "Where did you *find* her?"

"I circulated her picture to my contacts," he booms, "and one of them spotted her at the bus station!"

"Hey," I tell him between my teeth, "it's just me. You don't have to *announce* everything."

"And what are *you* doing here, young citizen?" he booms. "Isn't this facility for seniors only?"

Well, I'm not about to stumble through explaining *that*, so I just tell him, "I volunteer here." Then I turn to Mrs. Wedgewood and say, "People are going to be really happy to see you!"

"What day is it?" she asks.

"Tuesday."

"Oh my. Well, yes. I suppose I did get carried away. And waylaid."

"Look, I can take it from here," I tell Justice Jack, but he puffs himself up a little and announces, "The fellowship of this fine community tasked me with finding her, and it's my duty to see the mission to completion!" Then he adds in a regular voice, "But it would be nice if you opened the door."

So I pull the door open and let him push Mrs. Wedgewood through. Then I swoop in after them and call out, "Mr. Garnucci!"

Mr. G looks up from his computer. "Samantha? What's—" Then he stands up. *"Rose?"* He rushes over. "Where have you been?" And before she can answer, he looks at Justice Jack. "How did you find her?"

Justice Jack crosses his arms and inflates his chest. "All in a day's work, good sir!" Then he punches his fists onto his waist like he should have a cape billowing in the wind. "And now that she's in good hands, I'll be on my way!"

Now, since he has no cape and there's no wind blowing inside the Senior Highrise—well, not *that* kind of blowing wind anyway—he's forced to walk like a mortal out the front door. But still. Something about the way he whooshes out of a building makes you believe that he *could* fly if someone would just give him a cape.

Anyway, Mr. Garnucci is studying Mrs. Wedgewood, going, "Are you all right, Rose? You seem . . . pale." And while he's worried about her color, I just want to straighten out her wig, because the big black curls are all crooked and kind of sideways.

"I'm fine, Vinnie."

"Well, you gave us all a good scare."

She snickers. "Especially Sally and Fran, I'm guessing. Probably think I ran off with their money."

I snort. " 'Skipped town' is what they said."

"Skipped? Me?" She gives a little laugh. "That's a good one."

"Well, where have you been?" Mr. G asks her. "How did Justice Jack find you?"

"Is that that fellow's name? Well, I have no idea. When he first appeared at the bus station, I thought they were shooting a movie. Then he gets me in this wheelchair and whisks me away like I'm the president."

"He's been on the news a lot," Mr. Garnucci tells her. "So your neighbors asked him if he could find you."

She eyes him. "Did they offer a reward?"

"No . . . At least I don't think so."

"Figures," she grumbles. Then she takes a deep breath and says, "Can you assemble them?"

"Who?"

"The lot of 'em."

"The whole building?"

"No!"

Now, her wheelchair looks like an extra-wide model, but it's still not nearly big enough for her. She is wedged in tight, and what the chair can't contain is spilling over like a seismic eruption of muumuu. And somewhere inside all those flowery folds she's stashed *something,* because she's lifting up whole sections, looking for who knows what.

"Here!" she finally says, and out pops a big black purse. And I want to ask, What *else* do you have stashed in there? because all of a sudden the possibilities seem endless.

She roots through her purse and pulls out a notebook, then licks a finger and goes *thwip, thwip, thwip* through a bunch of pages until she gets to the one she's looking for. "Here's the list," she says, holding it out to Mr. Garnucci. "Get them down here."

This is how the Wedge works. She tells you what to do, and if you don't, watch out. I actually like it better when she's bossy than when she sweet-talks, because at least I know what I'm dealing with. When she starts spreading the sugar, I start to worry. Like, Okay, when are you going to throw spice in my eyes?

Anyway, Mr. Garnucci makes a few phone calls, and before you know it, the lobby's swarming with old people barking stuff like, "Where have you been?" and "Where's my money?" and "Why didn't you call?"

And it's starting to feel like a mob, so I finally say, "Hey! Hey, calm down! It's okay! She's here!"

They look at me like a bunch of angry owls. "Who is she?" Bun-Top asks, pointing at me.

"She helped Justice Jack bring Rose home," Mr. Garnucci says, and I toss him a look that says thanks, 'cause the last thing I want is a gang of ticked-off old biddies coming after me.

"Justice Jack!" the Prune Posse cries. "He's the one who found you?"

"I told you he was a fine young man!" Bun-Top squeals. "You have *me* to thank for this, you know!"

"So now what?" Screwdriver Sally snarls. "We need some actual justice!"

"Yeah!" the mob cries. "What did you do with our money?"

Now, I don't like how everyone's ganging up on the Big W when they haven't even heard what she has to say. It's feeling a lot like being in the principal's office, which, believe me, is not a good place to be. So I step forward again and say, "Maybe we can let her explain?"

Bun-Top's eyes narrow down on me. "What's this 'we' business? Who are you? Why is any of this *your* business?"

"Knock it off, Cynthia," Mrs. Wedgewood tells her. "She's just trying to help." She starts fishing through her bag again. "And listening *would* be a good idea."

Then her big, meaty hand pulls something out of her bag, and all at once the room goes quiet.

Except for the sound of dropping jaws.

TWENTY-THREE

The Prune Posse stands there with their eyes popped and their jaws dropped, looking at the Wedginator like she's just pulled a gun on them. But what she's taken out of her bag is really a big, bursting envelope of cash.

She thumps it onto her lap. "Vinnie," she says, holding out one hand, "the list."

Mr. Garnucci returns the notebook without a word.

"And get me a pencil," she commands as she rifles through her purse and comes up with a calculator.

Mr. G scurries off while everyone else stares, and believe me, they're not looking at her awful, crooked wig.

Mrs. Wedgewood snorts. "Yes, it's real, and, yes, you've all made a bundle." She accepts the pencil from Mr. Garnucci and mutters, "I just have to calculate my rake."

Now, I don't know what a rake is, and apparently neither does anyone else. But as she goes down the list, I edge in from behind. She's smelling pretty ripe, so it'd be more natural to back away, but I get as close as I dare to and try to figure out what she's doing.

In her notebook there's a list of names and two columns of numbers, and what she does is punch in the amount that's in the second column of numbers and multiply it by 0.75 Then she writes down that amount in a third column, counts out the calculated money, calls the person's name, and hands over a stack of cash.

It doesn't take long for me to catch on that the first column is the amount the person gave her, the second column is the amount they won, and the third column is the amount she's paying out.

Which means she's skimming twenty-five percent right off the top.

She doesn't seem to realize that I'm hovering behind her, because she barks at anyone else who gets close. "Get back, Sally, I need to concentrate!" "Fran, what did I just tell Sally?" "Ted, you'll get yours. Back off!"

When she's finally done distributing the money, I step away as she eyes Mr. Garnucci and says, "Bet you wish you'd believed me."

Mr. G nods like, No kidding, while the rest of the mob counts through their money, not quite believing their eyes.

Finally the Ted guy says, "But how'd you *do* it?"

The Wedge shrugs as she stuffs away her notebook and what's left of the money. "Told you. I got a tip."

"But *what* tip?" Bun-Top asks. "And where'd you go?"

"You probably don't want to ask too many questions."

"But why didn't you just use your own money?" Screwdriver Sally asks.

"She probably didn't *have* any," Ted says, and there's an edge to his voice that doesn't sound too friendly.

"Then what's all that green she just stuffed back in her purse?" Bun-Top says.

"Wait. Are you skimming off our winnings?" Screw-driver Sally demands, and I swear if she'd had a screwdriver in her hand right then, she'd have used it to do a stick-'em-up to Mrs. Wedgewood.

The Wedge looks at them and you can tell she's flabbergasted. "I nearly tripled your money," she tells them. "I can't take a percentage?"

"How much did you take?" Ted asks.

"What's it matter?" she growls at him. "I could have just returned what you gave me and you would never have known I had any winnings at all!"

"How much?" Ted demands.

"Twenty-five percent! And now I'm thinking I should have taken fifty!"

"Twenty-five percent!" the Prune Posse cries. "That's highway robbery!"

Then an old guy in the back with a five-day stubble shakes his cane and says, "No dealer gets twenty-five percent! Five, maybe ten . . . And you took twenty-five?"

Mr. G steps forward. "Everybody, calm down! Can we look at the positive here? Yesterday you thought you'd lost all your money; today you've got almost three times that amount! I'd be happy to give up twenty-five percent for that kind of return on my investment!"

"But she *could* have lost it all!" Bun-Top says. "And if she had, would she have given us twenty-five percent of her own money?"

Mrs. Wedgewood squints her beady little eyes at her. "What?"

"Go!" Mr. Garnucci tells them, shooing the greedy

grumps off. "Quit looking at how much she took and focus on how much she gave you."

Everyone else starts to move, but Bun-Top stands firm. "But she risked our money to make a ton of money for herself! She sure shouldn't get a quarter of it!"

"Go!" Mr. Garnucci barks at her. "Enough of this!"

So she leaves, too, but it's easy to see from the glares they all throw over their shoulders that they're feeling ripped off.

"Wow," I say, shaking my head. "That's really unbelievable."

Mrs. Wedgewood nods. "As my daddy would say, no good deed goes unpunished." Then she opens her purse again and pulls out two crisp one-hundred-dollar bills.

Now, for a second my heart skips a beat, because I think she's going to give them to me, but instead she turns to Mr. G and says, "Here, Vinnie. Sorry you didn't invest. I'm sure they've been driving you nuts."

His face lights up. "Why, thank you!"

She drills him with her eyes. "I trust you can keep the investments made here quiet?"

"Of course," he says with a smile as he plucks the money from Mrs. Wedgewood's fingers.

Suddenly her giving him the two hundred makes sense. She doesn't *have* anything on him, which is why she's bribing him to keep all this quiet.

He doesn't seem to really get that, though, because he asks her, "Would you like me to wheel you up?" like she's his new best friend instead of his resident blackmailer.

"No, Samantha can do that." She gives me one of her

beady looks. "You're here to visit your grandmother, I assume?"

I force a closed smile and nod.

"Then let's go."

Even when she's on wheels and not slippery with soap, moving Mrs. Wedgewood is a workout. I wound up having to give her my skateboard to hold because I needed to really lean into the wheelchair to get any movement. And when I *did* get her going, I couldn't stop and almost crashed her into the elevator door.

Talk about momentum!

Anyway, waiting at the elevator seemed to take forever. Probably because the Miffed Mob was using it.

Or jamming it because they knew the Big W had to use it to get home.

And while we're waiting, I can't help noticing that Mrs. Wedgewood's whole face is misty.

Make that *sweaty*.

And then I see that there are drips of sweat trickling down her temples.

"Thanks for taking me up, sugar," she says. "I knew you wouldn't mind."

Which I wouldn't if she had asked me instead of commanding me.

And also if she didn't smell so bad.

And since she's calling me sugar, I'm pretty sure she's gathering spice—thinking of ways she can put me to work for her that'll take me all night. So I try to interrupt her blackmailing mind with small talk. "It's too bad the rest of them couldn't just be happy that you won so big."

"Someone was sure smiling down on me," she says, wobbling her head. "At the track and at the casino. I was on an incredible roll." She turns her sweaty face my way. "I hadn't planned on staying so long at the casino, but the buffet?" Her eyes close and she lets out a happy sigh. "It was un-be-lievable. Unlimited tiramisu, crème brûlée, prime rib, lobster Florentine . . ." She smiles at me again. "It was out of this world."

The door finally opens, and as I bear down to push her in, I say, "Sounds like a foreign language to me."

"You must at least have had prime rib at some point?"

I want to wipe her face and yank her wig straight, but I just push the 5 button. "Nope."

She doesn't say anything on our ride up, but as the door slides open, she says, "You're probably too young to appreciate it anyway," and she's *panting*—like riding an elevator up five floors is real exercise for her.

"Well, here you go," I tell her as I roll her up to her apartment.

I take my skateboard off her lap and wait as she fumbles through her purse. "I can't find my key," she finally tells me.

"You want me to look?" I ask, 'cause really I just want to get her over the threshold and *leave*.

"I should be able to find my own key," she grumbles as she starts pulling things out of her bag and putting them on her lap.

First comes her notebook.

Then the envelope of "rake" money.

Then *another* envelope bursting with cash.

She must have heard my eyes pop, because when she realizes what she's just done, she says, "I won it with my rake. Not that I need to explain that to *you*."

"Hey, I'm just trying to get you home. It's none of my business and I don't care. Besides, it's not like any of them even thanked you."

Her head screws around and she drills her beady eyes into me. And at first I think she's mad at *me*, but then she says, "Not one thank-you, you're right."

"Well, Mr. Garnucci thanked you. . . ."

"He doesn't count." She goes back to digging through her purse, and out comes a brush.

A *brush*?

Next come perfume, baby powder, a wallet, and a little portable fan.

And that's when it hits me that she has no luggage.

No extra clothes.

And I'm totally grossing out over the thought that she's been wearing that same muumuu and undies for maybe a *week* when she says, "Here it is," and hands her key to me like I'm her doorman.

Well, door*girl*.

So while she packs up her bag, I unlock her apartment and prop open the door, then I come back around and push her inside.

The doorgirl does not get a tip.

Or, ironically, even a thank-you.

The doorgirl gets told to fetch a glass of water. The doorgirl gets told to help her to the couch and remove her stinky shoes. The doorgirl gets barked at to turn on the fan.

And finally the doorgirl gets told to run down to Maynard's for some Tums. "I'm all out, sugar," she says, handing me a twenty. "Please don't take too long. And save the receipt."

So, yeah, the doorgirl's more than slightly ticked off, but what can I do?

I take the twenty and tell her that I'll be back as quick as I can.

"Don't get sidetracked!" she snaps as I head for the door. "I really need those Tums."

So I hurry over to Grams' apartment, where I dump my stuff and whisper, "The Blackmailer's back—"

"She is?" Grams says, popping up off the couch.

"—and I've got to run down to Maynard's for some Tums for her."

"Wait! What happened? Where has she been?"

"She wasn't kidding about having a hot tip. Everyone tripled their money."

Grams gasps, "No!" and you can tell she's kicking herself. But she shifts gears fast and says, "So when are the police showing up?"

I laugh, 'cause I hadn't even considered that she might have done something really illegal. I mean, how could someone like the Wedge make a mad dash or escape?

Besides, the thought of a walrus in a wig doing some kind of *heist* was just ridiculous.

Anyway, I head for the door, saying, "I've got tons to tell you, but I'm starving and I have to get this done first. Garnucci knows I'm here, so I've got to leave anyway. I'll be right back!"

"Promise me you won't get sidetracked!"

I stop and turn around.

"Why does everybody tell me that?"

She laughs. "Why do you think?"

"Thanks a lot," I grumble, and then head out the way I'd come in, promising myself I'd prove them all wrong.

TWENTY-FOUR

You're probably thinking I got sidetracked.

Well, guess what?

I didn't.

What I *did* was almost get killed.

Now, if Maynard's freeloading son, T.J., had been working the counter instead of the Elvis impersonator, I might have had to go clear down to the supermarket, because T.J. likes me about as much as a chained dog likes a cat. Something about seeing me sets him off, and he will bark and snarl and snap at me until he finally drives me away.

So there was definitely the *potential* for a sidetrack, but Elvis was happy to see me. "Hey, little mama!" he calls from behind the counter. "How are things in Carny Town?"

Now, with Hudson's help, I had finally figured out that the Elvis clerk talks only in Elvis songs.

Well, almost.

He'll throw an extra word in now and then to tie together the lyrics or song titles, but pretty much everything he says is something Elvis sang. And it used to drive me kinda nuts, because I've never heard any Elvis songs—well, except maybe "Jailhouse Rock" or "Hound Dog"—so it was like he was talking in riddles.

No, not even riddles.

More like mixed-up phrases.

Nonsense that actually made sense.

In a weird Elvis-impersonator sort of way.

Even so, I'm always super-happy to see Elvis, because seeing him means I don't have to see T.J. Of course, Elvis doesn't know that. He just thinks I'm a happy camper coming in for bubble gum.

"Things are hoppin' in Carny Town," I tell him, and then right away I flash to the similarities between him and Justice Jack. Not what they do—just how they dress in costumes and prefer to be people they're not. "Have you heard about Justice Jack?"

"Didja ever? He's catchin' on fast!" Elvis says with a crooked Elvis smile. "Beginner's luck."

"Think so?"

He nods. "Watch him try to move from a jack to a king."

I laugh. "But you're the King, right?"

He laughs, too. "Doin' the best I can."

I grab the Tums and put them on the counter. "Seems like the two of you could be friends."

He shakes his head. "I got wheels on my heels, baby."

I stare at him. "Okay. What *does* that mean?"

He rings up the Tums. "I'm just a lonesome cowboy in a long black limousine."

I almost tell him, No, you're not. You're an Elvis impersonator working in a corner market! But instead I ask, "Can you translate, please?"

"My long-legged girl told me to get on the long, lonely highway."

"So . . . you had a girlfriend who broke up with you?"

He nods. "My honky-tonk angel turned out to be the meanest girl in town. I told her, 'Reconsider, baby, put the blame on me! Let's patch it up!' I said, 'Baby, I've been steadfast, loyal, and true! You're the only star in my blue heaven!' But she's a machine with a wooden heart, and now there's been too much monkey business." He shakes his head. "I'm afraid it'll be the twelfth of never before my blue moon turns to gold again, so it's viva Las Vegas for me."

I hand over the twenty. "You're moving to Las Vegas?"

"Cross my heart and hope to die. I'm movin' on."

"When?"

"Tomorrow night. It's now or never." He makes my change and snaps off the receipt, and as he hands them over, he sort of cocks his head and says, "You look like you're gonna sit right down and cry."

"I really liked you being here," I tell him.

He gives me a little shrug. "I slipped, I stumbled, I fell, and I'm leavin'. But that's all right, mama. Don't think twice."

"Well, I'll miss you," I tell him, then grab the Tums and head out.

"Hey, hey, hey!" he calls after me, and actually follows me to the door. "Before we go our separate ways, let it be me that gives you some sound advice."

"What's that?"

"As we travel along the Jericho road, anyplace is paradise."

He's looking like Serious Elvis now, so I nod as I keep walking and say, "Thanks."

But Elvis isn't done. "Keep a pocketful of rainbows."

"Will do."

And since I'm now at the corner and about to cut across a red light, he calls, "Always stop, look, and listen!"

I laugh. "Thanks!" And as I'm heading across the street anyway, he shouts, "By the way, my real name's Pete Decker! I'll get you passes to my show if you're ever in Vegas!" And since I'm so shocked to hear his real voice and his real name, I do something you should *never* do when crossing against a red light.

I stop, turn, and stare.

All of a sudden horns are blaring and zooming by and I'm running and jumping like crazy trying not to get killed.

"You almost had the steamroller blues!" he shouts when I'm safely across. Then he waves. "Bye, Sammy! I'll remember you!"

I wave. "Who could forget you?" Then I hurry up the sidewalk and sneak back over to the Senior Highrise.

Now, when I'd left the Highrise, I'd gone out the front door and waved real big and shouted good-night to Mr. Garnucci so he'd know that I was leaving the building. Which meant that I now had to sneak up the fire escape to get back inside. No biggie, but halfway up it hit me that I'd made a mistake.

A kinda *big* mistake.

When I'd come in with Justice Jack and the Wedge-o-matic, I'd had my backpack and my skateboard, but when I'd gone out, I didn't have either.

I tried to convince myself that Mr. Garnucci wouldn't notice something like that. Especially considering all the excitement about Justice Jack delivering the Wedge and then the big payouts and everything.

But still. It bothered me. I could just see him waking up in the middle of the night going, Wait a minute . . . !

So I'm a little preoccupied sneaking back into the Highrise, and I really just want to deliver the Tums and get home quick, but while the Wedgie Woman's checking her change, she says, "Don't rush off, sugar. Sit a spell."

So, great. Now I have to *visit* with her? Like doing her laundry and shopping and hoisting her off the bathroom floor isn't enough? Now I have to chitchat?

About *what*?

She can see me thinking. "Come on, sugar. It won't kill you to visit a minute."

I take a deep breath. "Mrs. Wedgewood, I have homework and chores to do, and I'm starving." And then, just because I've never actually admitted that I live next door, I add, "And I still have to help my grandmother with a few things before I go home."

"Home," she says with a cagey smile. "We both know what a long walk that is."

"Look, Mrs. Wedgewood, I don't mean to be rude, but I do have other responsibilities."

"Sit," she says.

I don't know how to explain it other than to say that there's something about two beady eyes, five chins, and a crooked wig that adds up to scary.

So I sit.

"Now, then," she says. "Tell me about your mother."

"My *mother*?" I try to pull it back a notch. "What do you want to know?"

"Well," she scoffs. "I know she's beautiful and self-absorbed and in denial about her responsibilities, so we don't have to cover that. I'm curious what her plans are for after *The Lords of Willow Heights* is off the air. Is she coming back to Santa Martina?"

This did not feel like a theoretical discussion to me.

This felt like she knew something I didn't.

And while the wheels in my head are whirring around trying to figure out which direction to go, Mrs. Wedgewood adds, "She's very good in her role, by the way. I like her better than the original Jewel."

"You watch it?"

She smiles. "Since it first aired thirty years ago."

My eyes bug out. "You're serious?"

"Of course. Which is why it's so sad to see it going off the air." She studies me a minute, then sighs. "She hasn't told you."

I just look down.

"And neither has your grandmother?"

The truth is, I'm mad. Why am I learning this from *her*? Why am I always the last person to know? But I don't want the Blubbery Blackmailer to see she's getting to me, so I try to cover. "Are you sure? Maybe it's just a rumor?"

"Oh, it's official, all right. And your mother and grandmother both know. They've had several heated phone calls about it. And you."

I stand up. "Look, Mrs. Wedgewood, it's a little creepy to think about you eavesdropping on us—on *them*."

"Can I help it if my ears are unnaturally receptive? I don't set out to listen, but the walls are paper-thin, and, sugar, your situation is intriguing. Like a real-life soap happening right next door."

I head for the door. "I need to help Grams, then get home."

"And home is . . . ?"

"None of your business," I snap.

Now, for me this is like setting loose a tidal wave of pent-up anger, but to her it's just a little ripple. "Come back, sugar. No need to get defensive. Can't you see we're a lot alike, you and I?"

I just stare at her with my jaw dangling.

"Sugar, it's obvious neither of us should be living here. I do what I have to to stay, and so do you. And believe it or not, I admire you and I have my concerns about your situation."

Now, I know she's a sweet-talking blackmailer. I know I should deny everything and storm out, but she actually seems sincere, so I just keep standing there, staring.

"How does your mother expect you to continue the way you have been?" she asks. "What are her plans for you? It seems she only has plans for herself. And what are your grandmother's plans for you?" She scoffs again. "Besides telling you to quit growing up so fast."

"Grams is a rock," I tell her.

"Oh, no doubt. But rocks stay put. They don't move

forward. Or soar. You need to soar, Samantha. You're smart and resourceful and you need to do something with your life."

Now, I complain about my mother all the time, but the Whale doing it and jabbing at Grams makes me want to harpoon her!

Besides, who is she to give me advice about doing something with my life?

About *soaring*?

But before I can figure out what to say, she sighs and adds, "I know you're not listening. I know you think I'm wicked. And you may not believe this, but I have not enjoyed my role in your life. But what else can I do? I do not want to wind up in a care home! I can't afford a good one, and even the good ones are just places to go to die!"

I give her a hard look. "I get that, but you don't have to do it the *way* you do it."

"What do you mean?"

"You don't ask for help, you demand!"

She laughs. "Like you would do all the things I need your help with if I just asked?"

"Look, Grams could have called Mr. Garnucci anytime and told him that you fall off the toilet and can't get up."

She gives me a hard look. "And I could have called any day to say you were living here!"

"You've made that threat every day since you moved in. The point is, *we've* never threatened *you*. You would have been out of here within a week if Grams had called Mr. Garnucci instead of helping you. And if you tried to get back at us, it would be easy for me to not visit for a week or two while he got you moved into an old-folks' home. Even if you sprang it on us, Mr. Garnucci knows I come to help Grams a lot, so he wouldn't be surprised to find me visiting. And since I have a massive wardrobe of two pairs of jeans and three shirts and absolutely no stuff, he sure wouldn't *find* anything." I shake my head. "Grams has never even *hinted* at turning you in, and the sad thing is, I would have been happy to help you. Nobody wants to live in a nursing home—I get that. The Senior Highrise is bad enough."

She just sits there like a wiggy walrus. So after a minute of her staring at me, I take a deep breath and tell her, "Look, you say you're concerned about my situation and I don't expect you to make it better, but could you please stop making it worse?"

She nods her head just a little, then whispers, "I'm sorry," and puts her arms out.

At first I don't understand the arms.

And then I do.

I try not to show how grossed out I am just thinking about it, but, really, there's no avoiding it. So I hold my breath and let her hug me, and when I resurface from the Stink Swamp, I smile the best I can, then escape.

And I'm planning to dive straight for the shower, 'cause, believe me, after you've been swallowed up by the Stink Swamp, there is nothing else on your mind.

Trouble is, Grams has the news on.

TWENTY-FIVE

The minute I walk through the door, Grams goes, "Shh!" like she's forgotten all about the payouts and the emergency trip to track down Tums. "The mayor's on!"

"Oh, good grief," I grumble as I head for the shower. I mean, come on. Who cares?

"Samantha!" She waves me over. "It's about the statue."

I stop short. "Did Justice Jack find it?"

"No! It's still missing."

I probably would have just gone and taken a shower, but right then the mayor says, "No, this is a personal reward. It is in no way connected to taxpayer dollars." His voice is very smooth. Polished. And in the back of my mind it sets off a little puff. Like a smoke signal. But before it can form into anything real, the *words* he's said register and snuff it out.

"He's offering a *reward*?"

"Five thousand dollars!"

I move in closer. "Wow."

All of a sudden Grams turns to face me. "Good heavens! What is that horrendous smell?" Her little rabbit nose wiggles in my direction. "Is that *you*?"

"Mrs. Wedgewood hugged me."

Her eyes nearly bug through her glasses. "She *hugged* you?" She leans away from me. "And you survived?"

"Grams!"

"Well, honestly! What is she doing hugging you?"

I grin. "You mean after putting the squeeze on us so long?"

"Yes!"

"Look, I have lots to tell you, but I have *got* to take a shower first."

She waves me off. "Yes! Do! Go!"

So while I shower and change into clean clothes, Grams heats up some leftover chicken and makes us soup and toast to go with it.

"Oh, thank you!" I tell her as I sit down at the kitchen table. "I'm *starving,* and this smells great!"

"Certainly better than you did," she says with an evil-granny grin.

"Hey! Who's always telling *me* to be nice?"

She lifts her nose a little, ignoring me, then dips her spoon into her soup like she's dining with royalty. "So tell me everything."

I've just taken a big bite of chicken, and while I'm chewing to clear my mouth, my mind flashes through my day—from the news about Lars and Sasha running off, to Billy showing up at Buckley's as the Deuce, to the Man in Black who turned out to be a Hollywood agent, to snooping at Pair-a-Dice, to Heather and her mother show-ing up, to shortcutting around the junkyard, to Justice Jack bringing in Mrs. Wedgewood, to the big Geriatric Goons payout, to the Elvis impersonator, to the Hug.

Finally I choke out, "Everything?"

She sips a little soup off her spoon. "Let's start with anything that has anything to do with Rose."

Well, that took us clear through dinner. And she was so riled up about the money she didn't make and my "dan-gerous conversation with that duplicitous ogress" that there was no sense in telling her about anything else. Com-pared to losing out on a big payday and my having shown Mrs. Wedgewood "all our cards," what did she care about Sasha and Lars? Or the craziness Billy had gotten himself wrapped up in?

"Look, Grams," I finally tell her, "things are better than they were, not worse."

But all she can focus on is one thing: "Did you ever come out and *say* you lived here?"

"No! But she knows I do! She's known all along! And by the time we were done talking, she seemed really sorry. So this is a good thing. Stop worrying."

She shakes her head. "I trust that woman as far as I can throw her."

We're both quiet a minute, then I wag my spoon at her. "Speaking of trust . . . what happened to our deal?"

"Our deal?"

"That we'd be honest with each other?"

"How have I not been honest?"

I just stare at her, and sure enough, she starts to squirm. Finally she tries, "What, exactly, are you getting at?"

"*The Lords of Willow Heights*? That it's been canceled?"

Her face collapses a little, but she also seems relieved. "Oh, that."

"What *else* is there?"

"Nothing," she says, a little too quickly. "Nothing at all."

I really want to push her on whatever it is she's hiding from me, but I decide to concentrate on one cover-up at a time. "So, what's Mom going to do now that *Lords* is canceled? What's Casey's dad going to do? He just moved there to be on that show!"

Grams tisks. "Canceled. After thirty years. Who would have thought?"

"I can't believe it stayed on the air *two* years, but that's not the point!"

She stands up. "I know, I know."

"So?"

"So your mother's auditioning for other parts."

"On what?"

She gives a little shrug. "She's vague about it."

"What a shock," I say with a snort.

And then Grams does what she always does when she wants to avoid discussing something—she makes up some excuse to go hole up in her room so she won't have to deal with me or my annoying questions.

Whatever.

It's not like I didn't have a ton of homework.

It's not like I *wanted* to talk about my mother.

So I cleared the table and powered through a language worksheet and then did the assigned reading and questions for science. And after taking a break to wash the dishes and clean the counters, I raided Grams' stash of shortbread cookies, poured myself a big glass of milk, and got going on my math. By the time I'd finally finished my homework, it was ten o'clock and I was completely wiped out.

I headed for the bathroom to brush my teeth and get ready for bed, and while I was in there, I could hear the Wedge thumping around next door. Please, I say in my head. Please don't fall off the toilet tonight, because I'm so tired that even the *thought* of having to hoist her up is about killing me. The whole time I'm in there brushing my teeth and washing my face and taking care of business, I'm sort of holding my breath waiting for the earth to quake, or for her fist to pound on the wall for help.

But when I'm done, what I hear instead is a little *tap-tap . . . tap* on the Wedgie Woman's wall.

Now, you have to understand, the Wedge *tapping* is like an elephant mewing—it's not something you ever in a million years expect.

So, yeah, I was caught off guard.

I mean, what did she want?

What did tapping *mean*?

Then there it is again, *tap-tap . . . tap,* and this time there's also her voice coming through the wall. "Good night!"

Good night?

I just stand there for a minute, blinking at the wall.

Her voice sounded nice, too.

Almost playful.

Like we were friends whispering at camp.

So finally I reached out and went *tap-tap . . . tap* back.

I didn't *say* anything.

I just tapped.

Then I went to bed feeling safer than I had since the day I'd moved in.

I don't think Dorito slept on my head, because I had no dreams about suffocating. Actually, I had no dreams at all. I was conked out, dead-to-the-world asleep.

Grams, on the other hand, looked like she'd been dragged through a knothole.

Or tossed down the trash chute.

Or left to tumble in a clothes dryer.

"Are you okay?" I asked when she staggered out of the bathroom the next morning.

"I had the worst night," she groaned, and instead of coming into the kitchen to make breakfast like she usually does, she slouched into a chair at the kitchen table. "All I could think about was Rose. She's got a vindictive streak, Samantha. And if she turns me in, what will we do?" She held her head between her hands. "Your mother's back to scrabbling for work, and she confessed last week that she hasn't saved a thing! Can you imagine? It's all gone to living the Hollywood lifestyle."

I was in the middle of putting together a peanut butter and jelly sandwich for lunch, and I stopped smearing jam. "Is that what she said?"

"Oh, she didn't call it the Hollywood lifestyle—she claimed it was an investment in her career. But it's just keeping up with the divas! She needs her beauty treatments and her name-brand clothes, and she insists she has to be seen dining at the right places to 'build an aura of success.'"

I shake my head. "Meanwhile, I live illegally with you in a government building and pack peanut butter sandwiches for lunch."

"Exactly! And what happens if Rose decides to become spiteful?"

I get back to making my lunch. "She won't, Grams. Everything's okay."

"How can you *say* that?"

"She tapped good-night through the wall last night."

Her eyes practically bug through her glasses. "She tapped good-night?"

"Uh-huh. It was . . . nice."

"And that's your *guarantee*?"

"There are no guarantees, Grams, but I have a good feeling about it."

"About Rose," she says, like I'm the most naive person on the planet.

"Yes. And—"

Just then the phone rings. It's so early that it has to be Holly or Casey or Marissa, but since the Senior Highrise is actually a multistory dinosaur cave and has no caller ID, just to be safe, I use a warbly old-lady voice when I snatch up the phone. "Hello, dearie?"

But it's not Holly or Casey or Marissa.

It's heavy breathing.

Heavy, *gurgly* breathing.

"Hello?" I say again, only this time I forget to use the old-lady voice.

"Sah—" the voice gasps. "Sah—"

And then there's an enormous crashing *thump*.

One we can feel ripple through the floor.

"Oh no," Grams moans. "She's down again."

I hang up quick. "Where's the key?"

She pulls it out of her pocket. "Here, but why are you so—"

I grab her by the hand and pull her along, dreading what we'll find next door.

TWENTY-SIX

I'd like to be able to say that I have no experience with
dead bodies, but unfortunately that's not the case.

I've seen six whole ones and a partial, and they weren't
all in coffins, believe me.

Oh.

And then there were the skulls.

And the giant refrigerator full of body bags.

But never mind about all that. The *point* is, I would
have been happy to go my whole life without seeing another corpse or body bag or skull, but the minute we found
Mrs. Wedgewood on the kitchen floor, I knew she was
dead.

I also knew she had not gotten around to taking a
shower.

"Oh my," Grams says, keeping her distance. "Is she . . .
gone?"

I get down on my knees and shake her. "Mrs. Wedgewood!"

Nothing.

I turn to Grams. "You call 9-1-1. I'll check for a pulse."

So while Grams gets on the phone and reports what's happened, I put two fingers against Mrs. Wedgewood's throat. And while I'm holding my breath, waiting for any sign of a beating heart, I can't help but look at her face. And it jolts me to realize that with the way she's lying and her peaceful expression, she looks like an angel.

Not one of those beautiful ladies with wings.

One of those fat little baby angels.

You know—a cherub?

Okay, so she's an ultra-mega-mondo-supersized version of that, but still.

"Anything?" Grams whispers over the phone.

I shake my head and switch to Mrs. Wedgewood's wrist. But the truth is, I can't be sure if I'm not finding a pulse because of everything it has to beat through to make it to the surface, or if there just isn't one.

Finally I put my ear up to her chest, and when I don't hear anything, I turn to Grams and shake my head again.

"There doesn't appear to be a pulse," Grams says into the phone, "but she's a very large woman, so we can't be sure."

I wave at her frantically and mouth, "No we."

"What?" she says, covering the mouthpiece.

"No we," I whisper. "They record everything!"

Her eyes get all buggy as she tunes back into what the dispatcher is saying. And after a minute she says, "Shouldn't I try to give her CPR before they get here? . . . No, I'm not, but maybe you can instruct me over the phone? . . .

Really? Already?" She starts waving frantically at me and mouths, "They're HERE."

So I get up and head for the front door, but when I peek out, there's Bun-Top stalking up the hallway.

I close the door quick. "I'm stuck!" I whisper to Grams, and like a trained rat, I dart for the bedroom closet.

Now, Grams' closet is stuffed with clothes, and the floor is covered with shoes and random junk. It's where I first unearthed the Awesome Dome of Dryness, and it's also where I unearthed the only connection I have to my dad—his catcher's mitt.

I used to carry the mitt around with me everywhere—usually crammed in my backpack—but since I'm not playing softball this year, I wound up putting it back where I found it. Maybe if I ever meet him, I'll dig it out so we can toss the ball around some.

Then again, maybe he's dead.

And who knows when I'll find out? According to my jobless, penniless, spa-pampered mother, I'm not mature enough to know who he is or where he is or even *what* he is.

Also according to my jobless, penniless, spa-pampered mother, it's just fine to dump me at Grams' and run off with my boyfriend's father.

But *anyway,* compared to Grams' closet, Mrs. Wedgewood's is practically empty. There are muumuus hanging from the bar, but there's actually space between them, and instead of stuff galore on the floor, there are only two pairs of shoes and one medium-sized cardboard box. It does *smell* a little, but other than that it's still a whole lot more comfortable than being crammed into Grams' closet.

I'd left Mrs. Wedgewood's bedroom door open, and I've got the closet door cracked so I'll be able to hear what's going on when the paramedics arrive, but then someone—probably Grams—closes the bedroom door.

Maybe because Bun-Top's barged into the apartment?

Whatever the reason, I'm stuck sitting there among the muumuus with nothing to hear and nothing to do. And after what feels like *forever*, I move the box so I can stretch out a little more. And after another forever, I try to use the box as a headrest and wonder what would happen if Bun-Top *is* in the apartment and she starts snooping around for things to steal and finds *me*.

And after *another* forever, I'm just bored out of my mind and *really* tempted to take a peek through the bedroom door, but I know that's a very bad idea. Especially since Mr. Garnucci almost has to be there.

So instead I open the box.

And what I see inside would have been a double dose of extra-boring since it's basically just files and papers, only at the very top of the papers is a box of chocolates.

And rubber-banded to the box of chocolates is an envelope.

And on the envelope, in big, flowery letters, is a name. *My* name.

At first I just stare at it feeling really, really strange. I mean, the morning had started out pretty much like any other morning, but one thing had led to another and now here I was, hiding in Mrs. Wedgewood's closet, staring at an envelope addressed to me.

It was kind of cosmic.

And, really, I didn't want to think about that too much.

Besides, what if this envelope and box of chocolates were for another Samantha? What if it was all just a big coincidence?

There was only one way to find out.

I opened the letter!

And right away I knew—it was for me.

December 9

Dear Samantha,

I've been thinking about our conversation and I've decided that simply saying I'm sorry for my behavior is not enough. You've done so much for me, and although I've been outwardly ungrateful, I've known all along that I've been blessed to have you in my life.

Words of gratitude won't change your life, though, so I want to put my money where my mouth is. The "helping" in this box may dwindle over time (since I may need to dip in for additional servings), but I'm hoping to leave you a feast, not a snack. (I've never been a fan of leafy greens, but even I have a taste for these!)

Understand that this is not to be used on Double

*Dynamos or even new clothes. (I think you look
darling in the ones you've got, even though they're
secondhand.) This is also not to be touched by your
mother or grandmother. This is for your college
education, nothing else. Put the complete amount in
the bank and leave it there. Then, when the time
comes, use it to pay for tuition or books or whatever
you need. However little or much it helps you,
promise me you'll bust out of here and make
something of yourself. You're smart, resourceful, and
caring, and I know you'll be great at whatever you
choose to do.*

Your grateful neighbor,
Rose Wedgewood

I was too overwhelmed by what she'd said to care
about how much she'd left. My hands were shaking and
my eyes were running, and inside I was a huge muddle of
regret.

I'd called her the Wedge. The Wedginator! Wedgie
Woman! The Whale! The Walrus! The Whopper! But
under all those layers of lard was a woman who'd given
more thought to my future than my own beautiful, nearly
fat-free mother.

I finally slipped the letter back inside the envelope,
wiped my eyes, and opened the box. And there, staring up
at me, were four stacks of cash.

All Benjamins.

And even though there were no chocolates left in the

box, I could smell that there had been. And it flashed through my mind how strange it was that chocolates that weren't even there could change a stinky closet into one that smelled so sweet.

How even after something's gone, it can still almost magically change things.

I sat there for the longest time thinking about that, and finally I took a deep, choppy breath and started counting.

One thousand . . . two thousand . . . three thousand . . . *four*.

Five thousand . . . six thousand . . .

And I'm just getting up to seven thousand when the door flies open. I totally spaz and jump and bump, but it's only Grams. "Oh!" she gasps. "You found it!" And for a minute I think she's been in on the Wedgewood College Fund. But then she says, "Quick! They're all after it!"

"What?"

"Just come!"

So I gather my box and the letter and scramble out of the closet to the front door. And after Grams has checked the hallway, she shoos me down to our apartment while she locks up Mrs. Wedgewood's.

"My lord!" she gasps when she's safely home. And she's so shaky that she can't even seem to make it to a chair somewhere. She just braces herself with her back against the door and her hands spread wide. "That was insanity! As if dealing with the paramedics and the police and seeing Rose taken away wasn't bad enough, everyone's attacking me because they think I have a key and will go back in there and find her money!" Her eyes get huge. "Do you hear that?" she whispers.

Well, since I'm actually *in* the apartment, not up against the door, I can't hear what's going on in the hallway, but apparently she can.

"They're back!" she whispers. "It's a miracle I got you out of there!" She motions for me to hide, then opens the front door and says, "Oh, good heavens!"

I recognize Bun-Top's voice as she calls back, "Good heavens all you want, Rita! If Vinnie's not posting a guard, we will!"

"So you're going to sit there all day, Cynthia? Because you think I'm a criminal with a key?"

"That's exactly why!"

"Well, I never!"

"Well, I never all you want, Rita! Everyone's taking a shift! We don't buy that bit about Rose leaving her door unlocked! Nobody leaves their door unlocked! You found her, and we know how! You have a key!"

"Suit yourself," Grams calls back, then closes the door and comes to where I'm crouched beside a bookcase. "Looks like you won't be going to school today."

I stand up. "Can we back up please? I take it Mrs. Wedgewood is dead."

"Oh. Yes."

"And people are already fighting over her money? It was *her* money!"

"They obviously don't see it that way. And it's not like Rose had friends here. Look at the way she treated *us*." She eyes my chocolates box. "How much is there?"

221

I stare at her a minute, then hand her the letter.

"What's this?"

"Just read it."

So she does, and about halfway through, she staggers over to a kitchen chair and kind of dissolves into it. "Oh my," she gasps. "Oh my."

I sit down across from her and watch while it all sinks in.

"Oh, I feel terrible!" she finally says. "Here you tried to tell me . . ." She shakes her head. "I feel terrible."

I take the letter back and put it inside the envelope. "I don't think this is supposed to make you feel terrible."

"And I'm worried!"

I laugh. "Of course you are!" I shake my head at her. "What about? That I have probably ten thousand dollars in a college fund?"

Her eyes bug out. "Oh *my*." Then she says, "No, I'm worried that even with that letter, they'll never believe she *gave* all that money to you. And they'll claim it was theirs! What if they issue a search warrant! What if the police show up and—" She gasps. "They'll find you, too!" She points to the box. "We need to get that out of here! We need to get *you* out of here!"

"Oh, good grief."

Suddenly there's a knock at the door.

"Quick!" Grams whispers. "Get in the closet!" Then she calls out, "Just a moment!"

But my stuff is all over the place, and it takes more than a moment for me to fly around and hide my half-made peanut butter sandwich while Grams makes it look like her couch is not someone's bed.

And while she waits at the door, I grab my backpack and sweatshirt and the box of sweet cash and do what I always do.

Ditch it into the closet.

TWENTY-SEVEN

I think it's probably from years of dealing with old people, but Mr. Garnucci always talks loud, even when he's inside a tiny apartment and there's only one other person in the room. And in this case that turned out to be very helpful to the *other* person eavesdropping from the closet!

Bottom line, he'd come to tell Grams that, even though *he* believed her, and even though Mrs. Wedgewood's things would be moved into storage the next day, just to keep the peace, he was having the locks changed right away.

"A brilliant solution," Grams told him. "Thank you. You can't imagine how fed up I am with their accusations."

He laughed, "Sure I can!" and that was it.

He was gone.

"I suppose you heard all that," Grams says when she lets me out. And before I can even say, Yeah, she laughs and says, "He'll be in the hot seat now."

"Mr. G will?"

She shrugs. "He'll be the only one with a key."

"Wait—isn't he always the only one with a key? I mean, when there's a . . . you know . . . a vacancy?"

She gives me a sly grin. "Just you wait."

Now, since I was being forced to miss school and was stuck inside the apartment, I decided to take the time to make myself some sugar-sprinkled biscuits that had strawberry jam baked inside. They're about as close to jelly-filled donuts as Grams'll let me get, and even better tasting if I can sneak dunking them in maple syrup. Which for once I could because Grams was too busy keeping an eye on what was going on in the hallway to pay any attention to what I was up to. Every few minutes she'd peek outside, and every few minutes she'd close the door and give me an update, which pretty much was always the same: "She's still there."

Finally I told her, "You're acting like Mrs. Graybill."

Well, *that* got her attention, because Mrs. Graybill was the nosiest neighbor ever. "I am *not* acting like Daisy Graybill!"

"Sure you are. She always had her nose in the hallway."

"Samantha! Take that back!"

"I'll take it back if you'll give it a rest! Looking out there every five minutes isn't going to change anything. Besides, they've got to know you're watching. It makes you look sneaky—like you're dying to get in there."

She knew I was right and sat down for some biscuits and tea. "So what are you going to do stuck inside all day?"

What's weird is that the very last thing in the world I usually want to do is the first thing that popped out of my mouth. "Homework."

"Didn't you do it last night?"

"Uh . . . I sorta ran out of time."

What I *didn't* tell her is that lots of times I run out of time, and lots of times I'm scrambling to get stuff finished during the class before the class it's due.

"Then by all means, do that!" she says.

And normally I do my homework at the kitchen table, but this time I didn't want to do it there. I knew Grams would be fidgeting and fussing, and I had this urge to *concentrate* on my schoolwork. It was like all of a sudden I wanted to do good in school.

Okay, right, do *well*.

It was a weird feeling—almost like I wasn't really me. But now I had a *reason* to do well.

A reason besides wanting to stay out of trouble, that is.

And who in the whole wide world could have predicted that the reason would have come from Mrs. Wedgewood?

Not me, that's for sure.

The first thing I did once I'd set myself up in Grams' bedroom and closed the door was reread Mrs. Wedgewood's letter. And the part I re-reread the most was the part where she said that I was smart and resourceful and caring, and how I should bust out of here.

It was the first time I'd really thought about busting out. Before, I'd always had this feeling that I had to go along with what other people decided, and that there wasn't much I could do about it. This was the first time I thought I could change things, the first time I really felt that how my life turned out was now on *me*.

I stared at the letter and let the idea sink in. I liked the feeling it gave me, and I didn't want it to become one of those thoughts that slips away. I wanted to let it sink in good and deep, so it was really anchored inside me.

And then, finally, I slid Mrs. Wedgewood's letter back inside the envelope, opened up my backpack, and got to work.

It was lunchtime when Grams knocked on the door and peeked inside. "Good heavens. You've been working this whole time? I thought maybe you'd fallen asleep."

"What's the latest with the Prune Patrol?"

"Samantha!" she scolded, but under it she was laughing.

"Well?"

"Well, the lock's changed, but I was right—Cynthia, Fran, and Sally are doing shifts now on Mr. Garnucci."

I closed my book and stood up, because suddenly I was starving. "I can't believe he didn't kick them out for breaking and entering when he had the chance."

She blinks at me. "You're right . . . .!"

I snort and head for the kitchen. "'Course if I hadn't come over when I heard you in Mrs. Wedgewood's bathroom, they'd be saying the same thing about you." And before she can tell me how what she did and what they did were not even in the same universe, I switch subjects. "But this means I'm stuck, right? Like, I may miss school tomorrow, too?"

"Maybe so."

"Then I need to get my homework."

She hesitates. "It's only a day or two."

"I need to get it."

She studies me a minute as I look through cupboards for something to eat. "Can you get in touch with Marissa?"

I shut the door with a little slam. "Not Marissa."

Her eyebrows go flying. "Are you two in a fight?"

"No. She's just an idiot who's having a great time with her new, happy friends and doesn't need me or my advice anymore."

"Oh, dear," she says quietly. "Sounds like a fight to me."

I look right at her. "In a nutshell? She's back to thinking Danny Urbanski walks on water."

"No!" she gasps. "After he kicked a man so hard he cracked his ribs?"

"Yup. One smarmy phone call from him was all it took for her to dump Billy." I throw my hands up. "She's sure Danny's repented. Turned over a new leaf. Started a clean chapter in his smooth-talking life."

"Any chance that's true?"

I eye her. "Oh, he's still smooth-talking, but there's nothing new or clean about it. He's already lied to Marissa and is still sneaking around with Heather Acosta."

Grams thinks about this a minute as I search the refrigerator, but, really, my appetite is gone.

"Poor dear," she finally says. "Being stuck on a loser will certainly get you lost."

I stop searching and turn to face her. "Wow, Grams. That's profound."

She blushes a little. "Profound? I don't know about *that*." Then she adds, "But here's what's important—she's been your friend since the third grade. As soon as she comes to, she's going to need you. Make sure you're there for her."

"Meanwhile," I grumble as I close the door, "I need to get my homework."

"What about Holly?"

"That works."

But the *way* it worked turned out to be super-complicated because Holly doesn't have a cell phone and Grams gets all flustered when she lies to "school authorities."

Apparently, she's okay with *me* doing it, though. I dialed the school myself and when I got the secretary on the phone, I pretended to be my mother. "Yes, Mrs. Tweeter, this is Lana Keyes. My daughter, Samantha, is home sick today, and I would like to have her friend Holly Janquell bring her any assignments and homework. Could you arrange that?"

"I'll do what I can," Mrs. Tweeter says, "but it's already quite late in the school day." Then she adds, "And most teachers list their assignments online."

"I do realize that, but unfortunately that's not an option for us at this time."

"You don't have internet access?"

All of a sudden I'm understanding why Grams gets flustered when she calls the school. I mean, what business is it of hers if we do or don't? But I try to keep my cool. "Service is down. And Samantha says some of her teachers use worksheets."

"I see. Well, I'll do what I can. Please tell her to feel better."

"Thank you. I will pass that along."

"Service is down?" Grams asks when I get off the phone. "What service?"

"Internet service. A lot of teachers post their assignments on the school's website."

"They *do*?"

Now, the fact of the matter is, I've sort of hidden this tidbit of information from Grams and my mom, because if they knew about it, they'd also figure out quick that my *grades* are on the site. All they need is a user name and password, and, *presto,* no snowing them about how I'm doing in school, or whether I've done all my homework.

So I just shrug and say, "Yeah, but we don't have a computer, so what can we do, huh?"

Still, after we finally ate some lunch and I got back to work, *I* started thinking about it. I mean, here I am in Grams' bedroom, surrounded by papers I'm trying to sort, not really sure if I turned some of them in or what, and suddenly I'm wishing that I *could* see the online grade book.

Suddenly I really want to know—what *am* I missing? How *am* I doing?

After a while, Grams peeks in. "Mr. Garnucci's called a meeting about Rose's money down in the rec room. Don't answer the door for anyone, okay?"

"Got it," I tell her. And after she's gone, I go to the phone and call the one person I know I can trust with, uh, *classified* information. "Hudson?" I whisper when he answers. "It's Sammy."

"Everything okay?" he whispers back.

"Yeah. Fine. I'm just stuck in the apartment and have to keep my voice down." I give him the quick lowdown on Mrs. Wedgewood and the Prune Patrol, and since I don't know how much time I've got before Grams comes back, I bite the bullet and get to the point. "I need you to do me a favor, and I need you to keep it confidential."

"Of course."

"Okay. Can you go to your computer?"

"Sure. What's this about, Sammy?"

"I need to straighten out my grades."

"Your grades?" He hesitates. "Did you and your grandmother have a heart-to-heart?"

"Nope. And she can't see what you're about to see. You said you'd keep it confidential."

"Is there a *problem* with your grades?"

"I get by just fine."

"So . . . why the sudden motivation?"

I take a deep breath. "I want to go to college."

"College? You're only in eighth grade!"

"Yeah, but they base what you take in high school on how you did in junior high, and they're probably not going to put me on the college track with the way things are right now. But I'm going to change that. I've got to figure out what I'm missing and how to raise my grades."

"Okay, then!" A short minute later he says, "I'm logged on. Where do you want me to go?"

So I kind of stab around in the dark, giving him information and directions until we have an account and a password. And once we're at the grade book, I stab around some more until he's found and printed the pages I need.

231

"I'm guessing you'd like these tonight?" he asks when we're done. "What do you say I bring over some Chinese takeout for dinner and do an old-fashioned clandestine handoff?"

"You're serious?"

"Unless you think Rita would have objections to my appearing out of the fog?"

I laugh at the picture in my mind of him wearing a spy coat with a flipped-up collar, holding a big manila envelope. "Oh, I'm sure she'd love that. Too bad you gave away your awesome coat."

"It looks like young Billy is putting it to better use."

My brain whirs around. "How do you know about that?"

He chuckles. "I've seen enough of your energetic friend to recognize him, even in costume."

"But . . . where did you see him?"

"In the paper. Front page. Nice article about him and Justice Jack patrolling the mall. I'll bring it when I come over."

"Hurry, would you?"

I was suddenly starving. And Billy on the front page of the paper?

This I had to see.

TWENTY-EIGHT

Right after I got off the phone with Hudson, I had the bright idea to have Holly hand off my homework to him. So I called her and asked her to set that up, and since she had worksheets for me from language and history, I was glad I did.

I also asked her to get a message to Casey through Billy, which I knew she would.

It's nice having a friend I can count on.

Anyway, when Grams came back from the meeting in the rec room, I sprang it on her that Hudson was coming over, and it sent her into a dusting frenzy. "A little notice would have been nice!" she gasped.

"Someone bringing over dinner *is* nice," I told her. "So, what was the meeting about?"

"Well!" she huffs. "Vince Garnucci sure gave them a scolding!"

"And?"

"And I think he got through to them. He told them that he had a master key to all the apartments for emergencies and that he has never, ever abused the responsibility—"

"Wait—he could come in here anytime?" It made sense,

but I'd never actually thought about it before. And thinking about it now was pretty . . . scary.

She flings my sweatshirt at me. "Which is why you shouldn't leave your things lying around. Ever."

"Okay, okay!"

"He also informed those vultures that he always has a licensed, bonded cleaning crew put the personal effects of a resident in storage for the heirs, and that he doesn't touch it. *And* he told them they had no right or claim to Rose's personal property, and that if they continued with their savage ways—"

"Is that what he said? Savage ways?"

She laughs. "Yes!"

"Go, Mr. G!"

She wipes the TV screen with the duster. "He said he would call the police and tell them exactly what was going on—that they were all beneficiaries of what was almost certainly illegal gambling—and that once the police were involved, all bets were off. He warned them that they might have to return their winnings *and* that the IRS would come after them *and* that the Housing Bureau would investigate and review their eligibility for residence at the Highrise. He said that he was a witness to all of it, and that after the miserable way they had treated him, he would have no problem testifying against them."

"Wow!"

"They scurried off to their rooms like roaches from the light."

"So do you think I'll be able to go to school tomorrow?"

She hesitates, then moves toward the front door with a

finger to her lips. "I guess Fran got the message," she says after she's checked outside. "She was here when I returned from the meeting, but she's gone now."

I eye her. "You think Mr. Garnucci will sneak inside tonight?"

She shrugs. "I'm not going to lose any sleep over it. But what this *has* done is make me realize that I should not leave this apartment unattended until the contents of that candy box are in the bank." She eyes me back. "And also that the two of us need to start being a lot more careful."

Dinner was delicious, but I was way more interested in checking out the big envelope Hudson had slipped me than in hearing a recap of the hijinks in the Highrise or watching Grams blush like a teenager every time Hudson paid her a compliment. So as soon as I'd finished eating, I excused myself and holed up in Grams' bedroom.

The first thing I pulled out of Hudson's envelope was the newspaper, and there it was, a huge, full-color picture of Billy dressed as the Deuce, grinning at me from the front page.

Justice Jack was standing a little in front of him in full hero gear with his gold-gloved fists punched onto his waist. And even though Billy was in his mask and bomber helmet and coat and stuff, anyone who knew him would recognize his goofy grin right away.

The headline shouted VILLAINS BEWARE! and the subtitle was CITIZENS SHOW VIGILANCE, VALOR.

It was mostly a puff piece about "a dynamic duo of colorful crime-watch characters" spiced up with Justice

Jack–isms, such as "Evil is the rust of humanity—it never sleeps!" and "We tag 'em, the police bag 'em!" and "All aboard the Justice Express!" There were no quotes from Billy. Just that he had "heartthrob looks and a personality to match."

I had to laugh at that. Billy was cute, sure, but a heart-throb?

Come on.

Then I looked again.

And I don't know—maybe it was the mask, or just the way he was standing with his chest sort of puffed out, but he *did* seem older.

And . . . handsome.

And kind of . . . heroic.

In a slightly goofy Billy Pratt way, but still.

I was really tempted to call Marissa and ask if she'd seen the paper, but as the night ticked away, I got more and more ticked *off* by the fact that *she* hadn't called *me*. I mean, she didn't know why I'd missed school. For all she knew, I had the flu. Or a broken arm. Or maybe I'd been hit by a car!

So I didn't call her. Instead, I made myself focus on the grade-book records Hudson had brought over. But every time I noticed the clock, it hit me that she still hadn't called, and it made me mad all over again.

Finally at nine o'clock I was able to block her from my mind, since that's our cutoff time for calling each other. And when Hudson left at nine-thirty, I moved my stuff out of Grams' room and let her go to bed while I kept working at the kitchen table.

It took me a while, but what I figured out with my calculator is that the difference between a C and a B can be one lousy five-point assignment.

It can also be the difference between a B and an A.

And I was missing a lot of lousy five-point assignments. And some ten- and fifteen-pointers, too.

I had A's in PE and drama, so I didn't have to worry about those, and even though I didn't know if some of my teachers would take late work, I started with science and either found, finished, or did whatever assignments were missing.

It was eleven o'clock when I was finally done with science, and I wanted to call it a night, but I still had history, language, and math to do. Plus the worksheets that Holly had picked up for me. So instead of quitting, I got a big glass of milk and some shortbread cookies and made myself keep working until midnight.

And even though I had more to do, when I finally crashed on the couch, I felt happy.

Like I'd just discovered that the boat I'd been drifting around in had a steering wheel.

And I was free to use it.

When Grams checked the hallway the next morning and gave me the all clear, I was ecstatic to get out of the High-rise. I swear, riding my skateboard never felt so good. And even though I'd only missed a day of school, it seemed like I'd been gone a *week*.

The weird thing about school is that you're supposed to be going there for an education, but so much other stuff happens when you're there that it's easy to, you know, *misplace* that reason. Especially when you walk into class and overhear someone like Heather in the middle of gossiping about a certain classmate who ran off with his home-schooled girlfriend.

How can you not be distracted?

"They got caught in Santa Luisa!" Heather was saying.

"Santa Luisa?" Angie Johnson gasps. "How'd they get clear up there?"

"Well, they had bikes," Heather says like a snotty know-it-all.

"That's still a long way."

"Spokes powered by looooove," Tracy Arnold says.

Heather swings off her backpack. "Yeah, well, I heard Sasha's parents are going to press kidnapping charges!"

"Kidnapping?" Angie says. "What, they think Sasha didn't pedal her own bike?"

All of them laugh, and then Heather shrugs and says, "Kidnapping, abduction, whatever."

Billy walks into class right then, and just like that, Angie and Tracy abandon the conversation and swoop over to him. "Was that you in the paper?" Angie whispers.

"Moi?" Billy asks, pointing to himself, and then flashes that unmistakable Billy Pratt grin.

I give him a no-no-no! sign, but Heather descends on *me* and says, "By the way, I just sent something to my friend to share with your friend. Want to see?" and shoves her phone in my face. She turns it sideways, too, so I can get the full picture. "It'd be more fun if you losers had your own phones, but whatever."

Now, I try to keep a poker face, but I can feel myself turn red around the edges. Partly because I'm embarrassed by what I'm seeing, but also because I'm *mad*.

Not that the picture has anything to do with me. On the screen, Heather's arm is stretched way up to take the picture, but she's lying back, giving the camera a totally smug grin while Danny's face is buried in her neck.

And let's just say that they're not exactly dressed for winter.

It's not easy to pull off, but I give her a confused look and say, "I thought Lars was with Sasha. What's he doing latched onto *your* neck?"

Her wrist snaps around and she looks at the picture. "That's not Lars!"

I grab her hand and turn it back. "Sure it is!" The final bell rings, so I let go and say, "Get your bicycle ready!" and take my seat.

What I can never quite believe about Heather is how bad-girl and tough she acts, but how the most ridiculous little curve can totally undo her. I mean, there's no way the guy in the picture is Lars Teppler. Even with his face not showing, it's obviously Danny. Besides stuff like hair, Danny's worn the same ring on the index finger of his left hand for as long as I've known him.

And his hand was definitely in the picture.

But still, as ridiculous as what I'd said was, it totally back-combed her. She kept looking at me during class, trying to get my attention so she could flash the IT'S DANNY, YOU IDIOT sign that she'd made.

I already knew what the sign said because I'd sort of

stretched up and seen it as she was making it. So when she was actually ready to *show* it to me, it was easy to ignore all her little coughs and dropped pencils and *psssst*s.

I mean, I was supposed to be concentrating on the lesson, right?

But see? That's the trouble with school. It's easy to lose track of why you're there. Risqué pictures of your archenemy, boys running off with girls on bicycles, your good friend turning into the Deuce, hate signs being flashed during class . . . How can factoring equations, or events that happened a hundred years ago, or the details of photosynthesis compete?

They can't.

So it's a good thing nobody tries to teach anything at lunchtime, because *nothing* could have competed with what happened then.

TWENTY-NINE

It took me half of lunch, but I finally found Marissa behind the drama building, bawling her eyes out.

None of her new, happy friends were with her, either.

She looked up when I sat down beside her, then threw her arms around me and buried her head in my shoulder. "I am such an idiot!" she wailed.

I heaved a sigh. "Yeah, you are."

She pulled back. "You've seen the picture?"

"Heather shoved it in my face during history."

"Last night he promised me—*promised* me—that they were just friends. 'Barely friends' is what he said!"

"So maybe she Photoshopped the picture?"

Her eyes get all big. "You think?"

I blink at her. "No! I'm just saying you *always* look for ways to let him off the hook."

"Oh."

"And you just did it again!"

"But . . . you know how vicious Heather can be!"

"Vicious, yeah, but not that clever. Or *competent*. There's no way she Photoshopped that picture."

She sighs, "You're right," then collapses into a blubbering

pool of heartache on my shoulder. "I am *such* an idiot!" And after she's bawled some more, she pulls back and says, "Go ahead. Say it."

The funny thing is that last night when I was mad at her, I would have been happy to snap, I told you so! But now . . . ? I just shake my head and say, "Nah."

Her face crinkles up. "Why didn't I listen to you? And I was mean to you!"

"Yeah, you kinda were."

"I'm sorry! I'm so, *so* sorry!"

"I'm sorry, too. I wasn't exactly *nice* about it." I heave a big sigh. "Just tell me you're done with Danny."

She nods. "Promise."

So we sit around a little more talking about Danny and how Heather should be the one who's embarrassed, and finally I stand up and say, "Come on. You need to get some cold water on your eyes before class. They are puffy!"

So I drag her out from behind the drama building, but before we can get to the bathroom, she stops short and says, "What in the world . . . ?"

It's Billy, with eight or nine girls following him, hanging on his every word.

He looks happy, too.

Really happy.

I laugh. "He's got heartthrob looks and a personality to match."

Marissa's face pinches up. "What?"

"You didn't see the paper?"

"What paper?"

"The *Santa Martina Times*. He was on yesterday's front page." Then real quick I add, "Well, 'the Deuce' was."

"What are you *talking* about?"

It hits me that I have the newspaper with me in Hudson's clandestine envelope. So I swing off my backpack and dig it out. "Here," I say, handing it over.

At first she just stares.

Then her jaw drops and she turns to me and gasps, "You're serious?"

"Yup."

She goes back to staring at the paper, and finally I nod and say, "My guess is we're not the only ones who recognize him." Then I add, "And I'm sure he's telling his new fans that he's going to be starring in a reality show, too."

Marissa's face practically flies apart. "A reality show!"

"Yeah, he shouldn't be talking about it, but knowing Billy, he can't help it."

"Sammy! What reality show?"

The warning bell rings, so I snatch the paper back and stuff everything away. "Wow. You missed out on a lot with your little trip to Dannyville."

"Sammy! Don't torture me—tell me!"

I study her a minute. "This whole thing with Billy being the Deuce started off as a way for him to get over you. He was really, really hurt by what you did."

"I *know*," she whimpers. She gives a pitiful look to where Billy is enjoying his harem and pouts. "Looks like he's over me now."

"That's a good thing, though, right?"

She says, "Right," but it's easy to see that she's kicking herself big-time.

I give her half a hug and say, "I can't be late to Rothhammer's—I'll catch you up in drama." I start toward the science classroom. "There is *so* much to tell you!"

"Can't wait!" she calls back.

Now, Ms. Rothhammer may be strict and serious, but she's a really great person, and she's probably my favorite teacher. So I felt a weird combination of nervousness and pride as I hurried to deliver my stack of makeup work to her before the tardy bell rang.

"What's this?" she asks.

"Missing work." I look her in the eye. "I'm sorry I've been slacking. I want to raise my grade. I want to get on the college track. Any amount of credit you decide to give me is fine." Then I kinda laugh and say, "I hope it's worth *something,* 'cause it was a lot of work!"

The tardy bell rings, which in Ms. Rothhammer's class means seated and silent, but before I scurry to my desk, she whispers, "I can't tell you how happy this makes me."

So I felt really good about that. And even though both Heather and Billy are in that class and there were plenty of reasons to get distracted, I made myself concentrate on the overheads and the lesson.

Heather must've noticed, because as she shoves past me on her way out, she says, "You're such a dweeb."

"Better'n being you," I call after her with a laugh.

And what's so funny is, she actually turns and sputters

like she wants to say *something* but can't figure out what, and then she storms off mad at *me*.

Whatever. I fall in step with Billy on the way over to drama and say, "Nice picture in the paper."

"I can't believe everyone's recognizing me!" he says, obviously thrilled that everyone's recognizing him. Then he drops his voice and says, "Justice Jack told me to meet him at headquarters after school. I think he's got something big planned. Maybe we'll be on the news!"

Now, I really want to ask stuff like, Did your parents see the paper? What did they say? Do you think being Justice Jack's sidekick is such a good idea? What *is* the deal with the reality show anyway?

But I don't want to choke off his happy mood. I don't want him thinking, Oh, brother, here comes that downer Sammy again.

Besides, when did I become the voice of caution?

So I just walk alongside him and let him be Happy Billy, and the only question I ask is if he could relay a message to Casey and tell him I'd pay-phone him after school.

"*Sí, sí*, Sammy-keyesta," he tells me with a goofy Billy Pratt grin, and whips out his phone.

I do kinda go Uh-oh when I see Marissa waiting outside the drama room, but Billy just walks past her with a "Cheerio, Marissa!" like nothing in the world has happened between them.

Marissa watches him go by like he's a-hunk, a-hunk of burning love. And it hits me how funny it is that yesterday she looked at him one way, and now she's all googly-eyed and drop-jawed over him.

And why?

Because *other* girls are.

Mr. Chester's usually pretty lax about students talking during drama. Probably because the class is huge and we work in groups, practicing our lines or making props. Every once in a while he blows a fuse—usually when he figures out that nobody's actually practicing, they're just talking—but mostly he's too caught up in one group to pay much attention to another. So during class it was easy to catch Marissa up on Pair-a-Dice and Buckley's and the whole Secret Agent Man thing, but it took longer than it should have because she kept interrupting me with questions and saying, "You've got to be kidding!" every seven seconds.

Anyway, I did a pretty good job of painting a picture of everything she'd missed, but when the dismissal bell rings, I find out that that's not good enough for Marissa. She latches onto me as we leave Mr. Chester's room and says, "You've got to take me there."

"What? Where?"

"To Pair-a-Dice!"

"Aw, come on. No. I was there on Monday and Tuesday. I've kinda had enough of the place."

"But I haven't seen it!"

"Look, I just told you all about it."

"That's like saying I don't have to see the *Mona Lisa* because you described it to me!"

I roll my eyes. "Trust me. Pair-a-Dice is not the *Mona Lisa*. It's a shed in the woods, okay? Not the kind of place you would ever want to go."

"It's in the *woods*?"

"Yeah, pretty much." I eye her as we leave Mr. Chester's room. "Bugs, snakes, spiders . . . you know."

"Did you *see* spiders and snakes?"

I laugh. "Oh, they're there. They're just hanging out waiting for you to show up so they can pounce." Then I add, "And Pair-a-Dice is not exactly down the street. You have to go past the junkyard to get there."

"There's a junkyard? Where?"

I do a little mental slap of the forehead, because of course Marissa McKenze doesn't know where the junkyard is. Her family lives out on East Jasmine. In a mansion.

I shake my head. "Look. You don't have a bike or a skateboard. . . . It took Billy and me almost an hour to walk there, and besides, I need to go to math lab."

"Math lab? Why?"

"Because I'm behind and I need help!"

She frowns. "Well, fine. I'll wait. And I don't care how far it is, I want to go."

I stop and stare her down with a scowl. "Well, I *don't* want to go."

"Pleeeeeeease?"

I keep scowling.

"Did I mention you're the best friend ever?" she says in a squeaky little voice.

"What?"

"You're the best friend ever."

"What?" I say, cupping my ear.

"You're the best friend ever!" she shouts. Then she spins around with her arms up, calling out, "Sammy Keyes is the best friend ever!"

I smirk and grab her by the backpack. "All right. Come on."

"You'll take me?"

"Yeah," I grumble, "I'll take you. After math lab."

I didn't have a clue what I was getting into.

THIRTY

Before going to math lab, I called home and told Grams not to worry if I was late—that I was with Marissa, straightening things out. Marissa did the same thing with her mom, and then I pay-phoned Casey. And I was excited to talk to him, but he sounded so bummed that I finally just came out and said, "You saw the picture, huh?"

"It's so awkward. Everybody's sending it around. What is she *thinking*?"

Now, I'm sure not one to jump to Heather's defense, but I found myself wanting to make Casey feel better. So I wound up saying stuff like, "Well, it's not like they were naked," and, "Look, she just did it to make Marissa cry," and, "She probably didn't think her friend would send it to anyone else . . . ," but none of it seemed to help. So finally I give up on that and tell him, "I promised I'd take Marissa out to see Pair-a-Dice. I have to go to math lab first, but any chance you want to meet us there?"

"Are you trying to get Marissa over Danny the way you got Billy over Marissa?"

I laugh. "Ironic, huh? I hope she doesn't turn into a

sidekick, too." I eye Marissa. "And she promised me she's over Danny for good."

"Man, I hope so."

"It might get kinda late if you've got to be back by five."

"I don't care. If I get reamed for this and Heather skates for that picture . . . ?" He fades off, then tunes back in and tries to sound more upbeat. "I'll be there. Get your jungle whistle ready!"

"It's always ready!" I tell him, and hang up the phone.

"Everything okay?" Marissa asks.

I head over to math lab. "Heather's picture is getting passed around the high school. Casey's kinda sick over it."

She follows after me, shaking her head. "Can you imagine having her as a sister? How embarrassing."

"I just don't get Heather. Why is she so . . . ?"

"Vindictive? Mean? Vicious? Nasty? *Possessed*?"

I laugh. "Yeah." Then I shrug and say, "Maybe someday we'll figure it out, but that probably won't be today."

Mr. Tiller runs the math lab, and he's one of those teachers who used to tell me he'd love to see me live up to my potential but finally stopped. So when I came through the door, his eyebrows went creeping upward. "Good to see you here."

"It's about time, right?" I laughed. Then I spun around. "This is me, turning over a new leaf."

So I concentrated on the stuff I was having trouble with and had him check my work. And when I understood one kind of problem and had a good example to work from, I went on to the next kind of problem until I knew how to do everything from three of the sections where I hadn't turned in homework. Then I packed up, thanked Mr. Tiller, grabbed Marissa—who'd also decided to get her math homework done—and got out of there.

"I've been thinking," I tell Marissa as we set off for Pair-a-Dice. "Heather did you a big favor."

"She what?"

"Think about it—how long would Danny have strung you along if she hadn't taken that picture?"

Her head quivers like it's shivering cold. "Can we *please* talk about something else?"

"Okaaaay." I think a minute. "How about your parents—what's going on with them?"

She groans like she doesn't want to talk about that, either, but then launches into a blow-by-blow of their fights and her mom's crying and her dad's storming out and Mikey's sleeping in the extra bed in her room. "They're a mess, he's a mess, we're all a mess. I keep thinking it'll get better, but it just seems to get worse. I heard Mom tell him that we have to move into a smaller place, but Dad said he could fix everything if she'd just give him a chance."

"Uh-oh. Does that mean gambling?"

"Probably," she says, all disgusted-like. "Why doesn't he get that he's never going to win?"

I shrug. "Because people do win."

"Oh yeah? Name one."

"Uh . . . Mrs. Wedgewood?"

"Wait—your *neighbor*?"

I take a deep breath and let it out in a great big gust. "She's not my neighbor anymore."

"What happened? Did she finally fall off the toilet so hard no one could help her?"

I eye her. "She died."

"What? Oh! I'm sorry. That was mean of me." She studies me a minute. "But you hated her, right?"

And it hits me that it is kinda strange how you can call someone the Wedginator and the Mighty Wedge and the World's Biggest Wedgie when they're alive, but after they're dead?

Well, it does seem . . . wrong.

But if it's wrong after they're dead, then it was wrong when they were alive, right? It's just you've run out of time to take it back. Or say you're sorry. Or give it any more *thought*.

It's like you've been swimming around in a pool of to-morrows and suddenly, *whoosh,* it's drained.

Thinking about that made me really glad I hadn't just told Mrs. Wedgewood off like I'd wanted to. I'd had that little last chance to take things back. Or at least *explain* things.

"Wow. What is going through your head?" Marissa asks. "You look so *serious.*"

I try to wave it off. "It's a funny story, really." Then I launch into Mrs. Wedgewood's disappearing and the Prune Patrol and the Senior SWAT Team out to get her with screwdrivers and credit cards. I go into all the details, too, and kind of jump around and act out the things Bun-Top and the others had said.

But the whole time I'm talking, there's a little voice in

my head telling me to be careful. Telling me not to tell Marissa about the candy money.

Telling me that telling her might somehow . . . backfire.

So I kept mum about the money.

"You weren't kidding it's far," Marissa says when I'm winding down about Mrs. Wedgewood. "And it's already getting kind of dark."

It was, too. Not *dark* dark. Not even dusky, really. But it was kind of cloudy and the sun was definitely saying See ya for another day.

"Well, there's the junkyard," I tell her. "We've got to go about halfway down those eucalyptus trees, take a right, then another right back up this way through the trees."

"A right and a right? That's like doing a giant U-turn. Isn't there a shortcut?"

I look at her and bust up. "You *want* to take a shortcut?"

"I want to get there already!"

I think about it a minute. "Well, Casey and I cut out through the trees and along the junkyard fence thataway, so you're right—it would be way shorter if we cut in through the trees on this side."

"Trees?" she says, like she's suddenly worried.

"Yeah, you know, those living logs that shoot up from the earth?" I give her a little shove. "You're the one who brought up taking a shortcut."

We're nearing the entrance to the junkyard now, but the gate is rolled closed and locked up tight. And all of a sudden the dogs I'd seen in the office when I'd stopped in before come charging at us, barking and growling and snapping like they're going to tear us apart.

"Ahhhhhh!" Marissa squeals as they slam against the chain-link. "Ohmygod, ohmygod, ohmygod! That one's got devil eyes!"

We run ahead, and the dogs do chase after us for a minute, but turn around well before we get to the end of the property.

"Why do junkyards always have vicious dogs?" she pants.

"You didn't even know we had a junkyard!"

"Well, I've been to the movies, you know! And why would anybody own a junkyard? Broken cars, mean dogs . . . Talk about stupid."

"Maybe they're actually smart. Maybe they had a bunch of dilapidated cars and the neighbors complained about the mess but it was too big to clean up so they put up a fence and a sign and started making money instead!"

"Maybe not," she snaps.

"You know," I tell her, "you always get testy when we're about to take a shortcut."

"I'm not being testy," she says in a totally testy way.

I laugh. "Oh, right. But the point is, we don't *have* to take a shortcut."

"Look, I want to *get* there already. This is taking forever! If I had known—"

"I told you it was a long way!"

"But why'd you have to go to math lab!"

"See? Testy. I'm not the one who wants to go here. I've

already been here twice. I know all about it. I'm also not the one without a bike or a skateboard. So if you want to go back, I'm all for it!"

"Sorry," she says with a little frown.

We're nearing the end of the junkyard property, so I say, "What's it gonna be? Shortcut or no shortcut?"

She doesn't say a word for about ten steps, then finally grumbles, "Shortcut."

So we turn in when we get to the end of the fence, and pretty soon we're zigzagging through the trees, going deeper and deeper into the eucalyptus forest.

"Are you sure you know where you're going?" Marissa whimpers after we've walked awhile. "It's really eerie in here."

"As long as we can see the junkyard fence, we're fine. There's this little, like, *seam* in it, and once I find that, I'll know where we are."

"What do you mean, a seam?"

"It's this twisty thing that holds two parts together."

She hurries to catch up to me. "How do you know about a twisty thing that holds two parts of a junkyard fence together?"

But then I see something.

Something that does not belong in a eucalyptus forest.

I stop cold and it doesn't take long for me to realize that there's only one sensible thing to do.

Grab Marissa and hide!

THIRTY-ONE

I drag Marissa behind a big tree, and she gasps, "What are you doing? What's wrong?"

I peek around the tree and watch as a truck moves carefully through the forest.

It's a shiny red tow truck with a flatbed, and even though we're too far away to read the fancy white lettering on the side, I know what it says.

TONY'S TOWING.

"That's the same tow truck Billy and I saw the first time we came out here. The guy stopped and told us the road was a dead end."

"So?" Marissa says as we watch it do a careful three-point turn, and that's when I notice that the truck has wide double rear wheels.

Duallies.

"So it's going to back up to that seam in the fence."

We watch, and sure enough that's just what it does. Then a big guy with curly black hair gets out of the driver's side, and in no time flat he's got that twisty thing twisted off the fence and has enough room to squeeze through the opening.

Marissa shakes her head a little. "Why would someone want a secret after-hours entry to a *junkyard*?"

All of a sudden the piece of buzzy meat that Casey and I had seen makes sense. "The dogs," I mutter. "He's trying to avoid the dogs."

"If he wants to avoid the dogs, why doesn't he just stay out of the junkyard? It's a *junkyard*. What's to steal?"

And that's when it hits me. The weird footprints. The gouge in the ground . . . Someone had dragged something heavy backward.

My heart starts pounding in my chest. "He's not stealing."

"Then what?"

"He's retrieving."

"What are you talking about?"

"Come on," I whisper, and hurry forward from tree to tree, closing in on the truck.

So there we are running along, thinking it's just us and Tow Truck Tony, who's long gone inside the junkyard, when all of a sudden a door slams.

We duck behind a tree and look at each other like two electrified owls. "Was that the truck?" Marissa whispers.

I nod. "Must've been."

"So is there another person?"

My heart is whacking away. "Must be."

"Do you think they saw us?"

"Must have."

But nobody shouts, Hey, you! and we don't hear any leaves crunching our way. So finally we hold our breath and peek around the tree, and sure enough, there is a second person.

Someone I know.

Like lightning, the things Officer Borsch had said about Justice Jack flash through my mind:

Petty crime has gone way up since he's decided to "help out."

Up, not down!

There have been ten stolen bicycles in the last two weeks!

Everywhere I turn, there's Jack!

I let out a little whimper. *"No."*

Marissa looks at me. "Do you know her?"

"That's Justice Jack's mom."

"His *mom*?"

"Maaaaaaan . . . !"

"Why are you so upset?"

"Because this means Justice Jack is a fraud."

"It does?"

And that's when the little puff of smoke that had been snuffed out days ago sparks to life and fireballs through my brain.

"It was all a setup! Every bit of it! The mayor didn't call him at Buckley's! It was probably *that* guy pretending to be the mayor."

"Well, who *is* that guy? Justice Jack's dad?"

I shake my head. "Jack's dad died. Maybe he's the mom's boyfriend?" My brain races as we watch Mama Jack do something that makes the bed of the tow truck tilt. "I should have known! I mean, what a coincidence—Jack's at

Buckley's with the Hollywood guy and the *mayor* calls? What are the odds of that?"

"What makes you think it wasn't the mayor?"

"I heard the real mayor on TV. He didn't sound anything like whoever called Justice Jack when he was at Buckley's." I shake my head. "Why didn't that click?" Then I add, "*Boy,* he's a good actor."

"Who?"

"Jack! None of what he did was for making the world a better place—it was to get a reality show! Stealing the statue must just be part of that."

"Wait—you're saying Justice Jack stole the statue?"

I nod toward where Mama Jack is now pulling on a large metal hook to unwind a cable that's anchored to a big red W-shaped brace at the back of the cab. "I bet they're here to get the statue out of its hiding place."

"Why not just hide it out here in the trees?"

"Anyone could stumble upon it out here. Someone walking their dogs . . . someone shortcutting home from school . . . And the junkyard's like a really secure prison. With man-eating dogs! Besides, you sure wouldn't want to get *caught* with that thing, right? And who's going to look in some back corner of a junkyard?"

Marissa shakes her head. "That statue seems like a crazy thing to steal!"

"Yeah, but it was the perfect thing to steal for publicity, and that's what they're after. They probably couldn't land a reality show by rescuing kittens and returning bicycles. They needed something bigger."

"But . . . to break into City Hall? That's risking a lot."

And that's when something else clicks. "Officer Borsch said the alarm didn't go off." I think a minute. "He said there was a broken window, but the alarm didn't go off, but . . ."

"But what?"

I hold my head. "*Billy* was the one who said, 'City Hall!' when Jack got the call at Buckley's."

"Did he see the caller ID?"

"Yes! Jack showed it to him."

"So . . . maybe it *was* the mayor?"

All of a sudden it feels like my brain is stumbling over big blocks. Like it wants to race but it can't because there's too much stuff in the way.

Could it have been the mayor?

And then Marissa says, "Or . . . maybe Billy's in on it?"

I look at her, horrified. "No!"

"Come on, Sammy. Can't you see Billy going along with something like this? He probably thinks it's funny."

"No. N-O, no!"

She shrugs and rolls her eyes, and we both sit there a minute thinking, until finally she says, "What if one of *them* works at City Hall?"

"Oh!" I look at her all wide-eyed. "Do you think *any* phone from *any* office over there would show City Hall on the caller ID?"

Marissa shrugs. "Probably."

I think about it another minute and something about it just *feels* right. "Thank you. That makes total sense."

It's definitely dusky now, but we can see movement on

the junkyard side of the fence. "There he is," I whisper. "And he's dragging something really heavy."

"He looks like a giant waddling penguin," Marissa whispers back.

We watch while Tow Truck Tony takes the hook from Jack's mom and loops the cable around something big that's wrapped up tight in a brown tarp.

"That's about the right size, don't you think?" I whisper.

"It seems kind of small to me," Marissa says.

"You're used to seeing it on the base."

"So they stole just the brass part?"

"Right."

She nods. "Okay. Then maybe so."

Once Tow Truck Tony's got the cable hooked on and secured, he goes over to the passenger side of the truck and pretty soon a noise starts and the cable pulls up, up, up, hauling the big tarp-wrapped thing onto the bed like a wrecked car.

"That *must* be the statue," I mutter. "What else could it be?"

"But what are they going to *do* with it?"

"Plant it somewhere and have Jack miraculously find it. Billy said there was something big going on tonight—this must be it." I hit my forehead. "Snakes in December—I knew there was something weird about that!"

"Wait—snakes? What?"

"Never mind," I grumble. "You think *you're* an idiot? *I'm* the idiot. I can't believe I let myself get sucked in by Justice Jack. I actually *believed* him."

"So, what are we going to do?"

261

A bunch of ideas flash through my head, but the only smart one is something I can't do. "It's so stupid that neither of us has a phone."

She snorts. "Tell me about it." Then she eyes me and says, "But speaking of stupid, I sure hope you're not getting any ideas about jumping on the back of that truck."

"It did cross my mind."

"No! You hear me? No! We don't even know that it's the statue!"

We watch as Tow Truck Tony levels the bed and then has Mama Jack help him connect some fat straps across their junkyard load. And when the straps are snugged down tight, Tony twists the secret entry closed and the junkyard sneaks get back in the cab.

I whisper, "If we jumped on the truck, we could look under the tarp and then we'd *know*."

"Oh, sure. How are we going to do that?"

"They'll be coming right by us to get out of here. It would be easy."

"How do you know they'll be coming this way?"

I point to an island of dirt just a few yards away. "See the tire tracks? Casey and I followed them last night. That's how we found the seam in the fence in the first place."

The truck engine fires up and Marissa starts to squirm. "You want us to jump on board like we're jumping a train?"

"They won't be going very fast. And there's no back window for them to see us. It'll be easy."

"But *why*?" she asks as the truck starts toward us. "Why put ourselves in danger over a stupid statue?"

Real casual-like, I say, "Did you know there's a reward?"

She snaps to face me. "A *reward*?"

I nod. "Five thousand dollars."

"You're kidding!" She blinks at me. "Do you know what I could do with five thousand dollars?"

I laugh. "Who says you're getting five thousand?"

She hesitates. "Well, twenty-five hundred." She looks at me, worried. "Right?"

I shrug. "Sure. But if we don't know where they're taking it and Jack magically discovers it before we can call the police, we'll get zip."

"But what if it's not the statue?"

"Then we'll jump off before they even know we're there."

Marissa's face sets up. Like all of a sudden the cement of a decision has *hardened*. She snugs down the straps of her backpack and looks at me. "I'm in."

I don't have one of those fancy backpacks with the skateboard clips, so real quick I loosen my backpack straps all the way and get Marissa to help me wedge my skateboard between my pack and my back so my hands are free.

The truck rumbles closer.

And closer.

I yank down my backpack straps and adjust the skateboard so it's not jabbing me so much. And as the truck rumbles by, I take a deep breath and say, "Ready?"

Marissa's fidgeting like crazy. "What if they see us in the side mirrors?"

"I think they're too busy driving through a maze of trees." I look at her again. "You in?"

She nods. "Let's do it!"

Then we jet out from behind the trees and run like mad to jump the truck.

THIRTY-TWO

Even though the tow truck wasn't moving very fast, getting on board was hard.

And *painful*.

That was probably mostly on account of my skateboard gouging my back and banging my arms as I ran and jumped and stumbled, because Marissa seemed to do okay but I was like, Ow! Ooooh! Aaaah! when I finally crashed to a halt beside her.

"You okay?" she asked.

I told her, "Yeah," but I must've been looking pretty pained, because she said, "You sure?"

I nodded. "I just hope they didn't hear us."

"They would have stopped by now, don't you think? And this rig isn't exactly quiet, so I think we're okay."

It must've been the reward money giving her guts, because normally Marissa would have been shaking in her shoes. But I liked her being calm, because I sure wasn't.

"Help me get this skateboard out. It's killing me."

"You sure?"

"I can jump off fine with it in my hand," I told her, struggling to get it out. "Come on. Help me."

So there we are, wrestling with my skateboard as we ride through the eucalyptus forest, rumbling along on the back of a tow truck, when I hear the jungle whistle.

"Oh, man!"

"What?"

"Did you hear that?"

"Hear what?"

"That whistle?"

And there it goes again: *Ah-ee-ah-ee-ahhhhh.*

"What is that?"

"That's Casey looking for me."

"You guys have your own whistle?" She shakes her head and rolls her eyes. "Sounds like the call of the wild."

"Yeah, well, I'm supposed to whistle back."

She gets the skateboard dislodged and says, "Probably don't want to do that until we figure out if this is the soft-ball statue. If it's not, we'll just bail off and you can whistle all you want."

So we dig at the tarp, but it's hard to get underneath it, especially with the straps cinched down tight. And I start to panic that we're totally wasting time because we're already jostling onto Sandydale Lane. "Man! I wish I had a knife!"

But Marissa's found an end of the tarp and is pulling it up. So I jump in and help her, and all of a sudden out pops a big brass hand holding a big brass softball.

"Yes!" Marissa whispers, pumping her fist.

Now, in the back of my mind I had thought that the tow truck would make a pit stop at Mama Jack's mobile home. I don't know why. I just did. And even if it didn't, I thought I could signal Casey with the whistle and get him to sneak on board with us. Trouble is, as soon as we hit Sandydale Lane, the truck starts *moving*.

I look at Marissa. "What's our plan?!"

"To get the reward!"

"But what's our *plan*? What if Tow Truck Tony's got a gun?"

Normally, this would have sent Marissa into Nervesville, but something about the reward is making her brave. "Justice Jack's mom knows you, right? She won't let him shoot you. It's just a stupid statue!"

"Which the most powerful man in the city wants back!"

"Which is why we'll be swimming in five thousand dollars!"

I hear Casey's whistle again, and this time I cup my hands together and whistle back. And as we barrel past Pair-a-Dice, I spot him on the side of the road.

Ah-ee-ah-ee-ahhhhh, I whistle again.

"Hey!" he shouts as we go by, but I'm afraid to shout anything back. And instead of doing something smart, I figure, Okay. When we get to the stop sign at the bottom of Sandydale, I'm jumping off.

But Marissa *is* apparently thinking, because she's got her backpack off and open and she's tossing a piece of rumpled yellow paper at Casey. It doesn't go anywhere *near* him, but he does see it and races to pick it up.

"What did you write?"

"Call the cops!" she tells me.

"Wow. That was quick thinking. And you were fast! But I'm bailing off at the stop sign."

"No, you're not!" she says, pointing her yellow pad at me. "We won't know where they're going! We'll lose the reward!"

"Marissa, this is crazy. I'm getting off!"

Trouble is, Tow Truck Tony doesn't even slow down at the stop sign. He just barrels through it and veers to the right, away from the main road.

"Oh, great!" I moan. Then I snatch Marissa's yellow pad from her, rumple up a piece of paper, and toss it over the side.

Then I do another.

And another.

Marissa gets all excited and starts helping. "Oh! Like Hansel and Gretel!"

I shake my head. "You are never this calm and collected when we're in danger."

"There's never been a reward before!" she says, all happy-faced. "And so far the only danger is the way this guy drives!"

After a few more turns and dozens of wadded papers, the eucalyptus trees have thinned way out and I have no idea where we are.

Plus, it's definitely dark now.

Plus, I don't see any houses.

We keep wadding papers and tossing them overboard, but I'm getting more and more worried about being hauled into the middle of nowhere.

And then all of a sudden we slow down and turn off the road.

"Oh, *man*," I whisper, and start wadding up papers like

crazy. "Casey and the cops'll never see these papers in the dark!"

"Those two will never see *us* in the dark," Marissa says. "Which means the minute they stop, we'll jump off and hide. And we'll know where they stash the statue *before* Jack miraculously finds it, and—ta-da!—we'll be rich."

Now, even though it's dark back where we are, I don't want to risk being spotted in the side mirrors. And since we're slowing way down and I'd really like to be able to see what's going on, I stand up, lean across the statue, grab onto the big red W brace, and look over the top of the cab.

Marissa jumps up, too, and as we jostle side to side over some potholes, she says, "What is this place?"

We come to a sign that says SVENSEN'S DAIRY, and straight ahead there's a really large rectangular building.

"If this is a dairy, where are the cows?" She sniffs. "I sure don't *smell* any, either."

"It must be abandoned? Or out of business?" We've slowed down even more, so I grab my skateboard and tell her, "Let's get off while we can."

"Already?"

"Marissa! Get scared, okay? This is not a good situation!"

She comes down from her perch. "All right, all right."

So we do a quick butt-scoot to the end of the bed, dangle our legs over the edge, and push off while the truck jostles forward over potholes. And both of us do land on our feet, but somehow we wind up falling over anyway.

"That was still a lot easier than getting on!" Marissa laughs, dusting off.

"Wow," I say, shaking my head at her. "The lure of money has a powerful effect on you."

"I've been broke since summer!" she says.

"I've been broke my whole life," I grumble. Then I grab her and start to head back the way we'd come.

"Wait—where are we going?"

"Back to the road! We need to either find a house or flag someone down and call the police."

"Casey's already found some way to do that, don't you think?"

"And told them what? Follow the wads of yellow paper?"

"But don't you want to spy on them and see where they hide the statue?"

"They're not hiding it, they're *planting* it so Jack can make his amazing discovery."

"What kind of amazing discovery will it be if it's clear out here? No one will know!"

"Oh, I'm sure they'll call the TV stations and the newspaper and have a huge entourage of paparazzi documenting his do-gooder phoniness." I shake my head. "What a con. What a *fake*."

"He's like the wizard behind the curtain."

I snort. "He's not Justice Jack, he's Joker Jack."

"The Sham Man."

"Captain Con."

She laughs. "That's a good one." But then she looks over her shoulder and yanks me to a halt. "So where'd they go?"

I look over my shoulder, too, and at first it does seem like they've vanished, but then I spot the truck pulling around the far side of the barn. "Over there! See them? They turned off their headlights."

"So maybe they're not going into the barn? Maybe they're going out . . . out there! What if they hide it in a field? What if we know it's around here somewhere but aren't sure where? What if we lose the whole reward because we don't actually *know* where it is?"

"Marissa! Get a grip! We're in the middle of nowhere by an abandoned dairy farm. Who do you think would find us out here? How long would it take for someone to discover our vulture-pecked bones, huh?"

She blinks at me.

That's all.

Just blinks.

So I grab her again and march her back to the road, and almost right away I see a light coming toward us from the left.

At first I'm excited because out in the middle of who knows where you might not expect a car to show up for ages.

But then I realize that it's not a car.

Well, unless it's missing a headlight.

"Is that a bike?" Marissa asks.

We watch another minute, and finally I say, "Maybe it's someone with a flashlight?" because the beam of light is kind of jerking around. The light is yellow, too. And flickery. And I'm getting the sinking feeling that whoever it is won't be able to help us call the police when I realize there's a *sound* getting closer, too.

A sound I recognize.

And, really, it can only mean one thing.

We're in some deep, dark, middle-of-nowhere doo-doo.

THIRTY-THREE

"It's Justice Jack!" Marissa cries.

Like this is a good thing.

"He's *in* on this, don't you get that?" I grab her by the arm and haul her off the road and behind the SVENSEN'S DAIRY sign, and then we watch the headlight jerk to the side from time to time as the High Roller roars toward us.

Finally Marissa says, "So what are we going to *do*?"

"I don't know! I sure hope Billy's not with him. He's driving like he's drunk!"

They're getting close now, and over the roar of the High Roller I hear someone shout, "There's another!"

It's not Billy's voice.

Or Jack's.

"Oh no!" I groan. "Casey's using our trail of paper balls to lead Jack right to us!"

But then we hear, "Dude! Over there! On the right!"

"That's Billy!" Marissa squeals.

And then, booming over the roar of the bike, we hear, "Never fear, young champions! We'll find them!"

"How are they *all* on that contraption?" I ask, because the only thing we can really see is the headlight. But then

Casey shouts, "There's one!" and as the High Roller turns onto the dairy property, we see that Billy's in the sidecar while Jack is scooted way up on his seat with Casey crammed in behind him.

I race out from behind our hiding place and shout, "Casey! Billy! Wait!"

The High Roller nose-dives to a halt and Justice Jack cries, "Hark! The sound of damsels about to be rescued!"

"We're not damsels and you're not rescuing us!" I shout at him. "I know exactly what you're up to!"

He totally ignores how I know exactly what he's up to and says, "You weren't abducted?" and even in the dark I can see the phony innocence behind the mask.

Casey swings off the High Roller and runs over to me. "What happened? Where's the truck?"

"Down there!" I say, pointing toward the abandoned dairy barn. "They've got the softball statue!"

"The softball statue!" Jack roars, and before I can explain a thing, he cries, "Thieving fiends! Prepare to be Jackhammered!" and tears off in the High Roller with Billy still in the sidecar.

"NOOOO!" I shout after him. "BILLY, GET OUT!"

"What's going on?" Casey asks, chasing after me as I chase after the High Roller.

"Jack's mother stole the statue!"

"His *mother* did?"

"Her and her boyfriend! Well, we think it's her boyfriend. And Jack has to be in on it!"

"Jack does? Why?"

274

"Everything he's done has been staged so he could get a reality show!"

Now, let me tell you, it's not easy running with a backpack bouncing around and a skateboard in your hand. At least Marissa can hold down her straps and keep her pack from bouncing. But I'm all bumping around and it's slowing me down, which is frustrating because it feels like Billy's in danger and I just want to get to him and warn him that he's sidekick to Captain Con.

And then it hits me that Casey doesn't have his backpack *or* his skateboard. So I ask him, "Where's your stuff?"

"I dumped it at Pair-a-Dice."

And just like that I'm dumping mine. "Marissa!" I shout, because she's a little ahead of us. "Ditch your backpack!"

She spins out of it and, *clomp,* it falls without her even slowing down.

"What's up with her?" Casey asks, because it's definitely not like Marissa to lead a charge.

"There's a big reward for the statue!" Then I add, "And maybe she's kicking herself over Billy?"

Since all Jack heard me say was, "Down there!" he doesn't go around the back of the barn where the tow truck had disappeared. Instead, he roars right up to the big barn door, leaps off the High Roller, and bashes the door in with his boot.

"Billy!" I shout. "Billy, he's a fake! He's conning you right now!"

But Billy either doesn't hear me or doesn't believe me,

because he leaps out of the sidecar and follows Jack inside the dairy barn without even looking back.

"The tow truck didn't go into the barn," I call over to Casey. "It went behind it."

"But we're following Billy, right?" Casey calls back.

"I am not getting cheated out of that reward!" Marissa shouts over her shoulder. "I didn't risk life and limb for nothing!"

So we charge over to the barn door—which turns out to be two big swinging doors—and all of a sudden there we are, inside this massive building that has a dirt *road* down the middle and long rows of open-sided stalls. The stalls are made out of metal pipe, and all together they look like some kind of stainless-steel rib cage.

Like the carcass of a huge alien robot, or something.

The reason we can see this is that headlights are shining toward us from the other side of the barn. At first I'm surprised that Tow Truck Tony did come inside, but then it hits me that of course Jack knew where to look. He's been in on the whole thing!

Jack's in the middle of putting on a big show, too. "Don't move, villains!" he cries as he strides commando-style toward the headlights. "You cannot escape the Golden Gloves of Justice!"

We can't see beyond the headlights very well, but I can make out a big waddling movement between the truck and the cow stalls.

Jack whips out his slingshot and commands, "Unhand that statue and move away or prepare to be pummeled by the Pellets of Pain . . . *t*."

Like a good sidekick, Billy whips out a slingshot, too.

"Billy!" I call as we move in on them. "He's a fraud! He knew they had the statue!"

"I knew no such thing!" Jack cries, and *boy* is he sounding indignant.

Billy pulls back the band of his slingshot and doesn't even bother to look over his shoulder at me. "A superhero has honor and valor! And he never lies!"

Well, Tow Truck Tony sure isn't paying any attention to Jack's commands. He keeps right on waddling, making his way into a cow stall. And Jack and Billy sure aren't paying any attention to me. They're cocked and locked and moving in fast.

And then Jack cries, "We gave them fair warning, Deuce! We have no choice. And . . . FIRE!"

Thwooop ! Thwooop! The Pellets of Pain . . . *t* go flying. Only I guess Billy hasn't had enough target practice, because his hits the truck, not Tony.

Thwooop . . . whack! Thwooop . . . ping! They fire again, and again, Billy's hits the truck, but this time Jack hits his mark. "Ow!" Tow Truck Tony shouts. "Ow!"

Thwooop . . . whack! Thwooop . . . ping! "Dang!" Billy cries when he hits the truck *again.*

"Stop it, you idiot!" Tow Truck Tony screams when he gets hit again.

"Surrender, villain!" Justice Jack booms, and when no hands go up, they fire again. *Thwooop . . . whack! Thwooop . . . ping!*

"Double dang!" Billy cries. "There's something wrong with my slingshot!"

277

And I'm not sure if it's so much the pain as it is the *paint* that's got Tow Truck Tony moving out of the cow stall, because his arms are crossed in front of his head, but what he shouts is, "Quit messin' with my truck!"

Thwooop . . . whack! Thwooop . . . ping!

"That's it!" Tow Truck Tony yells. "Sheri, your kid's an idiot and I'm done with this!"

And that's when Mama Jack appears in front of the truck. "Jack! Stop it! It's us!"

Inch by inch, Jack's slingshot lowers. "Mom . . . ? What are you doing here?" And then, "Is that *Tony*?"

And that's when it hits me—Jack really *didn't* know.

Jack's mom hurries up to him. "Tony got a tip that someone hid the statue out here, and they did! Look what we found!"

"She's lying to you, Jack," I say, running up to him. "*They* stole the statue."

"Why would we steal a stupid statue?" she says, but she's looking like a mom caught wiggling coins out of her kid's piggy bank.

I lock eyes with her. "Do you really want me to answer that?"

She gives me a pleading look.

Like, No.

Don't.

You'll destroy him.

But Tony's ticked off about his truck getting thwacked with paint and has no problem busting a wannabe superhero's bubble of righteousness. "Give it up, Sheri. This has gotten completely out of control." He rubs a paint splotch off his truck with a rag. "First the dogs, then the bikes, then the statue . . . How did you ever talk me into this?"

"But it worked!" she pleads. "We're *this* close to having a show!"

"Mom?" Jack says, and let me tell you, there's nothing booming or even halfway strong about his voice. "What are you saying?"

"Aw, honey," she says, moving toward him.

He takes a big booted step back. "Stop it! I'm not a kid! I'm Justice Jack! I take down criminals. I . . . I . . ." His face crinkles behind the mask. "Are you saying all my rescues . . . everything I did . . . ?"

His voice trails off, so Tony cuts in with, "Yeah. She set 'em all up."

"Not *all* of it!" Mama Jack says. "That purse snatching at the mall was legit!"

"But everything else?" Jack asks. "The bikes, the dogs, the *snake*?"

"Honey, look. You wanted to be a superhero. There was no talking you out of it! But you're an *adult*. I needed to find some way to turn your passion into your income. You don't want to be a loser living in your mom's trailer when you're forty! Or even thirty! And you've seen the junk that's on TV—it's a joke compared to your real life. You have such color and flair and passion for doing good in this world. What's your motto, honey? Come on, say it."

"It's a good world. Let's take it back," Jack says, but the life is totally gone out of him.

"See? You *are* a superhero! You just need a way to shine."

"I'm a fraud," Jack says, sounding really dejected. "I've been living a *lie*."

"No, honey. You've been living the life you dreamed of. You've been helping people. You've been making other people believe in doing what's right. Imagine all the people who are standing up for their neighbor because they've seen you do it!"

He shakes his head. "I didn't need you setting up crimes. I hate crime!"

"So from now on everything will be legit. You can't give up this reality show! All your young crime-fighting friends can be part of it!" She looks around at us. "Wouldn't you love that?" And before we can make a peep, she turns back to Jack. "Think of the opportunities that will come from having your own show! No more living in a trailer, no more—"

"No!" Jack shouts. "I'm not doing any *show*. All I wanted was to be a real crime fighter."

Tony spits on his truck and rubs. "Give it up, Sheri. All these kids know about it. It's over." He shakes his head. "I just want to know what we're supposed to do with this statue now."

"You're not doing anything with it!" Marissa shouts, and that's when I notice that she's nowhere near the rest of us. She's over in the cow stall, standing by the statue. "We're getting the reward and you're going to jail!"

"Wow," Casey says under his breath. "Not smart."

But Jack hangs his head and nods. "We deserve to go to jail."

"Wait a minute," I tell him, because goofy or not, the

guy's heart has definitely been in the right place, and it's not easy seeing someone's dream get shattered. "*You* don't deserve to go to jail. You didn't know what they were doing!"

"Doesn't matter. If I'm that stupid, lock me up."

Then slowly he takes off his helmet.

His mask.

His gloves.

"Noooo!" Billy cries. "Dude, you're my inspiration! My mentor! My *idol*."

"Sorry to let you down, Deuce," he says, and you can tell his heart is just a big lump of lead in his chest.

And the truth is, mine's feeling a little that way, too. I mean, watching a superhero give up is just . . . *sad*. And something about the whole situation feels *wrong*. I mean, maybe Jack's mom went way overboard trying to help her son, but to someone whose mother seems to have no interest in her, there was something sweet about it. A mom who would go through all that trouble to get her son a job doing what he loved?

Just thinking about it kinda choked me up.

Besides, aren't all reality shows staged?

Plus, I could see where she might think that instead of a reality show with a houseful of trash-talking egoheads, one with a guy who wanted to inspire good deeds and crime fighting might actually be something worth watching.

So, no. I didn't want to see her go to jail.

Or, for that matter, see Tow Truck Tony go to jail.

But how were we going to get the statue back to City

Hall? How could Justice Jack save face? Was there a way to return the statue and *not* let anyone know what had happened?

I looked at Marissa staking out her reward money. And Tony spit-washing his truck. And Jack with his head hung low from the weight of being mortal, while his mom stood by, holding her face while she cried.

And that's when I get an idea.

It's not perfect.

But at least it's something.

THIRTY-FOUR

Officer Borsch used to be so completely by the book. He would charge you with violating some sub-sub-sub-clause of the penal code and think he was being a good cop. But now he sometimes actually closes the book and looks at the whole situation, not just the violation.

Sometimes he even looks the other way.

So I was pretty sure that if I could explain what had happened and get Officer Borsch to see the whole picture, he would put away his ticket book and his handcuffs and find some way to help us.

When I explained my plan to the others, they all thought it made sense—everyone but Jack. He just wanted to hang up his utility belt and hide somewhere. But the whole plan depended on Jack, so I finally said, "Look, you don't want your mother to go to jail, right?"

"But she committed a crime!"

"Does it matter that she did it because she was trying to help you?"

"It's still a crime!"

"Nobody got hurt and the statue will be returned."

He just stands there shaking his head.

"And you don't want her to lose her job. Especially since you don't *have* a job. She's probably paying for your food and, you know, hero gear, right?" I look at Jack's mom. "I'm guessing you work at City Hall?"

She nods.

"So if they find out you're behind this, you're out of a job and maybe in jail." I turn to Jack. "Is that what you want?"

He heaves a sigh. "Punishment should not be relative." He sighs again. "But you're right. And I do need to get a job."

His mother tries cutting in with, "A reality show *is* a—"

"No!" he shouts. "It's bad enough being a fake in real life! I don't want to be one on TV."

"Give it up," Tony tells her. "He couldn't fake it for all the money in the world."

The minute he says that, it hits me that's exactly the reason I'd started liking Justice Jack. Sure he's over-the-top and full of bravado, but he means what he says. He may look like a cartoon, but underneath that he's *real*.

So I tell Jack, "Look, you have a big chance to do one last good deed."

He says, "What?" but it's more like, Who cares?

"You have a chance to get other people to carry the torch of justice."

He looks up at me for the first time since I'd started explaining my plan. "The torch of justice?" And I can tell that even without the mask, he's *Justice* Jack, and that the torch of justice has just become the Torch of Justice.

Once Jack was on board, I borrowed his cell phone to

call Officer Borsch, and once I'd laid down some ground rules with Officer Borsch—mostly that he couldn't ask too many questions—I told him where we were.

"How'd you wind up *there*?"

"See? You're already starting with the questions. Can you just meet us out here? And bring a big length of rope. And make sure there's not a lot of junk in your trunk."

Which, if you saw the size of Officer Borsch, you'd know was asking a lot.

Good thing I was talking about his squad car.

"Am I allowed to ask why?"

"We've got the statue."

"The *softball* statue?"

"Did another statue get heisted?" I ask. "What kind of protection are you providing the trusting citizens of Santa Martina?"

"Smart aleck," he mutters.

So after I knew the Borschman was on the way, I shooed Jack's mom and Tony off, and when the tow truck was gone, I had Justice Jack drive the High Roller back and forth over all the tire tracks outside the barn and inside, too, because I wasn't sure how hard the mayor would push the police to get to the bottom of who'd broken into City Hall, and dually tire tracks would be a decent clue to get them started.

And while Jack was confusing tow truck tracks with High Roller tracks, we all took turns calling home with Billy's cell phone.

Now, for Marissa and me it wasn't that hard to get out of trouble. We both just basically said, Well, if you'd give us cell phones like the rest of the world has, we wouldn't be scrambling around for ways to let you know where we are.

But for Casey? Boy, that didn't work at all! We could hear his mom screeching that he was grounded and that she knew, just *knew,* that he was "with that little witch."

So Casey said, "Mom! I'm with Justice Jack and Billy. We've found the statue, all right? The police are coming and I'll be home as soon as I can."

For some reason that seemed to quiet her down.

Which really surprised me.

But then Casey says, "Yeah . . . Yeah . . . Yeah . . . Well, I heard there's a reward, but I don't know if—"

And then his mom starts shrieking that if he's really found the statue and isn't just lying to cover up that he's "with that little witch," he'll come home with some reward money or be grounded for life.

Justice Jack had returned from scrambling tracks, and since it's loud and clear that Casey's mom is ticked off, Jack asks, "That was about the reward?"

"Uh, yeah," I tell him, trying to keep things simple.

"Money," Justice Jack grumbles. "It warps the thinking and pollutes the mind. It makes decent men turn to crime." He shakes his head. "There's no reward better than doing the right thing."

Just then Officer Borsch shows up, so we get him to park near the statue. Then I take him aside and explain the plan. And even though he starts asking questions about ten different times, each time I warn him, "There are some things you probably don't want to know."

286

After I've told him everything I can, we all heft the statue together and wedge it, foot-first, into Officer Borsch's trunk. The back end of the squad car sinks waaaaay down, and even when we've worked it in as far as we can, the statue is still more out than in.

Officer Borsch walks around it and says, "I don't know about this."

"The bottom's way heavier than the top," I tell him. "It won't fall out."

He sucks on a tooth. "I'm not worried about that so much as I am about bottoming out." He slaps the brass arm holding the softball. "And this needs a flag."

So he finds a red rag and straps it onto the softball hand, then ropes down the lid of the trunk and says, "We'll see how far I get."

"Uh . . . maybe it would help counterbalance things if we all got in the car?" I give him a little look. "Plus, we all could really use a ride home."

He looks around. "So how'd you get out here?" And when his gaze falls on the High Roller, I tell him, "Nope! Haven't been on it, cross my heart." Then I head for the double barn doors, calling, "My skateboard's outside! Hey, Marissa! Come on and get your stuff so Officer Borsch can give us a ride home!"

"I know you didn't ride your skateboard out here!" the Borschman hollers after me.

"You said you wouldn't ask questions!" I holler back.

So we retrieve our stuff and head for the squad car, but Billy doesn't follow us. He goes with Jack, straight to the High Roller.

"Hey!" Officer Borsch calls to him over the hood. "That's not a safety helmet!"

Billy knocks through the cloth of his bomber helmet. "Mine's built in, sir! Very convenient."

"Get in the cruiser," Officer Borsch tells him. "Enough lawbreaking for one day!"

Billy looks from Jack to Officer Borsch and back to Jack. "Go," Jack says to Billy, then gives his hand a mighty shake. "Proud to have had you on the Justice Team."

"Do you want me at the news conference?" Billy asks.

"You bet I do," Jack tells him, then turns to Officer Borsch. "You're going to help us set that up, right, Commissioner?"

"It's Sergeant Borsch, okay? Enough of the Commissioner nonsense."

Jack looks down. "You'll always be Commissioner to me, sir."

"Yeah, well . . ." Officer Borsch's eyes shift around a little and he waves him off. "Whatever. I'll set it up. The mayor, the news crews. Get your speech ready, and make it a good one." Then he looks at us and says, "What are you waiting for? Let's get this statue back to City Hall."

So we all pile in and lowride out of the dairy barn.

THIRTY-FIVE

Officer Borsch scheduled the press conference for the next day at three-thirty so all of us could make it and it still could air on the five, six, and eleven o'clock news. Marissa and I got there around three-fifteen, and when we peeked inside the City Hall foyer, we saw that the statue was already back on its big base.

There were news cameras set up outside the foyer near a podium with microphones, and a growing group of people was gathering. I wasn't sure Casey would be there, but he came running up to me a few minutes after Marissa and I arrived.

"Hey, you made it!" I said, and had the hardest time not giving him a very public hug.

"Only because Jack showed up at our door last night with my backpack and skateboard and totally floored my mom."

"He did?"

He laughs. "She has a thing about celebrities. She was all jelly-kneed after he left and she actually apologized to me."

"Was he wearing hero gear?"

He laughs again. "Oh yeah."

"So do you think your mom will show up *here*?"

"Oh," he says, looking around at the crowd. "Good point."

So I stay with Marissa on one side of the crowd while Casey goes off to the other. But we grin and wink and do little hand signals to each other while we wait, which makes Marissa go, "I hate the two of you, you know that?"

I smile at her. "You love us and you know it."

She looks like she's about to cry. "I can't believe I blew it so badly with Billy." She nods up at the podium, where Mayor Hibbs has just appeared all rosy-cheeked and jolly, followed by Justice Jack and Billy, who are both decked out in hero gear. "Look at him!" she gushes.

Well, Marissa's not the only one looking at the Deuce. There are girls everywhere swooning over the sight of him.

And then all of a sudden there's a familiar voice behind us going, "Quite a turnout!"

"Hudson!" Then I see that Mikey's with him, wearing his superhero Halloween costume. I laugh and slap five on him. "Spy Guy!"

"At your service, brave citizen!" Mikey says in the deepest voice a nine-year-old can make.

"How'd you hear about this?" I ask Hudson.

He laughs. "Oh, they've been teasing it on the news since early this morning. Your grandmother said she'd be here." He scans the crowd. "There she is!"

"Grams! Over here!" I call. And then I realize that Bun-Top and Screwdriver Sally and about six other members of the Prune Patrol are there, too. I look at Hudson.

"Good grief. I can't believe so many people care about that stupid statue."

"It's not the statue, it's Justice Jack." He gives me a knowing look. "People love a superhero."

And *then* I see that Casey's mom has found Casey, and that Heather is with them, too.

"Even *Heather*?"

He grins at me. "Especially Heather."

Well, if you ask me, Heather's like the Lex Luthor of William Rose Junior High—there's no way she would go all goo-goo over a fake superhero.

And yet . . .

I nudge Marissa. "Check out the way Heather is looking at Justice Jack."

"Whoa," Marissa says after a minute. "That's freaky."

All of a sudden Officer Borsch is up at the podium, welcoming people and introducing the mayor. He keeps it short and to the point, but then Mayor Hibbs gives a *long* speech that uses words like *community* and *pride* and *liberty* and *loyalty* and *unity*. He's reading it, too, which makes it seem like we're floating down a long, sleepy stream of patriotic mumbo jumbo until *finally* he says, "And now it is my great pleasure to turn the microphone over to the man who brought home the statue. Ladies and gentlemen, Justice Jack!" And the crowd goes wild.

Officer Borsch is standing beside me now and he gruffs out, "Jack came in for a one-on-one this afternoon. His conscience was bothering him."

"He told you . . . what?"

"Everything." He shakes his head. "I feel for the guy."

291

I raise an eyebrow his way. "Sounds like he's converted you, too."

"Yeah," he growls. Then he eyes me and adds, "And you know how tough that can be."

I laugh. "Yes, I do!" Then I ask, "So, what are you going to do?"

He raises an eyebrow my way. "There are things you're better off not knowing, and there are things you're better off forgetting." He goes back to watching the podium. "He asked me about joining the force."

"Seriously?"

"I don't think that would work in Santa Martina, but I'm pulling some strings to get him in an academy in Reno. They would love him there." He nods toward Squeaky and the Chick, standing off to one side of the podium. "Besides, they owe me and they know it."

The clapping and whistling for Jack finally die down, but when he booms, "Good afternoon, brave citizens!" the crowd goes wild again.

"Wow," I say, looking around.

Jack puts his hands up to quiet everyone. He doesn't read from a written speech, he just looks out at all of us and says, "It has been a noble cause, serving the citizenry of Santa Martina. I have seen you give freely to those in need, rise to your neighbors' defense, and dig within yourselves in service to justice. One man, no matter how competent his assistant"—he turns to give Billy a little bow—"cannot take on evil alone. Nor can one police force. We need *you*, the citizens of this fair city, to rally in defense of what is good and fair and just, and hold up a mighty shield against those who would have us cower in fear. Many small deeds add up to a collective good, so I ask you to rise above fear and do what's right." He takes a deep breath, which re-inflates his chest. "With the return of our city's symbolic statue, my tour as Justice Jack is over. It is now up to you to carry on the work I've begun here." He does a little head bob and ends with, "It has been an honor to serve you."

The mayor shouts, "Wait! What? You're quitting?"

As an answer, Jack peels off his helmet, his mask, and his gloves and hands them over to the mayor. And even though I can tell it's killing him, Billy does the same.

"Jack *Wesley*?" a woman from the crowd shouts. "Is that you?" And someone else calls out, "Dude, you've changed a lot since high school!"

Everything sort of goes chaotic after that. People start talking like crazy and girls are screaming out Billy's name and the mayor's all flustered and trying to figure out how this news conference could have gotten so out of control.

"Well," Officer Borsch says with a rare grin, "this is the first press conference I've actually enjoyed."

At first that surprises me, but then I see that it's the mayor he's got his focus on. "I can't believe you didn't warn him."

"Nah," he says, still grinning. "This was way more fun."

I thought about that grin of his a bunch that night. I thought about how Officer Borsch, of all people, went along with a cover-up.

Or, at least, an un-investigation.

I also thought about how Marissa was disappointed

293

that Billy and Jack got credit for returning the statue and we got none, and I wondered if she really could keep quiet about it, or if it would all eventually come out anyway.

But mostly I thought about Justice Jack and why a goofy guy in cheap hero gear could make you feel like it was possible to change the world. What was it about him that had that effect on people?

It couldn't be the costume.

It was a pretty corny costume!

And it couldn't be the booming way he talked or all his Justice-this and Justice-thats.

Try that at school and people would laugh you apart!

But the more I thought about it, the more I decided that what made people love Justice Jack was the way he *believed* the things he said. The way he believed that one person could change things by standing up, standing tall. Maybe that wasn't an actual superpower, but the way he put his whole heart and soul into it?

It *was* powerful.

Powerful enough to make *you* believe it, too.

And, you know, when you think about it, that may be the best superpower of all.

What do you think?

A few questions for you or your book club to ponder.

What did you make of Jack? Do you think, in the end, he influenced the hearts and minds of the people in town? What about his influence on Mikey? Was that a positive thing?

Why does Sammy not quite trust Justice Jack?

Why is Billy so eager to be Jack's sidekick? Would you want to ride in that sidecar?

Billy and Marissa make a pretty odd couple. Is that always a bad thing? Can opposites be good together?

Of course it'll never work if Marissa's still stuck on Danny. Why do you think she's so willing to give him second chances?

Mrs. Wedgewood is such a complicated person—she's devious and manipulative but, in the end, generous. Does the good in her outweigh the bad?

What does Mrs. Wedgewood see in Sammy that Sammy hasn't quite seen in herself? How has her gift already changed Sammy's thinking?

You won't believe what Sammy gets into next!

Here's a sneak peek at
Sammy Keyes and the Showdown in Sin City.

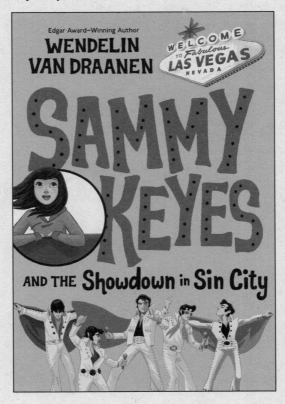

PROLOGUE

It's been more than two and a half years since my mother left me with Grams so she could move to Hollywood to become a movie star.

Or, at least, the Gas-Away Lady, and then a recovering amnesiac in *The Lords of Willow Heights*—a soap so popular it's just been canceled.

Yeah, it's been more than two and a half years since she promised me she would get settled and send for me "soon," but after about a year of broken promises and non-answers it finally sank in that I'm just a burden and an unwanted embarrassment—someone she wishes would just go away.

Or at least quit asking questions.

Especially questions about who my dad is.

But I have a problem with non-answers, and I have a problem with people who don't keep their promises. So when the call came from Casey, I snapped.

Enough, as they say, is enough.

ONE

Casey Acosta is my boyfriend.

He's also my archenemy's brother, and my mother's boyfriend's son.

So yeah.

It's complicated.

Especially since my boyfriend's mother hates me and *my* mother for "stealing her men." Never mind that Candi and Warren Acosta had been divorced a long time before my mother came into the picture, or that Casey's only fifteen and not exactly *property*—we've still "stolen her men."

Now, if anyone's got a legitimate complaint about my mother being with Candi's ex it's *me*. I mean, there are a billion other men out there for my glamorous mother to choose from—why Casey's dad?

But that's the way Lady Lana is. Grams may hate that I call her that, but I think it sums her up perfectly. She acts like royalty and doesn't care how what she does affects other people. For example, she doesn't think, Whoa, if I marry Warren, his evil daughter, Heather, will become my daughter's stepsister. Or, Hey, my daughter's boyfriend will become her stepbrother! How awkward!

No, she does what she wants and justifies it by telling me that Casey and I can't possibly last. That no relationship formed in junior high school does. That what she and Warren have is *real* and *mature* love . . . not just some silly "junior high crush."

Even though Casey's now a freshman in high school.

Anyway, since there seems to be no reasoning with wannabe royalty, I've just been hoping that her infatuation with Warren will blow over. Or that Warren will realize that he's in way over his head. My mom can be very . . . *snippy* when things aren't going her way, and since Warren was also on *Lords* and they're now both out-of-work actors, well, let's just say warning signs should be posted:

CAUTION: ENTERING SNIPPYVILLE
SLOW DOWN!
TURN BACK WHILE YOU CAN!

It's not like I obsess over them being together. I'd short-circuit if I did. Plus the two of them are way off in Hollywood, and I've got enough worries right here in Santa Martina. Like sneaking in and out of Grams' apartment every day, since it's for seniors only and totally against the law for me to be living there. Or like surviving junior high school. That alone takes major concentration and endurance, but with Heather Acosta lurking around every corner it's like fancy dancing through a minefield.

I've got Heather in half my classes—history, science, and drama—and then, of course, there's before school, break, lunch, and after school. And on a typical day, Heather greets me with a sneer and "Hey, loser," or "Outta my way, loser," or "Nice shoes, loser"—that last one being about my torn-up high-tops, which I'm hoping can last to the end of the school year.

True to form, Thursday during third period Heather went toward her seat and said, "Loser," as she passed by. She was texting, so I guess one word was all the multitasking she could handle. Plus she had a red paper clamped under her arm so she was probably also distracted by her "Love Connection" results from the Valentine's Day fundraiser the school was doing.

Everyone at school had filled out a survey in homeroom. It had questions about what you like to do, your favorite band, your best subject . . . stuff like that. The surveys were put into a computer, and that morning the results had gone on sale. For five bucks you could get a list of the top five people of the opposite sex that the computer thought you were most compatible with.

Everyone was buying their list, but I hadn't. It used to be that spending five bucks on five names would have been out of the question, because Grams is on a really tight fixed income and I don't get an allowance, let alone lunch money.

But for once I was flush. To make a long story short, I'd gotten a share of a big reward for finding a stolen statue, so five bucks was totally doable. But I hadn't bought mine because the whole computer match thing seemed kind of creepy.

Like I can't figure out who I like on my own?

And besides, I'm not looking.

I've got Casey.

Sure, I was tempted by the curiosity of it—just to see who was on the list. But I got over that when I saw what happened to other people.

Things got . . . awkward.

Like a *lot* of people, my friends Marissa and Dot bought theirs before school, and when Marissa tore hers open she whimpered, "Noooo."

"What?" I asked, moving in to see her list.

"How can Jacob Hogan be number one?" There were tears in her eyes. "And Rudy Folksmeir is number two?"

Not that long ago Marissa would probably just have laughed this off, but she's been an emotional wreck for months. In addition to boy problems, I think what's really got her completely stressed out is her parents. They used to be rich-rich-rich, but then they lost a fortune in the stock market and Marissa's father started gambling to try to make up for it.

I'm talking fly-to-Las-Vegas-and-get-rip-roaring-drunk gambling.

And even though he's joined Gamblers Anonymous and has tried to straighten things out, things are definitely not straightened out. Because of his gambling, they're "upside down" on their mansion of a house and may have to move. And last week Marissa's mom caught Mr. McKenze playing blackjack online.

So much for Gamblers Anonymous.

Anyway, Marissa's gone from rich-rich-rich to completely broke, and she's gone from going out with Billy

Pratt—one of the most popular guys at school—to having icky Jacob Hogan and Rudy Folksmeir in the top two slots of her Love Connection list.

"Hey," Dot told her. "Maybé you just don't know them very well. Maybe they're actually interesting and nice."

Marissa gave her a completely defeated look. "Rudy's favorite topic of conversation is *dirt*."

Which is true.

He's *way* into dirt biking.

Marissa leans over to look at Dot's printout. "So who did you get?" And even though Dot pulls back quick, Marissa sees enough to get upset. "You got *Billy*? There's no way you and Billy are compatible! You're quiet, he's a ham. . . ." She flings her arms in the air and shouts, "We want our money back!"

Dot, though, doesn't seem to want her money back. She just wants Marissa to pipe down. "Shh! It's not even anybody's business that we bought them, okay?"

"I have a question," I throw in. "If somebody's on your list, are you automatically on theirs?"

Marissa gasps. "I hope not!"

Our friend Holly has also just been standing quietly by, but since I've piped up, she does, too. "But it makes sense, doesn't it?"

Marissa whimpers, "So right now Jacob and *Rudy* are thinking we're compatible? What if one of them asks me to the Valentine's dance? What am I going to do?"

Holly shrugs. "Say thanks but no thanks?"

Dot adds, "Or just tell him you're going with your

friends." She looks around at the rest of us. "We're still planning to do that, right?"

We all kind of nod, 'cause that's what Marissa had talked us into. And even though it would be fun for me to go to a Valentine's dance with Casey, his psycho mom has forbidden him to see me, so a school dance is not exactly someplace we can meet.

Especially since Heather was sure to be there.

Instead, Casey and I had agreed to meet on Saturday for a Valentine's Day picnic at our secret spot—the graveyard.

Anyway, Marissa's still all worried, saying, "But . . . what if they *go* to the dance and *ask* me to dance?" She wags her Love Connection sheet a little and gives us a pleading look. "They're not the type to buy these, right?"

But it seemed like *everyone* was the type. Or, at least, couldn't resist. By lunchtime on Friday red sheets were everywhere, including poking out of Holly's back pocket. Only the corner was showing, but there was no mistaking the color.

"You bought yours?" I whispered, giving it a little flick.

She slapped at her back pocket. "Shoot."

I laughed. "It's not a crime, you know. Anybody good?"

She hesitated, then gave me a little smile. "Preston Davis?"

I smiled back. "Oh!"

"But now everything's weird! I can't even look at him without blushing." She rolled her eyes. "Is that stupid, or what?"

Which made me glad I'd resisted curiosity and not bought mine. *Everyone* was getting at least a little wigged out by their results—like they didn't know how to act around their friends anymore because they'd shown up on their Love Connection list.

And that's when I saw Heather pacing around, talking on her cell, waving a red paper in the air. "She's had hers since yesterday and she's *still* talking about it?" I laughed. "I wonder who's on her Loooooove Connection."

Holly chuckled. "Five poor schmucks who'd better hide quick."

"Or run fast!" Marissa added.

Dot shook her head. "Can you imagine?"

But then during science I noticed that Heather was texting under her desk. And I don't care *who's* on your Love Connection list, it can't be so bad that you risk texting during Ms. Rothhammer's class. She is strict and she always follows through with detentions, referrals, and confiscations. Everyone knows her rules are ironclad, and when it comes to cell phones it's real simple: text in class, lose your phone.

And believe me, if there's one thing Heather doesn't want to lose, it's her phone.

Now, Heather was being sly enough about it—her eyes were on the board while her thumbs were flying fast and furious under the desk—but still, it was dangerous.

So I started thinking that maybe what she was upset about was something bigger than having five "losers" on her Love Connection list.

Maybe it was something real.

I was dying to talk to Marissa about it during drama, but she didn't show up to class. She hadn't said anything about leaving school early, so I asked a couple of people if they knew where she was but got nowhere. Then Billy came up to me and whispered, "Pay-phone Casey the minute school lets out. He says it's important."

"Did he say anything else?"

He shook his head.

"Wait. When which school lets out? Ours or his?"

"Ours."

"But he'll still be in class!"

He shrugged. "I don't decipher, I just deliver."

He turned to go, but I grabbed him and said, "Do you know why Marissa's not in class?"

He looked around. "She's not?"

"Mr. Pratt!" Mr. Chester hollered at him. "How many times do I have to ask you to stay on task?"

"Sorry, sir!" Billy called back, and hurried off to the scenery he was supposed to be painting.

I really wanted to chase after Billy and ask him more, but I was pretty sure he didn't know any more. And then I noticed Heather lurking to the side of the stage and started wondering if maybe *she* did. She was still sneaking texts, and I could tell this wasn't just casual conversation.

She was *plotting* something.

And after Billy's message I started getting the sinking feeling that what she was plotting involved Casey.

And probably me.

TWO

The minute school let out I hurried over to the pay phone. It wasn't like I had to rush so I'd get to it before someone else did, since everyone else on the planet has a cell phone. But after watching Heather's texting get more and more intense during drama, and then having her singe me with her infamous Psycho Evil Eye as she bolted out of the classroom, I was dying to know what was going on.

"Hey, it's me," I said when I heard Casey answer.

"You okay?"

He sounded stressed, which made me look around for Heather. "Yeah . . . What's going on?"

"Heather didn't say anything?"

"She fried me with an evil eye, but that's all. What's this about?"

I could hear him take a deep breath, then let it out in a long, puffy stream. "Your mom and my dad."

For a split second I panicked.

Were they in an accident?

Were they *dead*?

Apparently Casey can read minds, because he says,

"They're fine." Then he adds, "But it looks like they're getting married this weekend."

"What?"

"In Vegas."

I yanked my jaw off the ground. "How do you know? Did your dad tell you?" But before he can answer I get totally ticked off. "This is so typical! Of course she wouldn't tell me! Of course she has to go off and be secretive and sneaky and not even think about how this is going to mess with my life!"

"If it makes you feel any better, my dad didn't tell me, either."

"She's a *horrible* influence on him!" Then I add, "But then . . . how do you know?"

I can hear him take another deep breath. "I overheard my mom talking to Heather about how she'd hired a private investigator."

It takes a minute for that to really sink in. "You're serious? Why'd she do *that*?"

He sighs. "She thinks he should be paying more child support than he is."

"So she hired a private investigator? To find out *what*?"

"I don't know. You know how she is."

"And he found out they're getting *married*?"

"He found out that my dad made a 'sizable purchase' at a jewelry store yesterday and bought two plane tickets to Las Vegas."

"For today?"

"Yup."

"But we don't *know* they're getting married."

"Well, it sure points that way, don't you think?"

I let *that* sink in, too, then sigh. "Yeah, it does."

"I tried confronting my mom, but she went into a tirade about eavesdropping and then accused me of still seeing you."

"What did you say?"

"Well, you know I can't admit it."

I sigh. "I know."

"So since she told me the usual nothing, I've been trying to reach my dad, but his cell's been turned off all day. You can try your mom, but I'll bet you won't get through."

"You think they've already left?"

"Yeah. And phones off is their Do Not Disturb sign."

All of a sudden I'm just *mad*. "She hasn't even told me who my real dad is, and now she's sneaking off to marry *your* dad?"

"My dad's not a bad guy, if that's any consolation."

"Well your stepmom-to-be is going to take care of that! He's already becoming just like her!"

He gives a little snort. "So true."

"I wonder if Grams knows."

"Would she tell you?"

"She may be good at keeping my mom's secrets, but I can't believe she'd keep *this* from me!"

"Okay. Well, if she tells you anything, can you let me know?"

"Via Billy?"

"Yeah."

Then I ask, "So what's your mom doing about it? Anything?"

"What *can* she do?"

"Fly to Vegas and cause a scene?"

He laughs. "She might if it would change things. But they're divorced, so that would be pretty over-the-top, don't you think?"

We're both quiet, and then he says, "Sorry for the bad news."

I hesitate but finally say what I'm thinking. "Is it going to weird you out too much?"

"Just don't start calling me your stepbrother."

I pinch my eyes closed. "I hate her."

"Why don't you find out if your grandmother knows anything." Then he adds, "And, Sammy?"

I choke out, "Yeah?" because I'm on the verge of crying. I mean, why couldn't I have a normal mom and a normal life? Why did things have to be so complicated and full of all this stupid *drama*.

And then Casey says something that pushes me over the edge. "I love you."

"I love you, too," I tell him in a really stupid blubbery way.

He laughs. "And don't worry. Nothing's going to change that." Then he says, "Keep me posted," and gets off the phone.